TRAINING SASHA

CLUB ZODIAC, BOOK ONE

BECCA JAMESON

ACKNOWLEDGMENTS

I'd like to thank my editor, Christa Soule, for the countless hours she spends on the phone with me working out my plots when my characters aren't cooperating! She is truly a gem. She deserves tremendous credit for making me dig deep and ask the hard questions.

As usual, a shout out to my cover artist, Scott Carpenter, for creating perfect covers and then changing them entirely when I decide the models fit better on book number two!

A special extra thank you to my daughter, Rebecca, for all her hard work on this series. I was pressed for time this month!

PROLOGUE

Sasha Easton had other plans that night, plans that didn't entail hanging around Club Zodiac with her brother Rowen's coworkers on her seventeenth birthday. The only reason she wasn't irritated by the party they'd organized was because she knew everyone would disperse to start their jobs one floor below at eight o'clock.

Rowen had been working at Club Zodiac three nights a week since shortly before she'd moved in with him five years ago when their mother died. His coworkers were also his best friends. And by default, they treated her like a kid sister.

Sasha loved them all. Every one of them had a hand in her formative years, everything from helping her with homework, to ensuring she had dinner, to scrutinizing her choice in friends.

Tonight was different. Not only were they gathered to wish her a happy birthday, but tonight was the night the new owner took over Zodiac. Sasha hadn't met him yet, but she'd heard the rumblings. She was anxious to get a glimpse of him if for no other reason than to discern whether or not the rumors about him were true.

If the gossip were to be believed, Lincoln Walsh was the entire package—tall, dark, and handsome. The way the female employees whispered about him with reverence indicated he also exuded power.

So, Sasha was filled with mixed emotions as she made her way around the breakroom above the club, greeting everyone with a gracious smile, anticipating the moment she could tear out of there to catch up with her friends, and a bit nervous about meeting Rowen's new boss.

The previous owner, John Gilbert, had retired. He was in his mid-sixties and had treated Sasha like a granddaughter from the moment she'd met him. After her mother died, he'd agreed to let her hang out in his office or the breakroom on Wednesday, Friday, and Saturday nights while her brother worked.

John adored her. He was always smiling and often laughing, the deep kind of chuckle that made his entire body shake. He provided a hug when she was feeling down. He filled her stomach with desserts his wife made. And he often slid her cash when no one was looking. *A lady should always have a few dollars on her.*

She smiled at the memories.

Tonight was a turning point for the club. She wasn't the only one feeling the tension. She would miss John, but she hadn't spent nearly as much time at the club in the last year since she'd gotten her driver's license and no longer needed late-night supervision.

She was standing in the back corner, talking with Carter Ellis —one of Rowen's best friends who went all the way back to their days in the army—when a hush fell over the room. She turned toward the doorway and lifted her gaze, and then her breath caught in her lungs.

No one had exaggerated when they spoke of the new owner. He was over six feet with thick, dark hair and dark skin that didn't come from the sun but rather from a gene pool that undoubtedly included someone of Asian descent. If that wasn't enough, he was also built in a way that indicated he worked out often and took pride in his body.

Lincoln Walsh entered the makeshift party with a friendly smile, greeting the staff with handshakes and nods. Easygoing while at the same time exuding an air of authority that belied his age, which she knew to be only twenty-five. He was young to own a club.

He was all Dom. Sexy as hell.

Sasha remained tongue-tied, unable to move from her spot across the room. She realized the foolishness of her strange attraction but couldn't stop the physical reaction taking over her body.

It was the first time she experienced true arousal. The first time she felt the tingling sensation in her clit. The tightening of her nipples. The wetness pooling between her legs.

Also for the first time, she felt a sense of self-consciousness. Glancing down at her white shorts and yellow camisole, she wondered how she looked to others around her. Probably young. She needed to think about getting some more grown-up clothes. Black maybe. No way would she ever impress a man like Lincoln Walsh dressed as if she were a walking advertisement for virginity.

Her hands grew sweaty and her mouth dry. Mesmerized, she stood completely still and waited for him to approach. When he did, she swallowed and licked her lips but couldn't manage to utter a word.

His eyes sparkled when he took her hand and held it in both of his. He winked at her. "Lincoln Walsh. You must be Rowen's sister."

She nodded.

"You look so young. I understand this party is for you. How old are you?"

"Seventeen," she murmured.

Lincoln's face froze, his smile fell, and then he dropped her hand as if she had the plague. "Seventeen?"

"Yes." It was difficult to utter that one word considering the total change in his demeanor.

Rowen approached from behind, coming up on Lincoln's side. "I see you met my sister."

Lincoln spun toward him, his face hard, his eyes scrunched together. "She's seventeen?"

Rowen frowned. "Yes."

"I thought you said she'd been hanging around the club for years."

"She has." Rowen let those two words draw out longer than necessary.

A hush spread across the room as Lincoln's words grew louder. "She's underage."

Rowen flinched. "I know that. She's not a member. She's my sister."

"She can't be here at all. It's against the law."

"She doesn't come into the club itself. She takes the stairs to the third floor and hangs out in John's office or the breakroom." The two floors that constituted the club itself and the offices were located above a strip mall with an unobtrusive entrance that led to the business above—Club Zodiac.

Sasha hadn't moved an inch since Lincoln had introduced himself. Mortification flushed her face. She fisted her hands at her sides and wished she could teleport to anywhere else on the planet.

"Well, not anymore. John must have had a screw loose allowing you all to let her stay up here these past few years. She needs to leave, and this is the last time she'll be permitted in the building for another three hundred sixty-five days." Lincoln turned around, marched out of the room, and shut the door behind him.

The silence was deafening. The dozen or so employees slowly started mumbling among themselves and then tossing uneasy smiles her direction.

Sasha felt like she'd been slapped in the face. Her cheeks were so hot she thought she might self-combust. The gorgeous new owner of Zodiac had acted like she was nothing more than a baby.

She left there two minutes later, shaking with embarrassment and anger, and vowed not to so much as drive by the place again for the entire next year.

CHAPTER 1

Five years later…

Sasha Easton stared up at her older brother with every ounce of defiance she'd schooled her face to deliver. She hoped her narrowed eyes shot daggers at him. After all, she was twenty-two years old, a college graduate, old enough to make her own choices. And she'd made her decision. "You can't stop me, Rowen," she growled.

He chuckled, infuriating her further. His stance had already royally pissed her off. The addition of his laughter only made things worse. He was currently leaning against his desk in his corner office on the upper floor of Club Zodiac. "The answer is no, Sasha."

She cocked one hip to the side, tapping her foot. "It's not your decision. I'm a grown woman."

He stopped laughing, stood taller, and tipped his head toward her. Damn her stupid genes for making her eight inches shorter than him. "What's this really about? Why the sudden interest in Zodiac, or BDSM in general?"

"If you'd ever paid attention, there's nothing sudden about my interest in submission. It's always been there, right beneath the surface. I've mentioned it to you on numerous occasions, but you wouldn't listen to me."

He took a deep breath. "You're young. I can understand why you'd be curious. Hell, I'm sure it's my fault. I never should have permitted you to spend your evenings here while I worked. I have no one to blame for that but myself. However, that doesn't change the fact that you're not cut out for this lifestyle, and there's no way I'm going to permit you to join this club."

"Fine. If you don't want me to join Zodiac, I'll get a membership at one of the other clubs in Miami."

His eyes narrowed further, his face flaming red with frustration. "Fuck no. Not a chance in hell." The vein on his forehead bulged.

She set her hands on her hips. "Are you listening to yourself? The double standard is atrocious. You were eighteen when you joined Zodiac. I'm four years older than that. So get off your high horse and stop being a chauvinist pig."

Rowen leaned in closer. "Don't go there," he gritted out. "You know I treat women like they're royalty. Don't you dare insinuate I think I'm superior. I have never once treated a woman as anything less than my equal."

Fury rose inside her, making her hands shake while flushing her cheeks a bright red to rival his. She glared at him, forcing herself to calm down before she spoke again. It wouldn't do any good to prove him right by acting like a child. If she wanted him to treat her like an adult, she needed to gather her wits and remain outwardly calm, albeit persuasive.

He was right about one thing—it was his fault she'd been introduced to BDSM in the first place, but she was also convinced she would have figured it out on her own eventually. Perhaps she would have wasted years of her life not being true to herself if she hadn't known at a young age she was submissive.

However, she couldn't really blame her brother for indirectly introducing her to the lifestyle. She'd been twelve years old when their mother died and Rowen had been forced to take on a baby sister who had no doubt been a pain in his ass.

Rowen had been twenty-two at the time. The ten-year age difference was vast. The two of them had different fathers, neither of whom were in the picture. Rowen's father had been killed serving in the military and then Sasha's father had skipped town the moment he'd found out her mother was pregnant.

Nevertheless, their mother had been a great mom, doing everything she could to provide for them and keep them fed and clothed. An aneurism had taken her life, leaving Sasha with no living relative other than her brother.

Sasha took a breath and forced her voice to calm. "I know you're an amazing man. You've always treated women with respect. I'm asking you to extend the same respect to me, Rowen. I'm not a kid anymore. You don't have to protect me. And I'm also not a private in your platoon, so drop the drill sergeant act too."

Rowen flinched. She'd hit a nerve with that last sentence. Not surprising. She'd had to point out his tendency to shout orders at her like she was his subordinate in the army many times since she'd moved in with him ten years ago. He'd only served four years, but the habits were engrained.

She also wasn't wrong when she played the age card. Rowen had been a member of Club Zodiac since he'd turned eighteen. He had frequented the place every time he was at home on leave, and when he started college upon his return, he'd taken a job working at the club to help defer some of his expenses.

Even at twelve, Sasha had been smart enough to know she was cramping his style. He'd thought Sasha was too young to be left in his apartment until the middle of the night. In the end, Rowen and John had struck a deal, and Rowen had reluctantly brought Sasha with him.

Sasha hadn't known what her brother did at the club at first.

She'd had no clue for at least two years. All she'd known was that she sat upstairs in John's office doing her homework and watching television every Wednesday, Friday, and Saturday night while Rowen tended bar.

It wasn't until one night when she was fourteen that she'd arrived late after studying at a friend's house and noticed how scantily dressed many of the patrons were. Rowen had found her in the entrance to the club, starry-eyed and tongue-tied. He'd ushered her straight up the stairs to the office and given her a firm lecture, rambling on about adult decisions and keeping her eyes on her education.

The two minutes she'd stood in the entry, seeing more than she ever should have seen, were imbedded in her mind for life.

From that day forward, she'd spent countless hours searching the internet and reading about BDSM clubs. She also started reading novels that featured everything anyone could possibly imagine related to dominance and submission. It intrigued her. It formed her. Now, it *was* her.

Rowen must not have liked the way she stood before him no longer speaking, because he ran a hand through his hair in exasperation. "Dammit, Sasha. Sit down." He pointed at the black leather loveseat against the wall of his office. "I need to check on a few things before we open. If you so much as move an inch..."

She watched his back as he stomped out of the office. She had no intention of sitting on his damn couch, mostly because he'd demanded it of her. Instead, she wandered toward the window and stared down at the traffic moving along the Miami streets below.

She needed to take this opportunity to regroup and gain the upper hand. Acting like a bratty teenager would get her nowhere. She leaned her forehead against the cool glass and closed her eyes.

Three years ago, Rowen and his friend Carter had bought into the business, joining Lincoln Walsh as part owners. Lincoln still owned a majority interest, but the club had grown and expanded enough that he needed more help. Rowen had an accounting degree, so he took over the financial side of things. Carter was a bodybuilder, so he became head bouncer and doorman.

And then there was Lincoln.

Sasha had a love-hate relationship with the club's head owner. She had never gotten over the way he'd treated her the night she met him, but neither of them had ever mentioned the incident again.

A full year passed before she saw him for the second time, and by then Lincoln, Rowen, and Carter were close friends. It wasn't surprising. The three of them bonded over their military background. Carter had joined the army at the same time as Rowen and then did two tours before getting out and coming to Miami. Lincoln had joined the army two years after his friends, also right out of high school. Sasha still didn't know why he'd left the service and ended up running a club in Miami, Florida, but his experience had drawn the three men together.

Lincoln hadn't changed one bit since the night she'd met him. He was just as sexy, domineering, and larger than life as he'd been the night of her seventeenth birthday.

Sasha rarely saw him over the years, partly because he intimidated her on a level that pissed her off. Partly because he'd treated her like a pariah the first time they'd met. But most importantly, it unnerved her to admit she was not only still attracted to him, but no man she'd ever met since that day had been able to live up to the standard Lincoln Walsh had set in her mind between the moment he'd stepped into the room and the second he'd dropped her hand after greeting her.

Over the years, Sasha had remained friendly with the rest of the staff. She no longer lived with her brother, but she regularly saw them at his house or whenever she stopped by the club. She'd known all of them so well before finding out what sort of club they worked at that she never once thought of any of Rowen's friends as anything other than regular people who happened to also enjoy some level of kink in their lives.

The door to Rowen's office opened behind her, jerking her back to the present. She spun around, startled from her memories.

Luckily, the person who stepped into the office and shut the door was not her brother. It was Rayne Bryant, her brother's on-again-off-again girlfriend. Apparently this week they were "on."

Sasha forced a smile to her face and stepped from the window. "Hey, Rayne."

Rayne frowned at her. "You okay? You look flustered."

Sasha sighed as she came to the loveseat and plopped down on one end. "I ought to. I've been arguing with my pigheaded brother."

Rayne chuckled. "Rowen? Pigheaded? Surely you jest." Rayne's voice was filled with sarcasm. If anyone knew how pigheaded Rowen was, it was Rayne. She lowered her sophisticated self onto the other cushion of the couch and crossed her elegant legs.

Sasha loved her. She had loved her from the moment Rowen first introduced them a year ago. Rayne was sleek and stylish for every occasion, even if all the two of them intended to do was rent movies and order pizza. Tonight she wore a black pencil skirt that fit her perfectly, a deep purple, silk blouse, and black pumps that were at least four inches high. If Sasha had to guess, she'd say Rayne had come from the law office where she worked as a paralegal while she put herself through law school.

Sasha knew for a fact that her brother adored Rayne. And the feeling was obviously mutual. There was one problem—Rayne had little interest in BDSM, and the subject had caused more than one heated discussion between them.

"What'd he do this time?" Rayne asked, her right hand draped casually across her knee, the dozen dainty, silver bracelets jingling. Her perfectly straight chocolate-brown hair was pulled back in a sleek ponytail at the nape of her neck, a silver clip holding it all in place.

If she were any other person, Sasha would feel inept and ridiculous in her presence. But she was just Rayne. She wasn't judgmental or pretentious. Never once had she made Sasha feel like anything less than her equal in the year they'd known each other.

"He still thinks of me as a kid he can boss around."

Rayne rolled her eyes. "I can see that. He sometimes talks about you that way too. I have to remind him you're a grown adult with a college degree, your own apartment, and a job. I think he feels a sense of responsibility for you that he's unable to let go of."

"I get that. He practically raised me. And I appreciate everything he's done for me in the last ten years. Without him, I have no idea what would have happened to me after Mom died."

All of that was true. And every time Sasha fought with her brother, she felt a sense of guilt. She owed him her life. He worked his ass off nights and weekends to support them. When he finished his college degree in accounting, he continued to work an extra job to save for Sasha's education.

She loved him. She knew he meant well for her. But he needed to back off.

Rayne sighed. "I'm sorry, hon. Is there anything I can do? I'll talk to him if you want."

Sasha shook her head. "Not this time. I can fight this battle. I don't need his permission to do anything. I just like to keep him informed is all. In a way, I think of him as a parent. But if he's going to continue to be an ass about my choices, I'll stop telling him my plans."

Rayne smiled. She was only two years older than Sasha. She was lucky Rowen didn't boss her around too. Although maybe he did. Who knew? "Stick up for yourself," Rayne advised. "Don't let him push you around. You know your mind. You're a mature woman with a fantastic head on your shoulders."

"I am." Sasha sat up straighter. This conversation with Rayne was exactly what she needed. As soon as Rowen returned to the office, she would put her foot down and let him have it.

CHAPTER 2

Lincoln was sitting behind his desk, facing the monitor and intently jiggling the mouse in a vain attempt to navigate the screen when he felt someone walk in, and he glanced up.

Rowen's eyes were serious, but he cracked a smile and pointed toward the desk as he shut the door behind him. "Who's winning? You or the mouse?"

Lincoln released the gadget he'd been close to throwing across the room and leaned back in his chair. "Needs new batteries. I'm just too lazy to go find a pair in the supply closet."

"Dude, that *is* lazy." Rowen ambled toward the desk and plopped down in the chair facing Lincoln.

"What's up with you?" Something was off. For one thing, Rowen looked like he'd like to hurl the mouse himself given the opportunity. And for another thing, he rarely shut the door behind him when he needed to speak to Lincoln.

They were business partners, but they didn't have many secrets that couldn't be shared with Carter or any other staff member who might wander by the open door.

Rowen tipped his head back, stared at the ceiling, and ran a hand through his hair. "Have a problem."

"Okay. You want to tell me about it, or shall I guess?" Lincoln teased, reading in his friend that some level of humor was going to be needed to diffuse his frustration. "I'm betting it has something to do with Sasha. I saw you downstairs arguing with her a bit ago."

Lincoln hated when Sasha sauntered into the club. He was pretty sure she did so to piss off her brother, but it got under Lincoln's skin too. She wasn't a member, so technically she needed to fill out paperwork and be approved before she could come into the main rooms, but Sasha seemed to think she was above the rules because she knew the staff and the owners.

She didn't come in often, at least not during business hours, but when she did, she caught the eye of half the room. Tonight was no exception. It wasn't simply because she was a beautiful woman with long brown hair that hung in ringlets halfway down her back. Hair that turned any man's head and gave him an instant hard-on. Nope. It had more to do with her choice in clothing and the way she presented herself.

Tonight she was wearing a pale pink sundress and tiny silver sandals. She held her head high and walked with authority. He had mixed emotions every time he saw her, including a half hour ago. Half of him rolled his eyes that she had the audacity to come to the club looking like she belonged at a sorority tea party. The other half smirked with pride that she was so confident that no one dared to fuck with her.

Everyone looked, including the women. The regulars knew exactly who she was and stayed clear. The newcomers and guests tended to size her up from head to toe with a bit too much interest for Lincoln's taste.

Sasha had no idea what she did to a man's libido. Either that or she thought it was all a game. In both cases, she was playing with fire.

Rowen sighed and lowered his gaze, pinning Lincoln with it. "Sasha wants to join the club."

Lincoln's entire body jerked. "What? Fuck no."

Rowen lifted his brows. "That's what I said. She's digging her heels in."

Lincoln shook his head. "Well, I'm the one who gets final say on anyone who wants to become a member, and you can tell her not to bother filling out the application because it would be a waste of her time. The answer is *no*."

Rowen chuckled. At least his anger was dissolving. "Have you spoken to my sister lately? She isn't the sort of person who takes no for an answer. When she wants something, she goes after it until she gets it."

"Do *you* want her to join the club?" Lincoln asked. He was fairly certain he knew the answer, but just to make sure they were on the same page...

"Hell, no. And I told her so. But she's headstrong. Says if we don't let her join Zodiac, she'll go to another club in town."

This time Lincoln jumped out of his seat. He set his hands on the desk and leaned forward. "Please tell me you're joking."

"Wish I could."

Lincoln spun around to face the window. The sun was dipping behind the horizon, but there was no way he could appreciate the purples, oranges, and reds tonight. He set his palms flat on the glass a few inches above his head, drew in a deep breath, and closed his eyes. "She can't join Club Zodiac, Rowen. It's out of the question. Let's call her bluff and see what happens."

It was the only option he could think of.

Sasha was smiling as she walked into the preschool where she'd been a lead teacher for the last year. She'd taken a short lunch break to run and grab sandwiches. She'd also used that time to call Marcus Pierson, owner of another local fetish club, Breeze.

She'd met Marcus a few times in the past. Rowen, Lincoln, and

Carter were friends with him. They didn't have a rivalry between them as some people would expect. Instead, they got together often and shared ideas.

Sasha had several options when it came to choosing a club to join, but she thought Breeze was the most logical first choice—after Zodiac—since she knew the owner was a stand-up guy. What she had feared was that Rowen or Lincoln would have already gotten to Marcus and blackballed her.

Apparently they had not. Thus the smile on her face.

Marcus hadn't balked at her request to visit Breeze. She was set for Friday night.

When Sasha reached the front desk, the school's receptionist—Ella—nodded at her. She was on the phone. Sasha lifted the bag in her hand and shook it to let Ella know she had returned with her requested sandwich. Sasha continued to the breakroom, knowing a starving Ella would join her as soon as she could get off the phone.

Sure enough, Ella came around the corner two minutes later and slid into the chair opposite Sasha. She grabbed her wrapped sandwich and then hesitated. "Where's yours?"

Sasha shrugged. "I had so many snacks this morning, I'm not hungry." Sasha lifted her water bottle and took a long drink, hoping Ella would leave it at that.

Ella narrowed her gaze. "You're lying. Nobody goes out to grab someone else food when they aren't getting anything for themselves. You gave it to that homeless woman who's always at the corner two blocks down, didn't you?" Ella's lips turned up in a slight grin.

"She needed it more than me. I have plenty of granola bars and pretzels in my desk. I'll be fine."

Ella laughed, shaking her head. "That's like three times this month. You do realize you can't save the entire world by giving away your food every day, right?"

Ella was wrong. Sasha had actually given the woman a

sandwich about ten times in the last month. Ella didn't always know. Sometimes Sasha bought extra. She sobered a bit to answer Ella's question. "I can't help it. It could have been me. If my brother hadn't taken me in when I was twelve, I could have been that woman or hundreds like her right here in Miami."

"You're the most kind-hearted person I know. But here's what I really want to know: Why the huge smile? You've had a shit-eating grin on your face since you walked in the door. Did you get a better-paying job somewhere else while you were gone? Because if you did, I'm quitting and going with you."

Sasha laughed. "No. Don't be silly. I love it here. Can't a person just be happy?" She wasn't about to tell Ella how excited she was about her upcoming visit to Breeze. Not that Sasha was worried about what her friend thought, but she wasn't even sure how she felt about BDSM yet herself. What she knew was that she'd lived on the fringe of the lifestyle for ten years, and it was time to break out of her perfect little mold and explore the aspects of BDSM she was curious about.

Maybe it would turn into something. Maybe it wouldn't. But she would never know if she didn't try.

Ella pushed away from the table and leaned over to give Sasha a hug. "Gotta get back to the front desk. Talk to you later."

Sasha smiled at her friend's retreating form. What *would* the woman think if Sasha decided to join a club and make it part of her life? Some of her trusted co-workers knew her brother was part owner of Club Zodiac, but probably none of them expected Sasha to come out of her shell and follow in her brother's footsteps.

She tapped her empty water bottle on the table, staring at it without seeing a thing. What was Rowen going to say when he found out she went through with her threat to visit another club? More importantly, what would Lincoln say?"

She chuckled softly, secretly hoping he flipped his lid. At least that way she'd know he gave a shit. In the recesses of her mind, she had to admit half the reason she was doing this was to get a rise out of Lincoln. Or at least attempt to.

She'd had a ridiculous crush on the man for five years. In return, he'd usually scowled at her. In fact, it wasn't until a year ago at her college graduation that she'd ever seen his face light up. Her knees had almost buckled when she caught him clapping, a huge grin wrinkling his eyes as she stepped down from the stage carrying her degree.

Had he been proud of her? It was the first time she'd allowed herself a glimmer of hope she might ever get him to notice her. He'd also handed her a huge bouquet of flowers later that evening at her graduation party and even congratulated her.

The memory of his hand pressed into her lower back for the brief second he'd given her his time was burned into her mind for eternity. Firm pressure from all five fingers. His palm resting right above her butt. The heat from that contact had lit a fire in her she'd forced to remain dormant from the moment she'd first met him four years earlier.

Her body had reacted the same way it had that first day. Nipples hard. Clit throbbing. Wetness dampening her panties.

He'd ruined every bit of progress she'd made in forgetting about him with that touch and his smile and his words and his flowers. He'd caused her to visualize him every time she masturbated. No, that wasn't true. She'd always used him as her source of inspiration, but after that day she'd begun to do so with more frequency.

Did other women masturbate as often as she did?

Lord.

Sasha jerked her head up, realizing she was sitting in the breakroom of her preschool daydreaming. Her face was flushed. Shit.

She hurried to get back to her classroom, but her mind wouldn't stop wandering. Would this experiment of hers work?

She hadn't told Rowen why she wanted to join the club so badly. He would have freaked. But Sasha had multiple goals in mind.

Sure, she was curious about BDSM. Had been for years. But jumping in with both feet at this point in time was a last-ditch effort to prove to herself if she could ever be the kind of woman Lincoln could be interested in. And the side bonus of this exploration? Seeing his reaction.

On Friday, Lincoln was seated at his desk again before opening the club when Rowen walked in. This time Lincoln had summoned his friend. He wasn't looking at his computer, and he didn't give a fuck if he even had a mouse.

Rowen sighed as he walked into the room.

"Shut the door," Lincoln growled.

Rowen's head lowered, along with his shoulders, as he eased the door shut with a snick. He came across the room on heavy feet and lowered into the chair across from the desk with a stiff jaw. "I'm not going to like this, am I?"

Lincoln shook his head. "I got a call from Marcus Pierson."

"Shit," Rowen hissed. Marcus was the owner of Breeze, their main competitor a few miles away. "Please tell me it was a social call."

Lincoln wished he could. "Hardly."

"Fuck," Rowen shouted. "The only thing worse than my sister joining my own damn club is my sister joining another club across town where I can't even keep an eye on her."

"We took a risk… and lost." Lincoln swallowed his frustration.

"So, I'll go over there tonight and drag her out."

"Nope. I'll go."

Rowen looked surprised. "You don't have to do that. I appreciate you making the calls to see if she followed through on her threat, but I can't ask you to go after Sasha."

"You didn't ask." Lincoln inhaled long and slow. "This way, you don't take the heat. She'd never forgive you if you embarrassed her in public."

Rowen's brow furrowed, then he slowly nodded. "Thanks, man. I owe you."

"You don't owe me anything. I just want her to be safe. I don't think it's wise for either of us to blow in there tonight and drag her out by the hair. She'd kill us. But I do want to watch her and see what she does. She's so green. She can't possibly know what she's getting into. Hopefully she just wants to watch and see what all the hype is about." He was banking on it.

"You think if we let her dabble, she'll realize how stupid she's being and stop pestering me?"

"That's what I'm hoping. I don't want her to test the waters without one of us keeping an eye on her, and I know you don't want to watch your sister playing at a kink club."

Rowen visibly shuddered. "It's not even the submission I'm worried about, but you're right. I don't want to see any part of her naked."

Lincoln smiled. "That's my point."

"Am I being unrealistic? She says I have a double standard. After all, I'm a Dom. You're a Dom. We enjoy submissive women on a regular basis. Neither of us views them as somehow weaker or less valued. Perhaps I should back off and let my sister make her own decisions."

Those thoughts had gone through Lincoln's mind over and over lately, even before Sasha had made her ultimatum. He'd known her for five years. He could easily believe she was intrigued by the lifestyle. After all, she'd been coming to the club since she was twelve.

Twelve.

It still pissed him off that John Gilbert had let an innocent young girl spend her formative years in a fetish club. Granted, he'd calmed down about the subject significantly after every employee assured him Sasha had never been inside the actual club. He'd also relaxed his view when he heard about her mother dying and her brother not wanting to leave her home alone at nights. Rowen should be commended for taking care of her.

Nevertheless, he wished at least one of the many adults involved in the decision to let her hang around in the breakroom three nights a week had figured out an alternative solution.

She'd been so young. Influential. How much did she learn about BDSM before most people ever heard the term? He feared she was desensitized at an early age and now wouldn't be able to form normal relationships with men.

Lincoln had watched her curiosity grow over the past several years. He'd seen this coming. There was no denying she was titillated by the concept of dominance and submission.

On more than one occasion when the club wasn't open, he'd caught her wandering through the main room, touching the edges of the equipment. The time he'd found her running a delicate finger around the inside of a pair of metal cuffs, all the air had sucked out of his lungs.

There was no denying she had submissive tendencies, but how much of who Sasha believed herself to be was authentic, and how much of it was learned from overexposure?

"Lincoln?" Rowen yanked him from his thoughts.

He shook his head. "I don't think you're being unrealistic. I think your sister wants to sow some wild oats or something." He leaned forward, putting his elbows on the desk. "You handle things here tonight. Carter will be at the front door. I'll go to Breeze and see what she's up to."

"And if she decides to do a scene with some stranger? What are you going to do?"

Lincoln considered that possibility. "I'm going to stick close by and make sure she's safe. If she wants to try out some apparatus with a knowledgeable Dom, I think it would be prudent to let her get it out of her system. Hopefully she'll realize it doesn't suit her and the subject with be closed without her ever knowing we intervened."

Rowen cringed. "I don't think I could stand by and watch her scene with *anyone*."

Lincoln forced a smile that was wider than he felt inside. "That's why I'm going instead of you."

CHAPTER 3

Sasha was so totally out of her element. She'd spent the day agonizing about what to wear that night, and now that she stood in the entrance to Breeze, she hoped she hadn't made a mistake.

Master Pierson, the owner, greeted her at the door with a warm smile and an outstretched hand. "So nice to see you, Ms. Easton. Welcome to Breeze. I hope you find it as enchanting as your brother's club. He didn't send you here to spy on us, did he?" Master Pierson's eyes danced with humor, tiny wrinkles tipping up at the corners.

She gasped at his comment and licked her lips. "No… Sir. I mean, my brother doesn't even know I'm here." *Unless you told him.* The entire BDSM community probably knew who she was. She was actually surprised they hadn't been given instructions to turn her away.

Did he really think she was a spy? If so, why had he granted her a visitor's pass?

Master Pierson tipped his head back and laughed. "I'm kidding. I'm sure if I were in your shoes, I wouldn't want to attend the same fetish club as my brother either." He took her gently by the arm and led her into an office off the entrance.

She tried to relax, still fretting over her choice in clothing while she tugged on the bottom of her short, tight, black skirt. She had purchased it and the black corset barely covering her small breasts earlier that afternoon. She rounded out the outfit with strappy, black stilettos she hoped wouldn't hurt her feet or cause her to trip and fall during the course of the evening.

Master Pierson pointed at a chair opposite an ornate mahogany desk, and she was grateful to sit before she lost her balance, half from the shoes and half from nerves. "I have a few documents I need you to look over and sign before you can play in my club. Standard stuff you've seen before."

She hadn't. Ever. But he didn't know that.

He cleared his throat and continued, leaning back in his chair, "Tell me, what brings you here tonight? Do you have a particular interest you'd like to explore? I'd be happy to set you up with one of my trusted Doms if you have a fantasy you'd like to fulfill."

Her mouth was dry, and she had to stuff her hands under her thighs to keep from shaking. "Uh… Well, I'm not sure. Mostly I wanted to visit the club and look around, if that's all right."

"Of course. You're welcome to wander around and watch all you'd like. As long as you don't disrupt anyone's scene, you're free to explore. We have a number of members and guests who like to watch. Some of them do so for months or years, either building up the courage to try something new or simply benefitting from the voyeurism itself. Nothing wrong with either scenario." He smiled.

She nodded. It wasn't as if she had no idea what to expect. She'd wandered through Zodiac many times in the past four years. She'd seen more things than most women would in a lifetime. But she'd never had the opportunity to watch at her leisure. Besides her brother, Lincoln was a stickler for the rules. He frowned at her the entire time she was inside Zodiac.

Tonight, she could relax and explore without Lincoln

breathing down her neck with disapproval. "Thank you. I appreciate your warm welcome."

"Well, I'll let you look over the paperwork and check on you in a few minutes." He pushed from his chair and silently left the room.

She sincerely doubted every guest got this kind of reception. But, like he'd indicated, she wasn't an ordinary visitor.

Although she'd never signed a contract of any sort to enter a club before, she had researched them online, and she was relieved to find this contract to be nearly identical to everything she'd read.

It was ridiculous that she'd never seen a contract at her brother's club, but he'd managed to keep her out of nearly everything pertaining to Zodiac for ten years. And he showed no sign he would ever let up.

She'd considered going behind his back and speaking directly to Lincoln, but then chickened out. The man hardly tolerated her as it was. No way in hell would he have permitted her to join the club without telling her brother.

Fifteen minutes later she had everything signed and returned to Master Pierson, and she found herself free to roam the club. It was a relief. Not one person stared at her strangely or shot her a disapproving glance as she followed Master Pierson deeper into the club.

Granted, it was possible her choice of clothing helped her blend in better than anything she'd ever worn at Zodiac. But she also suspected every employee and half the patrons of Zodiac had been given strict instructions to shun her. Successfully.

Master Pierson led her directly toward a woman standing to one side of the main room. "Sasha, this is Faith. She's one of the dungeon monitors tonight. You'll recognize our monitors by the red bands around their biceps."

Faith smiled briefly at Sasha. Her gorgeous blue eyes were mesmerizing, but they held a deep sorrow no one could miss.

"Welcome to Breeze," she stated before her gaze shot back toward the room, scanning.

Sasha stared at Faith for another moment, wondering what her story was. She was surprised to find such a petite woman working as one of the dungeon monitors. Not that there was any reason why a female couldn't fill the role, but this tiny blonde was about the same height as Sasha. She couldn't be more than five four. If anything got out of hand, no way would Faith be able to physically intervene.

The tell-tale arm band covered a black, fitted, long-sleeved blouse. Faith also wore snug black jeans and black flats. Ordinary clothing, except nothing was ordinary about this woman.

With a deep breath, Sasha turned her attention back to Master Pierson as he pointed out another dungeon monitor several yards away. "I'll leave you to it. If you have any questions, don't hesitate to find me or ask one of the monitors."

She nodded and then wandered into the main room and took in the various scenes already underway. The room was similar to Zodiac in many respects, which helped calm her nerves. The lighting was dim, the walls, tile, and ceiling all black. It was only ten o'clock so things were just getting started.

Setting her sights on a couple preparing to use a spanking bench, she decided to head that direction and observe. Harmless enough.

The woman was about her height, five foot four. She weighed more than Sasha, but she was obviously comfortable in her skin. Sasha had always been self-conscious about her small frame. No matter what she ate, she never seemed to fill out. She glanced down at her chest for the millionth time and tugged on the corset to ensure it still covered her small breasts. She'd been shocked when the woman at the fetish store had helped fit her into the bustier, giving her the first actual cleavage Sasha had ever seen on herself.

She had to admit the tight lace and satin garment made her feel sexy. Also a first. It gave her confidence.

Several people were gathered to observe the couple at the spanking bench, and Sasha joined them. The woman calmly removed every stitch of clothing at a nod of her Dom's head. She didn't exhibit any signs of self-consciousness, not even covering her breasts with a hand. In fact, she kept her gaze downcast and her legs parted when she finished disrobing.

Her Dom wore black leather pants and a matching vest that left his chest bare at the top, a sprinkling of hair visible. He was in his mid-forties, she judged, and his serious expression as he slowly circled his submissive made Sasha's panties wet.

She stood frozen in her spot while she watched the scene unfold. Mesmerized, and not a little aroused. The woman had long black hair, which her Dom gathered at her back and braided. After tying the ends with a strip of leather, he pointed to the bench.

They were comfortable with each other, and it was obvious they'd done this before because few words were exchanged between them and those were whispered into the sub's ear at a volume Sasha couldn't discern.

By the time the woman was situated on the bench, her torso resting on about six inches of padding with her elbows and knees on smaller padded sections, Sasha couldn't blink. Her heart raced as the Dom rounded the woman again and then slowly secured her ankles and wrists to the bench.

He then turned some sort of crank between the sub's knees that made Sasha flinch as it creaked and spread the sub's legs wider.

Maybe there was some merit to what Master Pierson had said to her earlier. Sasha couldn't imagine ever finding herself in the position this woman was in, but it was titillating as hell to watch. Her breasts swelled, and she crossed one arm over them to apply pressure to her aching nipples.

No one seemed to be paying particular attention to her, so she continued to watch the scene, lost in her own world, her arousal growing by the second.

The Dom reached into a large duffle bag at his feet and pulled out a flogger. It was clearly loved, with thick lengths of supple leather that looked soft enough to tease more than cause any real pain. Part of her was a bit frightened, but her damn clit jumped to attention at the same time.

No matter how much research she'd done over the years, she had no way of being fully prepared to watch a scene in person. She knew the names of every sort of kink toy available to man. She'd seen porn. She'd even masturbated to it. But watching it unfold up close was another thing. The few times she'd caught a glimpse inside Zodiac while it was open didn't compare to this experience tonight.

Shocking her, the Dom trailed a finger slowly down his sub's spine, through her butt crack, and lower until he swiped it across her sex. The woman bucked her hips the few inches she was able to move, a soft moan escaping her lips.

Her eyes were closed, and her mouth hung open in bliss. Interesting, because the scene hadn't even started yet. But Sasha fully understood. She too was about to orgasm just from watching.

The man trailed his fingertips all over the sub's body for long minutes as she relaxed her muscles and stopped fighting against the restraints. Finally, he stepped back, lifted the flogger in the air, and let it land on his sub's butt cheeks.

She didn't even flinch. Not surprising since the lengths of leather had barely touched her. In fact, the woman looked even more relaxed as if she'd been waiting for a massage all day and it was finally happening.

As the Dom set up a rhythm and artfully landed repeated thuds of the flogger against his sub's butt cheeks and then her shoulder blades, Sasha too was lulled by the rhythmic pattern. Her muscles lost some of their tension. She could watch this sort of scene all day.

She also thought it would feel nice to be the recipient of a flogging if this is how it always went down.

She glanced around the room. She was here to witness. She didn't want to spend too much time on the flogging scene.

Another corner caught her eye at the sharp yelp of a woman. Sasha lifted her gaze and then stepped away from the flogging to see what made the other sub wince.

This sub was also a woman. She was skinny and tall. Naked like the first sub. Her breasts were high and small. Her nipples puckered. She wasn't attached to a particular piece of equipment. Instead, she wore thick leather bands on her arms with eye rings, and they were attached to two lengths of chain that came down from the ceiling.

She was totally exposed in the center of the space. A blindfold covered her eyes, tied behind her head in a thick knot over short-cropped, blue-tipped hair.

A man was circling her. He was of average height and build. Bare feet. Jeans that were frayed at the ends. No shirt. His gaze was intense, and gripped in his hand was a crop—long and thin and black with a flat leather end. It sent a chill down Sasha's spine.

Another glance at the woman told Sasha she'd already received her first strike—right across her thighs. A red, angry welt had raised. The woman was gasping for breath, her head tipped back, her spine stiff.

Sasha couldn't imagine why anyone would do this. The flogging she almost understood. It looked like a soothing massage. Even she wouldn't mind experiencing it. But this crop? Never.

She crossed one foot over the other and squeezed her thighs together as she waited.

The Dom circled, making his sub wait. Anticipation being his goal.

When the hiss of the leather finally rushed through the air,

Sasha flinched, and she gasped when it hit its target. She immediately glanced around to ensure she hadn't reacted too loudly. No one was looking at her. Thank God.

The crack of the crop was much louder than the thud of the flogger. The result was much more evident too. Another welt rose, this time across the sub's butt cheeks.

Sasha bit her bottom lip, trying to understand the logic and failing. She was here to watch. Learn. Explore. No way in hell would she be attempting anything like this.

She gritted her teeth as another swoosh of the crop sailed through the air, this time landing across the sub's shoulder blade. Obviously the goal was to keep the poor woman guessing because the Dom didn't strike with any sort of pattern, rhyme, or reason.

It was time to move on.

Lincoln arrived at Breeze early. He was happy to find out he'd gotten there before Sasha. It made it easy for him to touch base with Pierson and slip into the perfect dark corner to take in the room while he waited.

Breeze was not much different from Zodiac. This spacious main room was dark with dim lighting. He knew there were smaller rooms for private scenes. Behind him there was also a lounge area for aftercare.

Had he made the right decision in not permitting Sasha to join Club Zodiac? He was starting to doubt the wisdom of that choice. It would have been easier to keep an eye on her in his own club.

His home away from home.

Sure, he'd been young when he bought the club—twenty-five— but what he lacked in age, he made up for in experience. He'd been inside clubs observing and learning since he was seventeen. He'd met his mentor—Master Christopher—that year, and the man had taught him everything he knew over the next several years. Even when Lincoln graduated from high school and joined the army, he still saw his mentor every chance he could when he was on leave.

Lincoln owed so much to Master Christopher. His love for BDSM. His affinity for sadism. His expertise with nearly every tool. Even his ability to fund the club. Master Christopher had not only taught Lincoln how to be the best sadist in Miami, but he'd also given Lincoln the gift of a sizable chunk of cash to purchase Club Zodiac.

Lincoln shook the nostalgic thoughts from his mind as he glanced around the room again. Thank God Marcus Pierson was a good man and friend. If he hadn't permitted Lincoln to follow Sasha around this evening, Lincoln wasn't sure how he would have managed this situation.

Suddenly, he spotted her. *Damn.* He did a triple take to make sure his eyes weren't deceiving him.

Where the fuck did she get that outfit? He'd never seen her wearing anything that resembled what she had on tonight. She was a preschool teacher for crying out loud. She wore pastel sundresses and crop pants and cute feminine sweaters and blouses. They made her look younger than she was… and pure.

Not tight black skirts and corsets.

If it hadn't been for her fucking awesome long brown hair, he never would have found her. As it was, as soon as he spotted her, he had to grip the edge of the wall he was hiding against.

Holy mother of God. The woman had no idea what she did to men. Every man in the place had taken notice. Many of them probably didn't know who she was. All of them were drooling and glancing.

Sasha didn't have a fucking clue.

Lincoln adjusted his cock and reminded himself for the thousandth time why he was there. He had a job. Keep Sasha safe. That description did not include lusting after her sweet body.

Rowen would punch him in the face if he saw how Lincoln was salivating.

Sasha made his heart pound. It took every ounce of energy he had to remain on the fringes of the room and let her be.

As Sasha moved from the innocent flogging scene to the far more hardcore cropping scene, he stood still, watching, waiting, stiffening. Not breathing.

In an ideal world, he intended to remain in the shadows, keep an eye on Sasha, and then slip out after she decided to leave. How long would she stay? Her body language told everyone in the room she was green. She flinched occasionally, blushed, crossed her legs, and even squeezed her breasts with one forearm.

Every move made Lincoln adjust his cock.

There was another man watching her too. Master Colin. Lincoln gritted his teeth as he watched Colin's gaze roam up and down Sasha's body as if he wanted to devour her.

Not tonight, Colin.

Colin was one of the good guys, though. It wasn't his fault a beautiful woman had come to the club. He probably didn't know who Sasha was. And it was entirely possible Pierson had asked Colin to follow her. It wasn't as though Lincoln could trail along behind her himself.

His intention was for her to never know he'd been there.

Make sure she's safe. Get out of here. Take a cold shower.

Whatever you do, do not approach her. It will end badly.

CHAPTER 4

Sasha was totally mesmerized by the next scene in front of her when someone touched her bare shoulder, making her twist around to find a hard male chest invading her personal space. She lifted her gaze to find a man smiling. "Master Pierson wanted me to check on you. Said you're new here."

She nodded. "I am. Thank you."

He glanced at the spanking scene and back at her. "You're intrigued. Have you ever been spanked before?"

She shook her head rapidly. "No. I… Uh… No," she stammered.

"You want to experience it? I'd be happy to give you a demonstration if you'd like." He lifted a hand to shake hers. "Master Colin."

"Sasha." She shook his warm hand, still trying to wrap her mind around his suggestion. Did she want him to spank her? Lord, she'd only been at the club half an hour. Was she ready for something like that?

Her heart had only moments ago stopped beating out of her chest from witnessing the previous scene with the crop. The spanking scene was far more her speed. At least to watch. There was a difference between witnessing and participating, though.

He didn't say anything else, clearly giving her time to consider the option. He was handsome. Thirty-something. Five ten maybe. Brown hair cropped short. He wasn't wearing fetish clothing, but instead blue jeans and a black T-shirt. Harmless.

She hadn't come to Breeze with any particular expectations, but now that she was presented with the opportunity to try something new, she decided to grab it. *You only live once.* "Sure. I, uh... I'd like that."

His smile grew, and he took her elbow and led her from the scene.

She was nervous. Very nervous. But as she glanced around, she spotted the club monitors in several corners of the room. Faith was following her with her gaze and nodded. There was no reason to be concerned. Besides, if Master Pierson sent Master Colin to check on her, she had to assume he was well vetted. She was safe. She blew out a breath and tried to calm her nerves.

Master Colin led her across the room toward a St. Andrew's cross, the giant wooden X looming larger than life. When they arrived, he slid his hands to her hips from behind and encouraged her to step closer.

She bit her bottom lip and closed her eyes, trying to gather courage.

Master Colin eased his hands up her sides and then her arms as he lifted them gently into the air. He set them on the cross and tapped her wrists. "Don't move," he whispered. She lifted her gaze to watch him remove a peg from higher up the wood and reinsert it at the level of her hand. He did the same on the other side and then spoke again. "Grab the pegs, Sasha."

She did as instructed, acutely aware of her chest rising and falling, hoping her nipples remained covered by the front of the corset.

"Now relax. I can sense you're a newbie. I'm not going to

restrain you physically. Instead, I want you to hold on to the cross on your own. Understand?"

"Yes, Sir." The word came out naturally.

"Any time you scene with someone, whether or not you know them, always use a safeword. I'm partial to *red*. Okay?"

"Yes, Sir."

"Perfect. Relax, Sasha. I'm not going to hurt you. This is just a demonstration. If you like it, you can ask someone to spank you harder next time. For tonight, I'll strike you lightly so you can experience the way it feels to have a hand on your bottom."

She nodded.

"Breathe, Sasha," he whispered close to her ear. "Deep breaths."

She tried, concentrating on inhaling and exhaling.

Meanwhile Master Colin stroked her skin.

She closed her eyes again, leaning her forehead against the cross. She didn't know this man. It seemed crazy to let a stranger touch her like this. But since her stubborn brother wouldn't let her play with the people she knew, she needed to suck it up.

Her mind wandered as Master Colin's fingers glided up and down her arms and then across her bare shoulders. She enjoyed the calming strokes, but couldn't focus on the person touching her. Instead, she found herself picturing someone else in his place.

Lincoln.

She wished she could think of anyone else on earth stroking her skin, but as usual, Lincoln filled her fantasy. He had for years. Five of them. Every time she closed her eyes and touched herself, she pictured Zodiac's owner controlling her.

It was irrational. After all, he didn't even like her. Sure, he'd eventually warmed enough to glance her way and grunt at her on occasion, but he obviously didn't care for her as anyone other than his friend's little sister. Perhaps his lack of interest was what attracted her to him. Call her crazy, but maybe visualizing Lincoln was safe.

Because it would never happen.

He was an apparition. A fantasy. Not someone real. A sexy body. A stern domineering face. Nothing else. Two-dimensional.

When Master Colin's hand smoothed down the fabric covering her butt, she gritted her teeth. Could she do this? She wanted to. She needed to experience new things.

"You okay, Sasha?"

"Yes, Sir," she murmured.

"I'm going to spank you now. Easy. It won't even leave a pink mark."

"Okay, Sir." She braced herself, trying to remain loose and probably failing.

When his hand landed on the upper swell of her butt, she blew out a breath. It wasn't bad. In fact, it didn't hurt at all.

"You okay?"

"Yes, Sir."

"More?"

"Yes, please, Sir." She wasn't sure she liked it, but she wanted him to continue.

Master Colin set a hand on her shoulder and gave her two more quick swats to the same spot on her upper cheeks.

She exhaled, finding the spanking to be oddly boring.

His hand moved lower next, and he swatted her bare thighs, harder, but not hard enough to hurt. When he rubbed the backs of her legs, she tried not to move. She wasn't aroused. She wasn't sure she even liked him touching her like that. She didn't know him, and his touch felt almost clinical. She was floating, sort of detached, as if she were watching instead of experiencing.

"More?" he asked, his lips close to her ear.

"Yes, Sir," she whispered. She had no idea why she consented to continuing this scene, but she forced herself to stay in the moment. If she didn't, how would she know what she liked?

Master Colin touched the bottom of her skirt with the tips of his fingers and slowly eased it up her butt cheeks. She pursed her lips, willing herself to let him continue.

When he had the bottoms of her globes exposed, he spanked her bare butt with his other hand.

Sasha yelped and jumped backward, releasing the cross.

"Sasha?" His voice was far away.

Panic filled her. It was hard to explain. It had nothing to do with the spanking. It was something else.

She couldn't face him. In fact, she was afraid she might fall in her high heels as she fled without glancing back. Unease crept up her spine as she rushed to the right of the cross and slammed straight into the hard chest of another man.

She set her hands on the man's pecs and shoved, needing to escape the room and her embarrassment. What was wrong with her?

She lifted her gaze, expecting to find a monitor or the owner in her space, but instead, the breath whooshed from her lungs, her eyes going wide. "Lincoln?"

CHAPTER 5

Lincoln was struggling to find his speech almost as badly as Sasha. He'd been watching her for almost an hour as she observed the flogging and the cropping and a spanking and then followed this stranger to the St. Andrew's cross. He couldn't believe how readily she'd agreed to do a scene.

With a total stranger.

Granted, Lincoln knew the man. If he hadn't been well-acquainted with Master Colin, he never would have permitted Sasha to do something so foolish. But under the circumstances, since Lincoln's main goal was to get Sasha to give up this ridiculous interest in BDSM, he forced himself to hang back and watch.

Lincoln also knew he wasn't being fair. He definitely felt a double standard when it came to Sasha that he'd never felt toward any other submissive, male or female. Except Sasha was not a submissive.

Master Colin had done nothing wrong. He'd followed every proper protocol, taking things slowly, reassuring her, giving her a safeword, checking in often. There was no way he could have read the apprehension Lincoln saw on Sasha's face.

For one thing, Sasha had hidden her expression with her hair. For another thing, she'd schooled her voice to give nothing away every time she answered him. She'd even managed to keep her body relatively loose. She had done her research, knew what to say and how to act. But she hadn't been able to anticipate her reaction.

What made her jump out of the scene? Was it the spanking? Lincoln didn't think so. Master Colin hadn't struck her any harder that last time than the previous swats. No. It was something else that triggered her. Maybe it was the clothes she'd worn? Or the position stretched out on the cross? Or had something flashed through her mind at that precise moment to set her off?

Lincoln could kick himself for waiting about two seconds too long to intervene, but on the other hand, no actual harm was done to her, and he had to hope she'd received enough of a jolt to give up this foolish desire to join a club.

Master Colin stood behind her, eyes wide, mouth hanging open. He was about to speak when Lincoln shook his head, cutting him off. He would assure the man he'd done nothing wrong later. For now, he just wanted him to back off.

Master Colin nodded and turned away, his expression filled with concern.

A petite blonde woman rushed forward from behind Sasha next, her brow furrowed. She wore the red band of the dungeon monitors. As she opened her mouth to speak, Lincoln shook her off also, hoping he communicated he had things under control with his gaze.

The blonde hesitated, frowning, not backing off.

Sasha set her forehead against Lincoln's chest and fisted his T-shirt in her hands at his sides. Her shoulders heaved. She was crying.

His chest seized. Dammit. Without thinking, he leaned down, swept her small body into his arms, and cradled her against his chest. With a nod to the blonde monitor, he spun around and headed to the aftercare room.

Seconds later, he was seated on a leather couch, Sasha's sweet body across his lap, her face still buried in his chest. He was relieved no one else currently occupied the room.

He tugged a throw blanket off the arm of the couch and wrapped it around her. If nothing else, at least he wouldn't have to continue to stare at her sexy body in the skimpy outfit she wore. When had she purchased fetish wear?

Tonight she was not presenting herself as someone who taught preschool by day and hung with her girlfriends or her brother in the evenings. Tonight she was a sexy vixen who had turned the heads of everyone in the club. Not that she didn't also draw an equal amount of attention in her usual innocent attire.

Lincoln had to get a grip on his growing erection before she realized what was pressing against her thigh. Dammit. This was not happening to him. He was here to rescue his friend's sister, not lust after her.

Surely his attraction had nothing to do with Sasha herself and everything to do with how she'd so innocently watched the flogging scene with wide eyes and pink cheeks, her arm crossed over her breasts to pinch off the swell of her nipples.

He'd nearly choked watching her react to the scene.

Yeah. He'd missed nothing. He wasn't sure he'd even blinked from the moment she'd entered the main room of the club.

When she'd moved toward the man wielding the crop, she'd tensed, flinched, closed her eyes. She had not been turned on. Her ardor had completely tamped down.

And then the spanking scene. It had been mesmerizing watching her entire demeanor switch back to curious as she loosened her frame and eased her legs apart. She undoubtedly had no idea she'd done so.

Meanwhile, Lincoln's cock had stiffened so hard it probably had zipper grooves along it. She was such an open book, her every reaction etched on her face. The way her cheeks pinkened or turned completely white. The way her eyes went wide or narrow. So expressive. So damn sexy. So innocent.

That innocence was what fueled him to protect her. She didn't belong in this world. Had she figured that out? He hoped so. Maybe she was titillated by it, but she needed to flush it out of her system and move on. Hell, *he* needed her to flush it out of her system and move on.

Lincoln knew Marcus well enough to know that he ran the same tight ship as Lincoln. He would be aware of everything and ensure that nothing got overlooked. In fact, the owner of Breeze leaned into the room at that moment as if he'd read Lincoln's mind. He would probably be grateful Lincoln had been there to save Sasha from her foolish self so he didn't have to deal with her himself.

Lincoln gave him a nod, letting him know he had it under control.

Marcus's eyes were drawn together, but his shoulders relaxed as he turned around and left them alone. It was early still by club standards. Most scenes were just getting underway, which meant few people would be seeking the solace of aftercare for a while.

Lincoln had never had this much contact with Sasha. *She's in my lap. I'm holding her entire body.* He could count the number of times he'd touched her on one hand, starting with the night he'd met her and taken her hand in his.

Not to say he didn't remember that moment five years ago. He did, with perfect clarity. He'd been drawn to her from the instant he'd entered the room. He'd known she was Rowen's sister. He'd also known Rowen was twenty-seven. At no point did it occur to him that his sister was ten years younger than him.

For the rest of Lincoln's life, he would regret the way he so rudely reacted to finding out she was seventeen. He'd hurt her. Badly. There was no doubt. He'd also looked like an ass in front of everyone in the room who had become his employees that day.

He could only explain his behavior as a reaction to shock and disappointment at finding out Sasha was not only underage, but knew nothing about the lifestyle.

Lincoln himself had only been twenty-five that day, but he'd lived enough life for a forty-year-old man, and he knew several things for certain—one of which was that he was a sadist. He enjoyed helping submissives find release through various levels of pain. He was well-known in the club and even in Miami for his play with masochists at whatever level they needed. Both women and men came to him to get their fetish fulfilled.

That was just where his interest lay. His kink ran deep. His desires unwavering. He'd known it was his calling since he was seventeen and sneaking into a club he had no business attending. The same age as Sasha had been when he acted like she was a child and chastised her verbally in front of everyone. But dammit, it was different for her. She was innocent. She'd become a preschool teacher for fuck's sake.

Sure, he knew half his issue with Sasha was aggravation with himself for not only lusting after her that first day but not being able to shake the desire in all these years.

The truth was, Lincoln was a sadist who needed a masochist in his life to fulfill him.

Sasha Easton would never be that woman.

She was the polar opposite. Soft and gentle. Loving and sweet. Maybe she could dabble in the fringe of the fetish world for an hour or two with the right partner, but she was no masochist. And she would scream and run if she had any idea what sort of fantasies he had. Several of which revolved around her.

His fantasies were just that—day dreams. Nothing more. Visions of Sasha on her knees submitting to him had plagued him for too many years.

The woman had some sort of hold on him he couldn't shake. But he'd never act on it. Never mention it to a single soul. He couldn't. She wasn't right for him. He certainly wasn't right for her. She was nothing more than a cute girl with a hot body which he had twisted into something totally unobtainable in his mind. In fact, he had intentionally never permitted himself to get to know her over the years in order to keep the driving need to own her at bay.

Own her? That thought scared the fuck out of him. He didn't own anyone. He played. He dominated. He sent his submissives home. He didn't keep them. He couldn't. His twisted needs wouldn't jibe with anyone else's. Especially not Sasha's.

The bottom line was he was selfish. He could not have her for himself, and he couldn't bear the idea of watching her submit to another Dom, so he needed her to get this idea out of her head and move on to live a nice vanilla life.

Admittedly, his thoughts confused him. Visions of Sasha were unlike any other images he had for other women. They made no sense. They boggled his mind. He'd pushed them aside. Every time. For years.

He squeezed his eyes closed and forced himself back into the moment, stroking his hand over the soft skin of her arm while holding her lower back to keep her from slipping out of his grasp.

"Sasha?" he whispered as he smoothed his hand up to her shoulder and out from under the blanket to cup her face. "Look at me, sweetheart." *Sweetheart?* Jesus.

She shook her head, burrowing tighter against him. "I'm so stupid," she muttered. "What was I thinking?"

"You were thinking you wanted to see what all the hype was about. It's natural. You were curious." He nudged her chin again, but she didn't budge. "You were also lucky. If I hadn't been here, you would really be in a bind right now."

That wasn't necessarily true. Master Colin could have handled things. He was a seasoned Master. He would have stopped the scene immediately and been sitting where Lincoln was right now.

Lincoln gritted his teeth at the idea of Colin holding Sasha or even touching her skin. It had been hard enough to watch the man stroke her arms and shoulder. Lincoln had nearly slammed a fist into the wall when Colin had lifted her skirt, exposing the bottom swell of her cheeks.

Sasha shuddered, her fingers finding his T-shirt and fisting the cotton again. "You knew I was going to be here."

He could barely hear her. "Yes."

She groaned, lifting her face finally. "Rowen's going to kill me when he hears about this."

He shook his head, meeting her gaze. "No, he isn't. He won't even know."

She lifted her brows.

"I mean, he knows you're here, but he doesn't have to find out the details." He wanted to wipe that frightened look from her face. He wanted to kiss her forehead. Hell, he focused on her full pink lips and considered kissing her right on the mouth.

Lord, Lincoln. Get a fucking grip.

She calmed slightly, swallowing. Her face was streaked with tears.

Lincoln lifted his hand and wiped them away with the pad of his thumb. He needed to administer aftercare like he would with any sub. "Talk to me about what happened in there, sweetheart."

Jesus, fuck, Lincoln, stop using that endearment.

She suddenly stiffened, her eyes wide. "Oh God. Do you think I messed up anyone else's scene? How loud was I?" She bit her lower lip, her face changing to one of concern and worry.

Here she was recovering after probably the most embarrassing moment in her life, and she was worried about other people?

Lincoln had to swallow his own emotions. Sasha Easton was an absolute angel. Her heart was golden. Her soul was so open and kind.

"Sweetheart, stop worrying. No one noticed. You weren't nearly as obvious as it must seem." He stroked his fingers through the hair at her forehead.

"What about Master Colin? Will he get in trouble or

something?"

Lincoln shook his head. "No. It's fine. I'll talk to him. Explain things."

She trembled. "Can't you just take me home?"

He smiled, cupping her face again and then easing his hand to the back of her neck to thread his fingers in her thick curls. They were as soft as he'd always imagined. Thick. Lush. He held still to keep from stroking his fingers through them. "Yes. After you talk to me. Surely you've done enough research to know a good Dom always guides his sub through the proper amount of aftercare."

"You're not my Dom," she pointed out.

He had to give her credit for being quick and sharp after her crying jig. "True, but I'm the Dom currently holding you in my lap. I'm also the Dom who is going to talk you through your reaction to that scene." *Until you realize you aren't cut out for the lifestyle and stop trying to play in clubs while giving me a heart attack.*

She blew out a breath and rolled her eyes. "It's no big deal. I shouldn't have rushed things. I panicked."

"When Master Colin spanked you? Was the swat too hard?" He knew it wasn't.

"No." She shook her head. "It wasn't the spanking. That part felt sort of clinical. I think… I think it was the way he lifted my skirt." She dipped her face from his view. "I didn't like thinking other people in the room could see my bare butt."

He stared at the top of her head, shocked. And damn, kinda glad. At least he wasn't the only one in the room who thought her naked body shouldn't be ogled by other people. *Why, big guy? You want to be the only one who gets to see her naked?* No. Fuck no. He couldn't go there. No one should be ogling Sasha naked. Especially not him.

However, maybe she was seeing the light. He could work with this. Convince her to give up this obsession.

She continued, "I guess I wasn't ready for that. Hadn't prepared myself mentally to be naked in public. I'll be more careful next time. Take it slower. Maybe watch for a few more weeks before I try to do a scene myself."

"Next time?" He spoke louder than he'd intended.

She lifted her face and furrowed her brow. "Yes. Please tell me you didn't come here to talk me out of joining a club or hoping I would work it out of my system." She pushed against his chest and leaned back, crossing her arms in a way that only drew more attention to her cleavage.

Lincoln swallowed, forcing his gaze from her chest to her eyes. Normally he enjoyed more than a handful of a woman's boobs. But somehow Sasha's smaller breasts were making his mouth water. "Of course not," he lied. "I came here to make sure you were safe. I told you that."

"My brother sent you."

"No. I volunteered."

She gave another dramatic eye roll, which pushed him over the edge.

He grabbed her chin and waited until she looked him in the eye. "If you roll your eyes like that again, you're going to get a much better taste of what it feels like to have your bottom spanked than what Master Colin demonstrated." The words were out of his mouth before he could stop them. His cock was also fully erect and insistent. *Fuck.*

Neither of those reactions were common for him. He was always in control of his words and his dick. Always. Or he had been until tonight.

Sasha's face turned bright red and her eyes went wide. She didn't say a word.

Damn if he didn't wish she would test him. Somehow he knew she would not freak out at the touch of *his* hand on her bottom the way she had with Colin. *Shit.*

"You with me?" he demanded, again without properly filtering his words.

"Yes, Sir." She swallowed.

He stopped breathing. Holy mother of God. Those two words, spoken to him from the lips of this sweet, innocent angel threatened to make him come in his jeans without contact.

He never reacted like that to a woman. Never. The dominance he practiced was separate from his sexual needs. What was this little minx doing to him?

He forced himself to pull it together, taking a second to give himself a pep talk. He didn't have the luxury of glancing away or closing his eyes. Nope. Because this sweet newbie was still staring at him with her wide gaze and questioning looks. Her breaths were shallow. Her face red. Her chest rose and fell, her breasts lifting with every movement.

He needed to get her to talk about the scene some more. Work it out. He understood the exposure, but that was the last straw. She had been stiff the entire time. "Now, tell me what you felt when Master Colin spanked you, before he lifted your skirt, I mean. What did you mean by clinical?" He'd watched the way she grew more and more uncomfortable with each swat of Colin's hand. It wasn't like Colin had hit her hard. There already wouldn't be any evidence of his palm print.

Not that Lincoln intended to see for himself.

She licked her lips and chewed on the bottom one a moment before answering him. "I didn't feel connected to him, I guess. I was sort of out of my body. Like it was happening to someone else. It didn't hurt or anything. I just didn't want…"

He waited, and when she didn't continue, he prompted, "You didn't want what?"

"A stranger to touch me like that," she finished, her gaze lowering again.

His heart thumped. She was killing him. "Okay, that makes sense. A lot of people prefer to be with someone they know when they're in intimate situations. Most people need to develop a rapport, build trust. That's true in any relationship, not just within the lifestyle. You don't know Master Colin." What the ever-

49

loving hell was he saying? He needed to be telling her she wasn't cut out for BDSM, not helping her think it was possible with someone else.

"Right." She seemed to ponder his ill-advised words. *Great.*

He needed to right his wrong. "Maybe you aren't cut out for this lifestyle. Not everyone is. There's no shame in preferring a vanilla relationship."

She scrunched up her brow and shot him a glare. "What are you talking about? It was one scene. I went into it too fast. I didn't know that man. He touched my bare ass. It doesn't mean I'm not submissive."

He sighed.

"Shit." She released her arms to shove on his chest again, scrambling to get off his lap.

He was so shocked by her sudden movement that he couldn't stop her. In moments, she was standing a foot away from him, the blanket falling to the floor. "You planned this." Her voice was louder. "You absolutely planned this. My brother helped you." She pointed a finger at him.

Her skirt was askew and had risen high on her thighs. Her corset was also crooked and precariously in danger of exposing her nipples.

He lifted both hands in defeat, palms out. To continue to deny the truth would only make things worse. "We thought—"

She fumed, nearly screaming as she stomped her foot and fisted her hands at her sides. "You thought you knew what was best for me. That's what you thought. Both of you. Don't act like my sexuality is something I should be ashamed of.

"I'm tired of everyone acting like I'm a child. It's growing annoying. I'm a grown woman. I'm not that seventeen-year-old girl you met in the breakroom five years ago. I'm not the girl you humiliated in front of the entire staff with your highhandedness and domineering ways." Tears ran down her face and her voice cracked.

Fuck. He'd really fucked up. He'd fucked up then, and he was still fucking up now. No matter what he thought about her or how hard he'd tried to ignore his weird attraction to her all these years, she was right. He hadn't meant to shame her, only protect her. And himself. He was an ass.

He needed to admit it. "You're right."

Her chest heaved, and she opened her mouth to continue her rant, but stopped short. "I'm right?"

"Yes." He was so totally going to kick himself later for even thinking his next words, let alone speaking them out loud, but he did it anyway. "You're right. I was a dick that night I met you. And you deserve to explore this curiosity you have with submission. No one should deny you the opportunity, nor the right to own your feelings. If you want to give submission a try, you should do so."

She stared at him, leery, her eyes narrowing.

His next words were going to get him killed by her brother, but again, he spoke them anyway, knowing this might be the only way. "Let me train you."

She paused, and then she stumbled backward.

He leaped to his feet and reached out a hand to grab her before she fell on her ass. Steadying her upright with both hands on her elbows, he silently shot himself in the head.

Yes. Rowen was going to have him executed.

He eased one hand up her arm and cupped her face. He lifted her chin while he continued to dig his early grave. "Look at me, sweetheart."

She looked completely shocked when she did as he told her.

"If you want to explore your submission, let me be the one to train you. It's the best scenario you're going to get. I'm safe. You know me. You won't have to worry about meeting someone who doesn't treat you with respect or who makes you nervous."

"*You* make me nervous," she interrupted.

He chuckled. "Touché." But this was veering way off track.

Train her? Good fucking God. He needed to right this. He could do it. *Make some demands. Do it now.* "The first behavior I'm going to insist you correct is this constant insubordination and that mouthy way you blurt out the first thing that comes to mind. If you accept my proposal, I want you to address me appropriately from now on. And, I expect you to think before you speak. No more lashing out at me verbally. I won't tolerate such insolence. Are we clear?" He lifted a brow, hopeful.

He wasn't even sure what the fuck he was hoping for. His stupid self wanted her to take him up on his offer. His more rational self pushed the boundaries with that last little speech in the hopes she would renege and turn him down. Now would be the perfect moment for her to back out.

Best case scenario, instead of digging her heels in, she would be horrified by his demands and tell him to go fuck himself.

She breathed in and out, seemingly wrapping her head around his sudden proposal. Finally, she spoke. "Yes, Sir."

Well, fuck. His dick jumped. He couldn't stop the next words from adding to the train wreck. "Good girl."

"My brother..."

He lifted another brow. Two seconds and already she was speaking out of line.

"Sorry, Sir. But..."

"Your brother... Well, after he screams at me and throws everything not nailed down around my office, he'll see reason. He'll understand this is the best way to help you find yourself in the safest environment possible." Would he? Because Lincoln didn't even believe his own words.

She nodded slowly.

"I realize there are a lot of details to work out. I want you to know my only intention is to train you. I won't take advantage of you. Do we have an agreement?"

She hesitated again, making his heart stop, and then, "Yes, Sir. We have an agreement."

CHAPTER 6

"You *what?*"

As expected, Rowen didn't take the news well at all. He glanced around Lincoln's office, grabbed the first thing he could get his hands on—a magazine off the coffee table—and launched it across the room. It hit the window, but unfortunately it didn't have the dramatic effect Rowen was going for.

"I can't believe you." He stomped in a haphazard circle, hands on his head. "This is my sister we're talking about, not some slave girl you picked up on the street corner."

Lincoln pulled his shoulders back and set his hands on his hips. "Watch it, Easton. I'm not some flunky asshole who wants to take advantage of your sister, and you know it. I've never had a Master/slave relationship, and I don't intend to start now."

Lincoln pointed a finger at his friend and continued. "And if I ever hear you imply your sister is for sale again, I'll beat the shit out of you myself."

Rowen spun around. "Please. Don't you dare lecture me. I'm not the asshole who followed her to Breeze this evening to ensure she lost interest in the lifestyle, and instead came back three hours later with a hard-on the size of Texas and some elaborate plan to train her to be his own perfect submissive." He leaned in closer. "She's not even your type, Walsh."

Yeah, Rowen was pissed. And Lincoln couldn't blame him.

The door to the office was pushed open, and Carter stepped inside, closing it behind him. "What the hell is going on in here? You two are yelling so loud the entire club can hear you."

Rowen faced their third partner and waved a hand through the air as he sarcastically brought him up to speed. "Lincoln here apparently hasn't gotten laid in a while, so he thinks it's a good idea to use my sister to remind himself what it feels like to have his cock inside a woman."

"Oh, for fuck's sake." Lincoln fumed. Rowen was going too far.

Carter shot him a wide-eyed stare.

Lincoln kept talking. "You know I'm not that kind of asshole, Rowen. So shut the fuck up and listen to reason. Sasha is hell-bent on exploring her submissive side. That leaves you with two choices, let her go find herself with random strangers in a club across town or let me gently guide her in a caring way that won't cause her any permanent damage when she realizes she isn't cut out for this lifestyle."

"He's got a point," Carter stated, leaning against the door and crossing his ankles, clearly prepared to watch the shit-show.

"He's got a hard-on," Rowen shot back. "I can't even remember the last time he got laid." He turned his gaze from Carter to Lincoln. "I'm not with my sister twenty-four seven and haven't been for years, but I think I can safely say that she's about as innocent as a twenty-two-year-old girl can be."

"Woman," Lincoln interjected.

"What?" Rowen yelled.

"She's a woman, dude. Your sister grew up several years ago. Stop thinking of her as a kid."

Carter spoke again, though perhaps unwisely. "He has another good point."

Rowen spun around to face their partner, who also happened

to be the club's head bouncer and thus significantly larger than either of them. "Whose side are you on?"

"I'm on Sasha's side. Someone has to be. The two of you have been acting like toddlers in here."

Lincoln exhaled slowly. Carter was right. He needed to pull himself together. Think. Maybe Rowen was right too. This entire idea was stupid and ill-planned. He never should have offered to train her. Hell, where would he even work with her? It wasn't as though he could do it here at the club under her brother's nose. And considering how she reacted at Breeze tonight, he didn't want her in a public BDSM club at all.

Rowen padded across the room and faced the window. He stared out into the night in silence for a long time.

"I'm sorry, man," Lincoln finally said. "I shouldn't have suggested it to her before running it by you. It just sort of happened. She was so adamant, and I was grasping at straws. I didn't expect her to accept my proposal. I just wanted her to see reason."

"You're a sadist, Lincoln," Rowen told the window. "Not the kind of Dom who trains service submissives."

"What makes you think your sister even knows which sort of submissive she is or aspires to be?"

Rowen continued to face the window, but his voice was calmer. "I don't think my sister's submissive at all. I think she's being rebellious to piss me off. What I know for sure is that she isn't a masochist."

"Agreed. But unless I work with her, she's not going to be able to figure any of this out in a way that we can guarantee her safety."

More silence.

Carter opened his mouth, but Lincoln stopped him with a hand. If the guy repeated that Lincoln had a yet another good point, Rowen would probably go through the glass.

Finally, Rowen turned around. He met Lincoln's gaze and took a deep breath. "Promise me you won't mess with my sister."

"Come on. You know me better than that. I'm always careful with my submissives. I've never once hurt any of them."

Rowen shook his head, gritting his teeth. "That's not what I mean, man. Promise me you won't *fuck* my sister."

Lincoln stopped short. He blinked as he caught on. "Of course."

"You train her. Teach her everything there is to know about being submissive so that in the event she decides she wants a Dom of her own, she'll know how to be treated with respect and dignity. You got me?"

"I got you."

He strung his next words out. "Better yet, do your best to make sure she doesn't want anything to do with the lifestyle at all so we can continue to sleep at night."

Lincoln nodded. That was his intent.

Rowen leaned in closer, his eyes so narrow they were mere slits. "You do not have sex with my sister. You teach her about the lifestyle and what a Dominant expects and how to properly submit. But you stick to D/s. Now is not the time to let your dick get in the way."

"You have my word."

CHAPTER 7

Sasha stared at her bedroom ceiling, watching the slow path of the stream of morning sunlight as it leaked into the room through a slit in the blinds.

She had not slept. Even though Lincoln had brought her home last night with strict instructions for her to sleep, she had been unable to rest. In her mind she replayed the previous evening over and over again, mostly ignoring the parts with Master Colin and focusing on a running reel of the things Lincoln had said to her.

It seemed surreal. By the time the sun came up, she assumed she had surely imagined most of it. Maybe she had passed out and dreamed their conversation.

A knock at the door to her apartment made her bolt upright. She glanced at the alarm clock. It was eight in the morning. Early for a Saturday. Who the hell would be at her door at that hour?

The knock sounded again.

Shit.

She flung her legs over the side of the bed and pushed to standing, grabbing the first thing she could get her hands on to cover herself. Flannel pants. She shrugged into them, hopping on one leg while she worked her way toward the bedroom door.

Again with the knocking.

In a moment of panic, she realized it had to be her brother, and she hesitated. Maybe it would be best not to open the door to him. The last thing she needed at that hour was a lecture on top of very little sleep, no coffee, and confusion clouding her ability to reason.

How much would Lincoln have told him about last night?

More knocking. Louder.

With a deep breath, Sasha padded to the door and yanked it open.

Shock raced through her.

It was not Rowen.

It was Lincoln.

And he had the audacity to look well-rested, showered, and ready to start the day. Dressed in blue jeans, a tight white T-shirt, and loafers, he was also frowning. He set a hand on the open door, pushed it wider, and stepped inside.

Sasha inched backward as he shut the door, still frowning at her.

"Did you even look through the peephole to see who was at the door?"

She lifted a shaky hand to her throat. Lincoln Walsh was inside her apartment. *Lincoln Walsh.*

"*Sasha.* I asked you a question." His voice was clipped.

She flinched. "Shit, Lincoln. I'm barely awake."

He leaned toward her, wrapped his big hand around the back of her neck, and repeated himself. "Did. You. Look. Through. The. Peephole?"

"No." She breathed. "Jeez. I assumed you were my brother."

He released her neck slowly. "Why would Rowen be here at eight in the morning?"

She threw up her hands. "Oh, I don't know. Probably to give me a ten-hour lecture about meeting up with strangers in clubs and letting them spank me?"

"He won't be bothering you."

"What?" She narrowed her gaze. Unless Rowen was killed in a mysterious accident in the middle of the night, he would so totally be up her ass before noon.

"I spoke to him. Last night."

She rolled her eyes. "I bet that went over well."

"I told you I was going to handle Rowen." He frowned again.

Had he? Anything he said last night might need to be revisited since she had been frantic and slightly out of her mind. This started from the moment she got dressed in that out-of-character, black corset and skirt and then didn't end until the moment Lincoln dropped her off at her apartment while rambling through demands. None of which she could currently recall.

Odd since she'd spent the entire night reliving the evening. But her memories focused on the way he'd held her in his lap. The unmistakable bulge in his jeans. The way he'd cupped her face. Forced her to meet his gaze. She recalled jumping up and arguing with him. She also remembered making some sort of commitment. But surely that last part was in her imagination.

Lincoln sighed. "I handled your brother. He won't be calling you today."

She wasn't sure if that was good news or bad.

Lincoln's eyes drifted to her chest. "Put some more clothes on, woman. Lordy," he mumbled. "You're going to be the death of me."

She glanced down to see that she was only wearing a thin white tank top, her usual sleeping attire. That and a pair of panties. At least she'd had the sense to pull on pants before she greeted him.

He turned around and wandered farther into her space, smirking, though she had no idea why. Still muttering under his breath, "She not only opens the door without seeing who's outside, but she does so wearing fuck-me clothes."

"Pardon?" She set her hands on her hips, forcing herself not to cover her chest. Fuck him for speaking of her like that. She was covered.

He ignored her question. "We need to talk."

She lifted both brows as she rushed past him, heading for her attached kitchen. "I need coffee." What the hell was Lincoln doing at her apartment on a Saturday morning declaring that they needed to talk? Until last night, they rarely spoken to each other since they'd met.

"Black," he stated from right behind her.

For a second, she was confused, and then she looked down at her mug in her hands and realized what he was saying. Fine. She could make him coffee. Why not? She couldn't speak or think properly in front of him, but she could hand him a cup of black coffee.

He blessedly stepped away, but only a few feet to stand in front of her fridge.

She glanced at him to find him touching the edge of a finger painting under the alphabet letter magnet holding it to the fridge. "You're an artist?" he teased.

"Uh, no. If I attempted to use paints, mine wouldn't look that good. One of my four-year-old students did that." Sasha turned back to the coffee pot and willed it to run faster. Small talk?

"And you hung it up?"

She glanced at him again. His head was cocked to one side, his eyes drawn together. "It was for me. She asked me to." What was causing the confusion?

His smile warmed her before he left her alone in the small kitchen to wander back to her family room. When the coffee was done, she found him sitting on her couch.

She returned and handed him a mug as he pointed at the armchair across from where he sat. "Sit. But before you do that, go put on a sweatshirt or something." His grin had disappeared. He was back to all business. Serious. Frustrated?

She jerked her gaze to his, took a sip of her coffee, and dug her heels in. How dare he come into her home before any sane person was out of bed on a Saturday and start ordering her around. "I'm fine where I am," she stated, head held high. "And it's warm in here. I don't need more clothes. But thanks for your concern."

Bossy much?

The answer to that was yes. He was bossy. He was a Dom. She was well aware of that. But he wasn't *her* Dom. So he could go fuck himse— *Fuck.* Was he her Dom? She really wished she could remember more of their conversation last night. She took another sip of coffee, hoping it would help.

Lincoln's glare penetrated through to her bones.

She lowered herself onto the chair, tucked her legs underneath her, and hoped the compromise would appease him.

He leaned forward, set his mug on the coffee table, and propped his elbows on his knees. Hands clasped together, fingers worrying each other, he spoke again. "Did we or did we not come to an agreement last night?"

She gulped back nerves and tried to keep her hands steady by wrapping them both around her mug. "I might have been a little distracted. Can you remind me what we agreed upon?" Perfect. Not too bratty. Not whiney. Not angry. Just looking for clarification.

Did I agree to let him train me? Fuck. "Shit," she muttered.

"I think it's coming back to her," he said. It was the second time he'd referred to her in the third person. Weird. Sarcastic. Domineering. Rude. He continued though, "Enough cussing. I don't want to hear it coming from your sweet lips. Understood?"

She flinched. "Cussing?"

He narrowed his gaze, pinning her deeper into the chair. "Sasha, don't cuss. It's a simple request. You've said *shit* two times since I arrived and once last night. Don't do it anymore."

She pursed her lips.

"Sasha?"

Her eyes widened. What more did he want from her? Lord, this was weird.

"Are we clear?" he prompted.

"Sure," she blurted out, rolling her eyes. "Whatever."

A vein in Lincoln's temple bulged, his eyes piercing her with venom.

Shit. And damn. It was all coming back to her. She had made some sort of arrangement with Lincoln Walsh last night. It definitely involved eye rolling. And he also might have mentioned addressing him properly.

It seemed prudent to scramble to repair the damage and then request more details. "Sir. I'm sorry, Sir. I'm not quite awake, and I seriously don't remember everything you said last night. I was... distraught."

He hesitated, and then he relaxed slightly and leaned back against the couch, crossing one ankle over his knee. "Perhaps I should recap our agreement last night and see if it's still something you're interested in pursuing."

She blew out a breath. "That might be a good idea."

When his eyes closed on a slow inhale, she hastened to add, "Sir."

He smiled. "That's better."

It was. In more ways than he could imagine. Because she found herself aroused by the idea of pleasing him. What the hell? She squeezed her thighs together and tried not to squirm. She should not be aroused just because he approved of something she said. Nor should she be aroused at this hour of the morning.

"Do you want me to train you, Sasha?" He held up a hand. "Don't answer that right now. I can see mornings are not your friend. Just listen to me. I have basic requirements any Dom would insist upon. I know you're new to the lifestyle, exploring, and I'll try to be understanding of that fact, but you're going to have to put forth serious effort if you want me to work with you."

She nodded, deciding it was best to keep her mouth shut.

"First of all, you'll address me as Sir. Always. Without exception. Not because most Doms would expect that from a submissive twenty-four seven, but because I want you to live fully in the role while you're learning. It's confusing to new submissives to waffle back and forth between both worlds—D/s and vanilla. Understood?"

"Yes. Sir." The one word was weak. Strained. She watched his intensity and knew he was being totally serious about this. He was willing to train her. Lincoln Walsh was going to train her to be submissive. Holy shit. *Shoot.*

"I have expectations. One of them is that you not cuss. It's not something I normally demand of other subs, but it suits you."

"Why?" she blurted. What made her different?

He lifted a brow and waited.

"Sorry. Sir. Why, Sir? Why don't you want me to cuss?" It was the strangest request.

"You're the poster girl for innocence, Sasha. You work with preschool children. You wear conservative dresses and dainty sandals. Your hair is loose and curly and unruly like a flower child most days. Cussing doesn't suit you. Don't do it."

"Okay, Sir." Listening to him describe her in such detail made her sex clench. She was wet. It shocked her that he'd been so observant. And she was intrigued by the way he saw her. Did everyone see her in that same light? Some pure, sweet, innocent girl? She needed to speak her mind over one issue that was bothering her, though. "May I say something, Sir?"

"Yes. Thank you for asking politely." He was softening. He looked pleased.

Her nipples puckered. *Shit.* "I don't like it when you refer to me as a *girl*. I'm a grown woman. It makes me feel stupid and too young to know my mind."

He set his fingers on his lips and tapped them several times, thinking. "Sasha, when I call you a girl, it's not meant to be derogatory. It's a term of endearment common in the lifestyle. It's not that I don't think you're grown up. I can see perfectly well that you're a woman in every sense of the word." His gaze roamed to her chest and stayed there a moment.

She processed his words. So intense. Apparently he did not see her as a girl. Good.

He continued, "I don't think I'm capable of altering that habit. It's imbedded in my brain. Can you perhaps accept that I'm in no way trying to belittle you when I say it?"

Since he put it that way... "Yes... Sir. Thank you for clarifying."

He smiled. "See? Compromise? You might find it interesting to know I had this same argument with your brother last night."

She lifted a brow. "What?"

Lincoln grinned. "He kept referring to you as a girl. I came to your defense and pointed out to him you are indeed a woman. For all the good it did me."

"Thank you?"

He smirked. "Nevertheless, like I said, in the lifestyle, girl is often a term of endearment. Even if I did agree to refer to you by any other term, you won't find many Doms in the lifestyle who don't use it, so I suggest you get over yourself."

"Okay, Sir." She found it curious that he'd gone to such lengths to explain himself. Perhaps he was the perfect person to train her.

"Now, in order for your training to be most effective, it would be helpful if you had a chunk of time you could devote solely to this endeavor. Do you have any vacation time coming?"

"This is the last week of school before the kids go on summer break. I was planning to look for a summer job to augment my income."

"Perfect. So Friday is your last day?"

"Yes." The word wobbled. What was she getting into?

Part of her couldn't imagine a better proposal. Being trained as a submissive by one of the best in the lifestyle who also happened to be smoking hot and figured often in her dreams? She couldn't ask for a better arrangement.

And yet... Could her heart survive this experiment? What if she failed and disappointed him? What if they were both disappointed? What if she fell in love with him and he turned her away after they were done?

Yes. She definitely needed to hold her heart close to her if she agreed to this arrangement.

"Good. That gives you a week to think about this proposal. I want you to be sure. You have seven days to change your mind. If you decide you want to go through with it, I'll pick you up Saturday morning one week from today and bring you to my house for the duration. If you need help paying your rent or utilities while you aren't working, I'll cover them. Understood?"

"Yes, Sir." She gripped the mug so tight it was a wonder it didn't shatter. The coffee had long since gone cold, but she couldn't risk setting it down for fear she would spill it all over if she moved.

"I'm a firm Dom, Sasha. Do not think this will be a walk in the park. I'm demanding. I won't go easy on you just because you're new. In fact, I'll expect more from you than I would anyone else since we don't have to tiptoe around the disadvantage of not knowing each other. I'll be harder on you."

She gulped. How well did she know him really?

At least enough to know he would never hurt her. He was her brother's best friend. Rowen would kill Lincoln if anything happened to Sasha.

"I'll expect you to obey me in all things. I will punish you when you're disobedient. You have my word that I will not mark your body in any permanent manner. I will not pierce you or brand you or change your skin in any way. I will not have sex with you.

"I will spank you. I will also introduce you to a variety of toys for both your pleasure and your punishment. I will tell you what to wear and what to eat and when to sleep. Your job will be to learn to give up control to another person and submit obediently to a Dom's will.

"If you can accomplish that to my satisfaction, I will consent to your insistence that you're submissive and let you join Zodiac or another club. I'll even go to bat for you with your brother and get him off your back. After we're finished, I'll make sure you're free to live your life as you please without interference. I'll even help you find a permanent Dom if you desire.

"However, in exchange for you submitting to my training, you have to agree to accept my decision in the end. If I think you're not suited for the lifestyle, I want you to back off gracefully and stop giving Rowen a heart attack. Are we clear?"

She wasn't sure she was capable of speech, but she managed to get her lips to move to utter a soft, "Yes, Sir."

"If you have reservations, voice them. If you have questions, ask them. I'm sure you're overwhelmed right now. Make a list. Do some research. Email me or text me throughout the week."

Did he not realize she had been researching BDSM for years? She didn't comment. "Yes, Sir." He'd thrust so much information on her at once, she wasn't sure she fully heard it all. Her ears were ringing.

"I'll type all this in an email for you, Sasha. I don't want there to be any misunderstandings between us."

"Will you be taking me to Zodiac, Sir?"

He shook his head. "No. Not during your training period." He didn't elaborate.

"How long will my training last?" She stared at him. Was he talking days? Weeks?

He stared back, one brow lifted.

"Sir. Sorry, Sir."

"Perhaps a few weeks. Maybe a month."

She nodded slowly. *A month? In his home? Doing his bidding twenty-four seven?* It was nearly impossible to keep from squirming at the idea.

"I don't want to put a time limit on it because it will give you a false sense of finality. It depends on how you respond."

Depends on what? She didn't ask that question. Instead, she nodded. Maybe she could figure that out online. See what other Doms required.

Lincoln suddenly stood. He stepped toward the door and set his hand on the knob. His departure was so abrupt she couldn't even get her legs unfolded to see him out.

He turned around to face her again. "Lock the door behind me, Sasha. And for God's sake, don't open it without seeing who's out there from now on."

"Yes, Sir." She uncurled herself and got up, heading toward him in order to do as he'd instructed.

"You have my number and my email?"

"Yes, Sir." She stopped two feet from him.

"I'll expect to hear from you this week. Text. Email. Several times. Don't hold back. No question is too stupid."

"Yes, Sir."

He started to turn back around, and then he paused again and faced her, cocking his head. His voice was calm. "There are many types of submissives, Sasha. Some like restraints. Some like pain. Some like to be marked. Some submissives are service-oriented and get pleasure from doing for their Doms. Some are bratty and derive pleasure from being punished.

"And some…" he hesitated again, taking one large step toward her and grabbing both her wrists at her sides, "…are sexual submissives. Their focus is on reaching orgasm. They turn themselves over to the Doms to decide when and where and how they're permitted to achieve that goal." He squeezed her wrists with his fingers to emphasize his point.

He stood so close to her she could lean forward if she wanted and set her cheek on his chest. Feel the warmth. She could smell his clean scent and whatever shaving cream he used from this proximity.

He penetrated her with his gaze, waiting.

She shuddered. Her entire body shook with the force of his

words. Was she a sexual submissive? Is that what he was implying? If the reaction of her body at his pronouncement was any indication, he was probably onto something. She'd never been hornier than she was right at that moment. Every inch of her was on fire, begging for release. The itch to touch herself was intense. Her sex throbbed. Her clit swelled. Her breasts were heavy. A ball in the pit of her stomach curled tighter, threatening to spring loose and leave her flying all over the room in a thousand pieces.

Half of her couldn't wait for him to leave so she could flee back to her room and masturbate. She needed the relief. At this rate it would take her about two minutes to get off.

He spoke again. "I can't be sure if you're even submissive at all yet. I have my suspicions. But I do have one demand I'd like you to adhere to this week. I have no way of ensuring you obeyed me since I won't be seeing you, but I'd like you to give me your word."

"What…" She licked her lips, her mouth so dry now she might need to drink the cold coffee. "What would you like me to do, Sir?"

"Keep your hands off your pussy and your tits."

Her face flamed at his words.

"You heard me. Don't masturbate this week. If you have toys, leave them in your drawer. Do not touch yourself any more than what's required for hygiene purposes. Understood?"

Holy shit. *Shit. Shit. Shit.* "Yes, Sir."

He chuckled, startling her with his mood change. "I can practically hear you cussing inside your head. And that's fine. Can't stop you from thinking every four-letter word in the book. But don't utter them out loud. And don't masturbate." He lifted his brows as he released her wrists, and then he turned around and exited the apartment without glancing back again.

Sasha stared at the door for so long her legs cramped. She wasn't sure she could even process what he'd said, and she sincerely hoped he did send her an email detailing the conversation. If not, she would be toast.

One thing she was clear on was that she was so aroused it was a wonder the room didn't self-combust. Was she a sexual submissive? Perhaps. But how was she ever going to find out if he didn't intend to have sex with her? She shuddered at the thought that she might spend weeks or an entire month horny and unfulfilled.

Wait. What did he mean exactly when he said he wouldn't have sex with her? Sex was a broad term. Was he talking about penetration? Because she could think of a lot of creative ways to enjoy her time with him that didn't necessarily involve intercourse.

More importantly, how was she going to go an entire week without masturbating? It wasn't as though she felt the need to get off all day every day. But she did like to pull out her butterfly at least once a day. Usually when she went to bed. It helped her sleep if she had an orgasm first. She had no idea if she was an anomaly or not. It wasn't like she asked other women how often they made themselves come. It was hardly something she could bring up in the teacher's lounge at the preschool.

But something was different.

Yep. It was the demand that burrowed under her skin and left her feeling like she might come without masturbating. If this was what it felt like to submit fully to a Dom, she was totally going to ace this test.

The question was, what would happen to her heart in the meantime, and how would she ever survive leaving Lincoln, let alone permitting another man to dominate her after he was done?

CHAPTER 8

Five days later...

Lincoln stood inside the house he was currently renovating, staring out the back window at the patio. The floor beneath him had been stripped down to the concrete. He wasn't concerned. He had a good team of construction workers on this project.

He'd flipped so many houses in the last few years, he'd lost count. So far he hadn't ever taken a beating. What had started out as more of a hobby to bring in extra money, had turned into a lucrative business he was proud of. He enjoyed the thrill of finding run-down homes for auction, turning them into gems, and selling them for far more than he'd invested.

When Carter had become a partner in Club Zodiac, he had also become the construction head for Lincoln's side business. The man knew his shit. And what he didn't know, he didn't fuck around with. He found the right men and got the job done.

It was Thursday. Lincoln hadn't seen Sasha since Saturday. He'd had a hard-on for her the entire time, and that worried him. This entire arrangement had him up nights. Thinking. Planning.

Taking his cock in his hand. He knew he was a hypocrite ordering Sasha not to touch her sweet pussy while he jerked off more than once a day. But damn. The thought of her coming to him on Saturday with all that pent-up sexual frustration made his dick hard every time.

Carter's voice penetrated his thoughts. "Dude, we'll get this house flipped a lot faster if you move out of my way so I can lay the tile in this room."

Lincoln jerked around to face his friend and found Rowen standing in the stripped kitchen too. His eyes were narrowed. He looked concerned. "You worried about making a buck on this money pit, or are you thinking about my sister?"

Damn, he was sharp. Lincoln decided to turn the tables. "Neither. I was thinking about watching the game later tonight. You guys coming over? I've got cold beer. We can order pizza."

Carter was stacking tile in the center of the room as he responded. "Sounds good."

Rowen's eyes narrowed further. "If we're watching the game later tonight, why did you ask me to come by here now?"

Busted. The stupid game had been an afterthought to cover his tracks. Now he needed to backpedal. "Because we all need to sign the lease renewal on the building, and I promised the landlord I'd get it to him this afternoon." He held out a manila folder to prove his point. The lie was small. Their landlord didn't need the papers specifically today.

Since when was Lincoln lying to his friends to cover up his thoughts about a woman? *Since the woman in question is Rowen's sister.*

Rowen took the folder from Lincoln and pulled a pen from his pocket, but he was still glaring. He wasn't buying Lincoln's story. "I'll get back to you about tonight. Need to check with Rayne. She's... Never mind. Tell me what you have planned for Sasha."

Nope. Rowen wasn't going to let this go. He also had something going on with Rayne. Not a surprise. He always had something going on with Rayne. Lincoln wished Rowen would get his head out of his ass once and for all where his girlfriend was concerned and either cut her loose or make a commitment. He didn't want to interfere, but he suspected Rowen was stringing Rayne along, and Lincoln didn't like it.

Lincoln was a total fuck. Ironic that he would judge Rowen while he himself was in way over his head with Rowen's sister. At the moment, Lincoln couldn't imagine how long this farce was actually going to last. He'd told Sasha a few weeks or a month. That had been a lie to make her nervous. What he really needed was for her to see the error of her ways and safeword out of his house as fast as possible.

Right now, he needed to address the constant tension that had gotten between him and Rowen over the last five days. They'd been friends for years. Lincoln didn't want to ruin it over a woman. "Dude, my goal is to train your sister. Help her establish if she's cut out for this lifestyle. Nothing else. I gave you my word I wouldn't sleep with her. But I'm not going to give you a nightly play-by-play either like you're a prefect or the head boy."

Rowen snickered. At least Lincoln had broken the strain between them. "Did you just make a Harry Potter reference? What are you, thirteen?"

"Fuck you. Everyone loves Harry Potter. But that's beside the point. The point is that you're gonna have to trust me and back the fuck off."

"I'm not sure I can do that."

"Too damn bad. Either trust me or she'll find someone else to train her. You want her to try her luck at Breeze? Maybe Master Colin is available. He seemed to like her the other night."

Rowen growled. He actually *growled*. "Fine, Professor Snape, but don't make me have to kill you."

Carter laughed. "Are you two done acting like a couple of teenagers? I need to lay the tile now. Get the hell out of my kitchen." He made sweeping motions with his hands, ushering them toward the carpeted area of the attached family room.

Lincoln's phone buzzed in his pocket, and he rushed to tug it out of the tight denim with more haste than he should have. For the last five days, he'd kept the cell attached to his hip, literally, at all hours, eagerly awaiting contact from Sasha as if he were the teenage boy both of his best friends accused him of being.

Sasha texted him at least once every day with a question or comment. He wasn't sure if she did it because she liked to interact with him, she genuinely required a response to her inquiries, or she thought it might be funny to tempt him with her increasingly erotic questions.

He glanced at the screen, grinning when he saw it was from her. And then his face flushed, and he nearly dropped the phone on the carpet.

Sir, is a spreader bar used to keep a woman's pussy exposed? And if so, does it strap on at the thighs or the ankles?

Jesus. He was fairly certain by now she was making this shit up with increasing levels of sexual innuendo to get under his skin. And it was working. Dammit.

How the fuck was he supposed to respond to that?

Rowen interrupted him as he held his thumbs over the screen. "What the fuck is up with you?"

Lincoln pocketed the phone. He would have to answer her later.

Carter was staring at him too. "Your face is red, and you're grinning like a lunatic."

Rowen's gaze narrowed again, every effort to calm him down a few moments ago disappearing entirely. "Please tell me that wasn't my sister."

"It was." He didn't want to lie.

"And?"

"She's trying to kill me. Don't worry about it. I'll handle it. I said I would. And I will. I've got to get back to Zodiac. I'll see you guys tonight?" He asked that question as he rushed for the front of the house. He didn't wait around to hear their answers. The last thing he wanted Rowen to notice was the fucking hard-on once again bulging the front of Lincoln's jeans.

It was Friday afternoon before Sasha fully internalized this was real. Her preschool was closed for summer, and she was going to Lincoln's home tomorrow to stay with him indefinitely while he trained her to be a proper submissive.

She still couldn't wrap her head around what that really meant. She had no idea what he would expect of her except that she wasn't permitted to cuss and she needed to learn to address him as "Sir."

She also knew he didn't intend to sleep with her, though she hoped she might convince him otherwise. She'd certainly done everything she could to tempt him in the past week. At first she had dug deep to come up with questions that sounded educated and reasonable.

Do you like your submissives to keep their head bowed?

How do you feel about ropes?

Will I be expected to wear a ball gag?

What sort of nipple clamps do you use?

Are vibrators used internally?

She'd come up with something new every day in an effort to

engage him in the hopes she would get to know him better. She'd failed, seeing as every answer was clinical and brief. After pulling out the last stop yesterday, she knew she was doomed.

The contrived question about spreader bars had made it difficult for her to keep her fingers away from her clit as she typed it. And his response? She'd nearly come in her seat without touching herself. Thank God she'd been at home and not in front of her students.

Sasha, if we get to the point that I need a spreader bar to keep your legs open wide enough, whether it's attached at your ankles or your thighs is going to be the least of your concerns. Do I have your attention now?

She shivered every time she re-read his response. God, how she wished she could read between the lines, see what his expression had been when he typed that.

Did he have any idea what it had been like for her to sit on his lap wrapped in his arms? Like a dream. She had to text him every day at least once in order to remind herself he was even real. The spark she'd felt the first time she'd met him had burned hotter with every contact she'd had with him and then flickered into a flame the night of her college graduation when he pressed his palm into the small of her back. And that flame became an inferno when he held her against his chest at Breeze, brushing her hair from her face.

Being in Lincoln's arms had not come close to comparing to the reaction she had to Master Colin's touch. She didn't have to dig deep to wonder why this was the case.

Sasha was not Master Colin's submissive. She belonged to Lincoln.

Currently, she needed to stop thinking about tomorrow and concentrate on today. She still had packing to do, and she needed to let her neighbor know she was going to be out of town for a while.

She headed next door first, took a deep breath, and lifted her hand to knock on Mrs. Lopez's door. She knew most of the other people living on her floor, but Mrs. Lopez was the sweet old lady next door who wouldn't ask questions.

Or maybe she was mistaken...

The door opened to an older Hispanic woman whose face lit up as she ushered Sasha inside. "Hello, dear. How are you? I haven't seen you in several days. I hope those sweethearts of yours haven't given you a cold."

"No. Not lately. I've been lucky." Sasha stepped inside.

"Come in the kitchen, *mija*. I just made fresh tortillas. Can I tempt you with some? There are way too many for one woman."

Sure enough, the apartment smelled fabulously of the doughy goodness that was Mrs. Lopez's tortillas. Sasha's stomach grumbled. Not only did Mrs. Lopez have fresh tortillas steaming in their round pottery dish on the table, but she also had a cast iron skillet filled with carnitas simmering on the stove.

Before Sasha could decline, Mrs. Lopez had her seated with a glass of water and a plate full of food. "Ma'am, living next door to you is the best decision I've ever made."

The older woman chuckled. Sasha knew she'd been alone for several years. Her husband had passed away ten years ago, and her children both had families of their own in different cities. Feeding Sasha made her day. She would never deny the woman this pleasure.

Mrs. Lopez finally waved a hand between them as she settled at the table across from Sasha, not filling a plate of her own. "I haven't let you get a word in edgewise, *mija*. What did you stop by for?"

Sasha swallowed the delicious bite in her mouth and wiped her lips on her cloth napkin. "I wanted to let you know I'm going to be out of town for a while. I was hoping you could grab my mail and water my plants. I didn't have time to stop the mail, unfortunately."

Please don't ask me too many questions.

Mrs. Lopez clapped her hands together. "How exciting. Where are you going?"

"Oh..." *Why did I say out of town? Shit.* "Well, I don't have a destination in mind. I was going to head for the beach and then take some time to rest. It's been a stressful year with the kids. I need a break to read and relax."

Mrs. Lopez pouted. "The beach. That's like ten minutes from here. How about the mountains?" She perked up as if she were a travel agent.

Sasha took another bite to keep her mouth occupied for a minute. After swallowing, she met Mrs. Lopez's gaze. "That's not a bad idea. I think I'll do that. Thanks."

Mrs. Lopez reached across the table and patted Sasha's hand. "I'd be honored to water your plants and grab your mail while you go find yourself, *mija*."

Thank God Sasha hadn't taken another bite before those words were spoken. If Mrs. Lopez had any idea how close to the truth her words were...

CHAPTER 9

Lincoln was nervous. He'd never been this nervous in his life. In twelve hours he would pick up Sasha and bring her to his home.

He sat in his office chair, but he wasn't facing the desk. He was staring out the window at the darkness.

He knew several things after a week of communicating with Sasha by text and email. They hadn't spoken on the phone. He'd never encouraged that, and she'd never asked or attempted to call him.

He hadn't wanted to influence her with his voice. It was much easier to remain detached if he only sent her typed messages. Perhaps it was a cop out, but he stuck to it anyway.

She was curious. She asked all the right questions and some he was certain she threw in to get a rise out of him. He answered them.

She was ready.

And he feared she was indeed the submissive she believed herself to be.

There were so many problems with this scenario, and he had twelve hours to address them and get his head on straight before he picked her up. First and foremost, he needed to remind himself repeatedly that this was a temporary arrangement.

Sasha was not his. She never would be. It didn't matter how attracted he was to her, he still would never have her. For one thing, Rowen would kill him. For another thing, it was becoming more and more apparent based on her curiosity about the lifestyle that she might be a sexual submissive.

The sort of questions she asked told him everything he needed to know. She never asked about floggers or whips. She asked about ropes and bondage and vibrators. She asked about butt plugs and nipple clamps. Her curiosity ran toward sexual fulfillment. And she wasn't shy about her questions either. At least not in text or email.

Perhaps she wasn't nearly as innocent as he envisioned her. At least not in her mind. He still felt confident she was inexperienced. And she certainly would never be the kind of submissive he needed, nor could he be the kind of Dom she might need. In the end it didn't matter if she was submissive or not. He still needed to guide her out of the lifestyle.

Was he a selfish asshole? Yep.

He had no idea if she would be as open and inquisitive verbally in person. He would find out tomorrow.

What was he thinking? He couldn't go through with this. He needed to recuse himself and find another Dom who could give her what she needed and wanted. Someone who could train a sexual submissive. Someone like Carter.

Lincoln winced. For the millionth time. The thought of any other man touching her made him physically ill. Somehow after years of keeping himself at arm's length, he'd crossed a line. Holding her in his lap last weekend had changed him. The feel of her body in his grip. The way her heart raced. The way she licked her lips. The way her eyes widened when he spoke… Everything she did in that brief encounter changed him. He shuddered every time he imagined her with another Dom. If anyone even

79

attempted to so much as hold her hand, he would probably flatten them with his fist.

This bothered him more than anything. He had no business feeling so possessive of Sasha Easton. His partner's sister. *Keep reminding yourself, asshole.*

After dropping in on her unannounced last Saturday, he'd had trouble focusing the rest of the weekend. She'd been half asleep, her hair a mess of curls, her brain muddled, and her damn tank top hiding nothing. His cock had stiffened and remained that way for the rest of the day.

Lincoln was not the kind of Dom who played with sexual submissives. *Ever.* And he sure didn't train them. He was a sadist. He sometimes worked with other sadists. He sometimes worked with masochists. He didn't fuck the women he did scenes with in his club. He was well-trained in the use of many types of whips and floggers and crops and even rope bondage and paddles. Hell, all sorts of equipment. He used them to help many different subs achieve the release they needed.

He vetted his subs heavily before he ever touched them, and then he gave them what they required. He didn't get off on it. Not sexually anyway. He didn't even get hard. He kept his sex life separate from his BDSM world and always had.

The problem was he would never find a life partner with his particular limitations. He'd realized the dilemma years ago and had reconciled with the fact. A permanent woman was not in the cards for him. He knew this because he'd put it to the test several times over the years.

He'd occasionally scened with the same woman for weeks or even months at a time. He'd tried to combine his sadistic tendencies with a sex life over the years. It never worked. The two were mutually exclusive. There had been a few women who enjoyed having sex with him after a scene, and he put a lot of effort into combining the two, but they didn't mesh. Even if he knew he was going to sleep with a woman later that evening, he still didn't get off on striking her beforehand.

What he craved was unrealistic. He wanted a woman who enjoyed being flogged into subspace without sexual interaction whom he could later take to his bed and fuck into submission. That woman didn't exist.

And she certainly wasn't Sasha.

Something was seriously fucked up in Lincoln's mind.

What was he thinking training a sexual submissive in a twenty-four seven arrangement? Lordy.

It wasn't that he wasn't qualified. He totally understood the ins and outs of such an agreement. He even taught other Doms about the role. But he didn't participate himself. He was better suited to training other Doms how to be better sadists or even subs to be well-behaved masochists.

He should be appalled by the idea of taking on such a boring task. And yet, he was not only excited with the prospect, but his cock hadn't stopped throbbing for the entire week.

A noise behind him made him twist his head around to find Carter stepping into his office. The enormous man grinned. "Tomorrow's the big day, huh?"

Lincoln turned back to the window, not responding.

Carter shut the door and came more fully into the room, putting himself between Lincoln and the window. "You okay?"

Lincoln sighed, lifting his hands up to lock them behind his head. "No. And if you tell Rowen that, I'll have you shot."

Carter chuckled. "My lips are sealed. In over your head?"

"Totally," he admitted. He released his hands to run them over his face. He needed to talk to someone. Carter was his best option. At least the man was into the same things he suspected Sasha would enjoy. "I think she's a sexual submissive."

"Ya think?" He chuckled again, putting a hand over his belly. "Dude, I could have told you that years ago."

Lincoln winced. "Really?" How had he not noticed? He knew the answer. He had intentionally not paid attention.

"I think that's why Rowen's so freaked out. He can't stand the idea of his sister having sex, let alone with a Dominant. It sends chills down his spine. He's not just her brother. He's more like a father to her. Nobody wants to picture their sister or their daughter splayed open for a man. I'm sure most dads stuff the idea of their daughters having sex to the back of their minds and assume it's missionary and only for procreation."

Carter was right.

"If Sasha had come to Rowen and asked him to flog her or arrange for someone else to do it, he probably would've consented. But he's a sharp guy. He knows his sister's tastes run in a different direction."

Lincoln nodded. "I can't do this." He looked at the floor. "I've been sitting here for two hours trying to figure out how to bow out gracefully and still save face."

"You have an alternate solution?"

"No. That's the problem." Lincoln toed the carpet with his shoe, aiming to dig a hole in it clear to the floorboards. He inhaled a long breath and lifted his gaze again. "The only person I would hand this over to would be you."

Carter nodded slowly. "But you won't."

"No."

"Have you stopped to consider what that means?"

Lincoln groaned. "Too many times."

Carter snorted. "It's okay, you know."

"What is?"

"Falling for a woman. Even the great Lincoln Walsh is permitted to be human. I'd give my right arm to meet someone so obviously devoted to me. I'd move heaven and earth to make sure she felt cherished every day of her life."

Lincoln flinched. "What are you talking about? What makes you think Sasha's interested in me in particular? This is nothing but an arrangement to teach her what submission means. That's all."

Carter didn't laugh again. If he had, there was a chance Lincoln would have decked him. "You really believe that?"

"What?" He regretted asking immediately.

"Dude, you've spent so many years trying to put her off and make sure she knew you wanted nothing to do with her that you couldn't see how she worships you from across a crowded room."

Lincoln did more than flinch this time. His entire body tensed. "That's crazy." Right?

"Is it?" Carter lifted a brow.

Was she into him? If so, this situation was way worse than he suspected. Forget his personal concerns with training her. He'd spent the better part of the week worrying about how hard his dick was. What about her motives?

Lincoln stared at Carter for long moments. Fuck. He knew Carter spoke the truth. He'd seen it with his own eyes—countless times. She would jerk her gaze away when he caught her looking at him in a crowded room. He could count the times they had been in the same place. It didn't happen often. He hadn't allowed it to happen often, but when it did, she took his breath away.

Last year at her college graduation party, he'd seen her devotion in her eyes. He'd felt her trembling when he set his hand on her lower back, watched her face flush as she struggled with the words to thank him for the flowers.

But that wasn't the only poignant example of Sasha wearing her feelings on her sleeve. One night, about six months ago, he'd witnessed her totally lose her ability to rein in her emotions. Every time he thought about that night, he winced. It had been innocent enough, but the look on her face haunted him to this day.

He'd done a scene with a masochist whom he'd played with many times. That night Bethany had propositioned him afterward. And he'd taken her up on the offer. As they were leaving the club, Sasha was entering.

Bethany had been wearing high heels, fishnet stockings, and a tight spandex dress that hid nothing. She was holding Lincoln's elbow and leaning into him, laughing at something he'd said. Fun. Playful.

As Lincoln opened the door to Zodiac, Sasha nearly collided with them.

It was late. Rowen's car had been in the shop. Sasha had come to pick him up. When she saw Lincoln in the entryway with Bethany, she'd been unable to hide her shock. She gasped, eyes wide, bit her lower lip, ducked her gaze, and raced past them.

Lincoln might have been able to pretend he was mistaken about her reaction if it hadn't been for Bethany. "That was awkward." She gripped his arm tighter. "You want to go to her?"

Lincoln had jerked his gaze from where Sasha disappeared to look back at Bethany. "Sasha? No. Of course not. She's fine. I don't know what's up with her tonight, but Rowen will handle it."

Bethany had lifted her brows. "Lincoln Walsh, are you that dumb?"

Apparently so. Instead of taking Bethany home, they'd gone to a diner and gotten coffee. They hadn't discussed Sasha again that night, but the mood had been ruined.

Yep. Lincoln was an idiot.

He'd simply been in denial. And he was concerned about how many other people noticed. "Does Rowen know?"

Carter shook his head. "Don't think so. Never discussed it with him. He's probably in as deep denial as you are. But I bet half the rest of the staff knows and they're picking out china patterns as we speak."

That was going too far. Lincoln shoved to standing and paced away from his friend and business partner. "Come on. That's insane. Sasha is... Sasha. Rowen's sister. Maybe she had a childhood crush on me at one time, but surely she doesn't anymore. Hell, she spent most of the time we were together at Breeze last week yelling at me." *Please tell me it was just a crush.*

"So you're saying she's a brat?"

Lincoln stopped pacing to lower his head and shoot daggers at his friend. "No. I'm saying she's not into me like you think. She just needs someone knowledgeable to train her and help her realize if submission is right for her. That's all. I was there. I offered," he continued to lie.

"And now you regret the decision."

"Right."

"Why?"

"Because I'm not into this sort of thing." Lincoln's voice rose. He threw his hands in the air again. "I'm a sadist. I don't do sexual submissives. And I certainly don't do bratty ones." *Oh Lord. Did I say that out loud?*

Carter fought hard not to smirk or possibly grin, but his eyes gave him away.

"Stop being such an ass. I don't need your kind of help right now. I need to get out of this and pair her up with someone more qualified to train her to be what she needs." He stomped over to his desk and flipped through the ledger on top as if he might spot the perfect Dom among the pages.

"What are you so afraid of?"

"Me?" He jerked his gaze up again. "I'm not afraid. I just don't want to do her a disservice."

"Uh-huh. You realize anyone in this club would hands-down say you were the most qualified to train any sub, no matter what they needed or how much experience they had."

Lincoln cocked his head. "Don't be ridiculous."

"What are you afraid of, man?" Carter repeated.

Lincoln knew the answer. Deep down he'd pushed it to the back of his mind all week. He was afraid of falling for a woman who couldn't fulfill him in every way he needed. He was afraid to let himself be vulnerable to that kind of hurt. Because if he let

Sasha's sweet self get under his skin, he would be destroyed when she eventually left him. And so would she.

In the end, no matter how attracted to her he was, he was still a sadist. And she was still not a masochist.

"I think you have your answers," Carter whispered. "How about if you take it one day at a time and see what happens? Cut yourself some slack. Maybe things aren't as fucked-up as they seem." With those parting words, Carter left the room, shutting the door with a soft snick.

Was he right?

Did it even matter?

Lincoln was still screwed. He could no more get out of training Sasha than he could take a rocket to the moon. So, he was just going to have to lock his emotions up tight and hope to convince her she was totally wrong for the lifestyle. Failing that, he would have no choice but to train her to be the best submissive she could be and let her go when she was ready.

That second possibility made him cringe, but he needed to face the possibility. After all, he certainly couldn't keep her for himself. Carter might think the idea was obvious and simple, but Carter was wrong.

CHAPTER 10

Sasha was a ball of nerves threatening to explode Saturday morning.

Lincoln was picking her up at nine, and she couldn't concentrate on any one thing to get ready. She hadn't slept much in days. There were bags under her eyes. And she was a nervous wreck.

She'd spent an hour in her apartment's one small bathroom putting on makeup she didn't ordinarily wear to cover the purple evidence of her lack of sleep and ensure she looked her best. Why she wanted to impress Lincoln she had no idea. The man had made it clear repeatedly this week that their arrangement was strictly professional. Dom training sub. Nothing else.

Except for that one text. She shivered every time she remembered his words.

Sasha, if we get to the point that I need a spreader bar to keep your legs open wide enough, whether it's attached at your ankles or your thighs is going to be the least of your concerns. Do I have your attention now?

No matter how many times she read those words, she couldn't

come up with a single explanation that didn't include sexual innuendo. It gave her hope.

She secretly prayed he was full of shit with the rest of his cold, precise answers and she could convince him otherwise as soon as they were alone together. The only other evidence he might be feeding her line after line of crap had been last Friday night. She'd felt his hard-on pressed against her thigh when she'd been on his lap. That had to mean something, didn't it?

She was still stuffing clothes in her suitcase when a knock sounded at the door. "Shit," she muttered. She wasn't ready. She had no idea what to bring or how much. He'd given her no indication of what she might need. So, she'd grabbed dresses and skirt and shorts and pants and a wide variety of shoes.

It was too late to finish now. She needed to go open the door so he didn't start the first hour of their arrangement angry. She rushed through the apartment and yanked open the door.

Lincoln stood there looking almost exactly as he had a week ago today. Same dark expression of disapproval on top of jeans, loafers, and a—this time maroon—T-shirt. "Sasha," he warned, already pissed.

"What, Sir?" How was she already on his bad side?

He pointed at the door.

She followed his finger to the peephole. What was he, psychic? "Oops."

"Yeah, oops." He stepped inside and shut the door. "You're going to have to take this far more seriously if you want me to train you to do anything at all. I haven't even begun to list my requirements, and you can't even do the one simple task you were given." He leaned closer. "The most important one because it involves your safety."

She shuddered. "Sorry, Sir. I promise I'll do better." It was going to be difficult however, if he insisted on glaring at her like that all the time. There was no reason for him to be angry.

He glanced around the room. What did he think of her space?

She had only been in this apartment a year. It was smaller and older, but it was all she could afford. Her only goal was to prove she could make it on her own. To her brother and herself. So, she had second-hand furniture and not much of it.

"Where's your suitcase?" he asked.

"On my bed." She nibbled her lower lip. "I'm not done packing actually. I don't know what to bring."

He gently took ahold of her arm and led her across the living room and into her bedroom. This was one room she had put a few extra dollars into. It was her sanctuary. She had a queen-sized bed and a nicer mattress. Her bedding was pale pink and fluffy. Comfortable.

He didn't comment on her space. Instead, he sighed when he saw the mess of clothes piled on the bed, only half of it in the suitcase. "Here's what's going to happen." He turned to face her. "You're going to go into the bathroom and wash all that makeup off your face while I pack your suitcase. When you're finished, I'll hand you something else to wear." He pointed at the bathroom door. "Go."

She stared at him. He didn't like her makeup? Her lip quivered. Or her choice in clothing?

"Sweetheart, this is not going to go well for you if you hesitate every time I give you an order."

She spun around, fled the room, and barricaded herself in the bathroom. Maybe this was a mistake. What was she thinking? She leaned against the bathroom door, her body trembling from the reprimand. She hated displeasing him. So far that was all she'd done.

She wiped the tears from her cheeks and pushed off the door. She could do better. She wasn't going to fail. That was undoubtedly what he wanted. He'd probably plotted with her brother all week to figure out how to get her to cry uncle the quickest.

Rowen knew she was capable of crying at the drop of a hat.

She was a pleaser. She hated disappointing people. He would have told Lincoln how to get her to put an end to this before it even started.

She wouldn't fall for it. She would do this. Fuck her brother and his meddling. Not only was she going to enjoy every moment in Lincoln's presence, but by the end of their time together she intended to prove to him she was submissive enough to be what he needed. No matter what that was, she could do it. She had to. Her entire world was tied up in the success of this plan.

Lincoln Walsh was hers. He just didn't know it yet.

With renewed energy, she washed every bit of makeup off her face and dried it on a towel. Her hair hung in messy loose ringlets all around her shoulders and down her back. As usual. Couldn't be helped. If she wasn't mistaken, Lincoln liked it that way. She'd caught him staring at it on more than one occasion over the years when he didn't know she was watching.

With a deep breath and a commitment to impress Lincoln with her obedience, she opened the bathroom door.

He was leaning against the bed. Her suitcase was sitting on top, closed. There was no evidence of clothing anywhere. He'd either jammed it all in or put it away somewhere in the room or closet. She decided not to ask.

He held out one of her sundresses. "Go change. You'll wear this. Nothing else."

She reached for the thin white dress, wondering how he'd even found it in her closet. It was older. She hadn't worn it in a while. For one thing, it was too short and for another thing it was too see-through.

She started to point that out when the rest of his instructions sank in. *Nothing else?*

No bra? No panties? Just the skimpy dress that would hide nothing?

She swallowed as she took it from his hand. She could do this. If he wanted her half-naked, fine. Even better. She snatched the dress from his grasp and spun around to once again enter the bathroom.

This time she took very few minutes to change, dropping her favorite yellow sundress she'd worn to impress him in the hamper and trying not to think about the fact that she also shed her bra-and-panty set. Also her favorite. Also worn to entice him. Also left behind.

Her heart was racing when she stepped out of the bathroom. Her nipples were hard peaks. Wetness leaked from her sex. How embarrassing. Did he expect her to walk to the car dressed like this?

She knew the answer immediately.

He handed her a pair of white, strappy, flat sandals.

She squatted down to slip them on, and then she righted herself, unsure what to do with her hands.

"Ready?" he asked.

"Uh, I think so." She glanced around.

He didn't move to leave however, and she finally looked at his face. It was firm, a brow lifted.

"Sir. I'm ready, Sir," she amended. She really needed to get that right and fast or he was forever going to be angry with her.

"Let's go then." He lifted her suitcase like it weighed less than a pound and headed for the door.

She sincerely hoped it *didn't* weigh less than a pound or she was going to be in so much trouble.

At the door, Lincoln turned toward her. "Purse? Phone? Charger?"

She grabbed her purse from the couch. "Got it." It wasn't much. She'd always preferred simple. A small clutch she could toss over her shoulder that had little more in it than what he'd named. Plus some lip gloss he probably wouldn't let her wear, though that still baffled her.

He reached out a hand as he stepped into the hallway. "Keys." It was a demand. Not a question.

She handed him her keyring.

He locked the door and pocketed her keys. Interesting. That one small action had enormous implications. She wouldn't be returning to her apartment without asking for them. That was obvious.

She'd never been more self-conscious than she was on the walk down the hall, the ride in the elevator, and the short trek across the lobby and parking lot. Thankfully, they had managed all of that without running into any of her neighbors.

She felt totally naked. It was probably all in her head. But she still thought anyone who saw her would know she wasn't wearing any undergarments.

Lincoln stowed her suitcase in the trunk of his sleek black sports car and opened the passenger door. He took her elbow as she entered and pointed at the seat belt. "Buckle up." As if she wouldn't have done so on her own...

Not for the first time in the past week, she had to ask herself —*what the hell am I doing?*

She breathed deeply, forcing herself to calm down as he rounded the hood of the car. This was Lincoln. No need to freak out. What was the worst that could happen in his care? She might lose herself. He might break her. Or she might find herself. And he might fix her.

What he wouldn't do was hurt her. She knew that. Not physically. She needed to trust he wouldn't do anything to harm her emotionally either.

The worst thing that could come out of this experience would be solid confirmation he was right and she wasn't cut out for this lifestyle. And, of course, a broken heart.

Lincoln drove to his house in silence. In fact, she began to wonder if everything with him was going to be a series of psychological games. Silence. Demands. Punishments. The list went on in her head.

She'd never been to his house. Not once in five years. Rowen had. Many times. So had Carter. They had events and parties there. She was never invited. This was a first.

She had to admit she was surprised to find he lived in a gated neighborhood in a large ranch home that had to accompany a hefty mortgage. She had no idea if he did anything besides run the club. Her brother did. He was an accountant. Carter did something in construction. But Lincoln owned the majority interest in Zodiac. It was possible he didn't have another job or he had other money.

Lincoln opened the garage with a remote she never saw located somewhere in the car and pulled into the semi-darkness. It was large. In addition to the sports car she was currently seated in, he had a black SUV parked in the garage.

What stood out to her above all else as she stepped out of the car was how pristine the garage was. If he kept his home half as tidy as this garage, it would have to be a shrine.

Two minutes later, she was proved correct. Not one thing was out of place in Lincoln's home. And she didn't get the impression he'd tidied up for her arrival. It was way too clean for that. He kept it this way.

After holding the door open for her to enter his kitchen, he set her suitcase down and took her purse from her shoulder. Luckily he placed it on the counter next to the fridge and didn't rush off to hide it somewhere. And then he spoke his first words. "I'll expect you to call or text Rowen once a day to let him know you're okay. Everyone who goes with a Dom to his home should have a plan in place ahead of time with a friend or relative they have to check in with." He lifted a brow as he eyed her, his glare indicating without a single syllable that she'd already fucked up by not arranging such a thing.

That irritated her. Firstly, because how the hell did he know she hadn't made such an arrangement? And secondly, he was not a stranger she met last week on the street. He was her brother's best friend and partner.

She held her tongue and nodded.

"Aside from contacting Rowen, you're not allowed to use your phone without permission. Understood?"

"Yes, Sir." Who would she call? Mrs. Lopez to check on her plants? She almost laughed. She had friends at work, but she wouldn't utter a word of this even to Ella, the school's receptionist. She shuddered at the thought of telling any of them she was at a Dom's house training to be an obedient submissive.

The second thing that stood out to her was that he wasn't going to waste time or mince words. No easing into this arrangement. She was his trainee, and he meant business.

He picked up her suitcase. "Follow me."

She followed as he demanded, heading from his enormous sparkling kitchen into his equally fabulous family room. Where the kitchen was mostly white with stainless steel appliances, the family room was mostly dark with a black leather sectional, luxurious gray carpet, and a dark wood, built-in entertainment center. The end tables were the same mahogany as the entertainment center, and the lamps had gray shades in the same tone as the carpet.

He needed color.

She didn't tell him that.

She followed him down the hallway. He pointed to the first door on the left. "Guest bath." The first door on the right next. "Office." She glanced inside to find he kept his office as tidy as the rest of the house. Anal much?

They continued down the hall, pausing at the second door on the left. "Guest bedroom. There's an attached bath." He pushed through the open door and padded across the room to set her suitcase next to the dresser. "You'll be sleeping in here."

Why did that disappoint her so much? It wasn't as if she expected him to sweep her into his own bed and make mad passionate love to her during her stay. He'd made that abundantly clear. But a girl could dream.

The room was not as bland as the others she'd toured so far. Although the queen-sized bed was covered with a fluffy, white comforter, it had several colorful pillows on it, strategically placed. *Please tell me he doesn't take care of this house himself.* It would be too weird to picture him arranging those pillows so that they had a balance of size and colors.

Again, she held her tongue.

The floor was hardwood, but an oval area rug was a braided weave of bold colors that matched the pillows. Impressive.

The bed was four posted, and she fought the urge to shudder at the thought of what he might do with those four posts. How many women had stayed in this room? Again, she said nothing. It was becoming a habit, and she was rather proud of herself for holding back her questions.

He nodded toward her suitcase. "I suggest you leave that closed and hang on to the mystery. Yeah?"

"Yes, Sir." She shivered. What the hell had he packed for her? Too much? Or too little? There weren't many other choices. Which reminded her that she currently wore nothing but the flimsy see-through dress. She crossed her arms as that truth emerged in her mind.

Lincoln chuckled. "Come with me."

She followed him back to the family room, wondering why the tour had ended without including the rest of the rooms, notably the master bedroom.

There was a wall of windows covering the back of the house along the open kitchen/family room floor plan. And the backyard was spectacular. She didn't know how she'd missed it on the way through. "Wow," she uttered before she could stop herself.

"It's gorgeous, isn't it?" he asked, not commenting on her indiscretion.

"Yes. It is, Sir." She wandered closer, taking in his covered patio equipped with an outdoor kitchen, a teakwood table and chairs, and a full outdoor living room set. The brown wicker loveseat and rocking chairs had dark green cushions, and the entire display faced the amazing in-ground pool. He even had a rock waterfall on one end that fed into a hot tub.

She wanted to go out there and experience the beauty for the duration of her stay, but he hadn't given her permission.

The grass beyond the pool was perfectly cut with rose bushes and a few new trees artfully placed around the yard. The fence was high and wood. Private. How had she never been here? Her brother hadn't even mentioned the place.

"We'll go out there later. Don't worry. Come."

She turned from the window at his command and shuffled toward where he stood next to the sectional.

"Kneel on the floor." He pointed at the place he wanted her and waited.

She'd expected this. Anticipated it, even. And she lowered herself onto her knees, keeping them shoulder-width apart, clasping her hands behind her. She hoped he would be impressed.

"Good girl. You've done your homework." He set his hand on her shoulders and pulled them back a few inches. "Keep your shoulders back and your chest high."

She swallowed. Her head was tipped downward, her hair acting as a curtain to hide her face. Her view was of her nipples, dark and puckered. Great. How many people had seen them in the parking lot?

With her legs spread open, she became aware of her sex, currently leaking more than she would like.

"You'll spend a lot of time in this position. It's standard in the lifestyle. Any Dom you're with in the future will expect something similar."

She flinched at his reminder that this was temporary and she would move on to another Dom when he was finished with her. Little did he know that would never happen.

Call her crazy. Call her insane. But this lifestyle didn't extend to others. It was for him alone. Subconsciously, she'd always known that, but after scening with Master Colin and then sitting in Lincoln's lap, she knew for certain. She wouldn't tell him of course, but she'd become more certain of it over the past week of introspection.

For years she'd considered herself submissive. Ever since she first realized what Club Zodiac actually was at the age of fourteen, she'd been intrigued. She had never dealt with the usual shock other people felt when they learned about the slightly under-the-radar lifestyle because it was all so normal for her. Her moment of shock had come at fourteen.

Young? Yes. And she knew it pissed Lincoln off. But it was what it was, and Sasha had never considered herself to be harmed from the knowledge. If anything, it molded her to be open-minded. That couldn't be a bad thing.

She had been titillated and intrigued by what she saw and learned early on, but that didn't make her submissive. It made her horny. She'd learned to masturbate young and owned her first butterfly vibrator as soon as she was eighteen and old enough to walk into a fetish shop.

Granted, by then she'd already met Lincoln, so her libido had kicked up a notch, and she'd needed an outlet for it. Her fingers did the trick in a pinch, but a vibrator was so much quicker and more effective. What would Lincoln say if he knew she'd masturbated to his image for all these years? Until this past week. Damn him.

As far as submission was concerned, she'd learned that while she enjoyed reading about it and the way it made her feel to research it or lose herself in romance novels, she didn't think she would like to be publicly humiliated or flogged. The scene she'd done last Friday had made her uncomfortable.

Although she would do anything in the world Lincoln asked of her, she doubted his training would later extend to other Doms. It was jarring to realize, and she opted to keep that revelation to herself.

He was going to spend their time trying to figure out what sort of submissive she was, when the truth was she was *his* submissive. It was that simple.

"I like the way you're inside your head today, little one. It pleases me you've managed to control your tongue and your temper."

"Thank you, Sir." She kept her gaze lowered, but straightened her spine.

"I expect you to obey my every command at all times while I'm training you. It's more efficient and less confusing while you're learning. Understood?"

"Yes, Sir." She tried to keep her voice from shaking. Every demand he gave made her sex clench and her breasts swell further. Did he know that?

"I'm going to push you. Part of our exploration will entail figuring out what sort of submissive you are, if you're even submissive at all. So, I'll be guiding you in a variety of directions and watching how you respond.

"But I don't want you to worry about your safety or your boundaries. I would never ask anything of you I didn't believe you could accomplish. You've made it clear in our emails and texts what your hard limits are. I won't cross those without consulting you first. As time goes by, you might loosen your convictions."

"Thank you, Sir." Was he right? She'd given him a list of things she would never consider doing. She found it hard to believe she might take any of them back. She'd done her best to research and think hard on every detail and only included the parts that made her completely come out of her skin.

Obviously no permanent marks or brandings or tattoos or piercings. That went without saying, and he'd already pointed those things out last Friday. In addition, she'd declined to experience a whip, a violet wand, and ball gags. The whip made her cringe every time she imagined the sound alone. The violet wand was a mystery that involved more electricity than she could stomach. And the thought of having her mouth forced open wide made her gag impulsively. She might be able to endure a bit or something smaller, but not the ball gag.

He circled her several times. Slowly. Unnerving. Intentional. She hoped she didn't spend all her time psychoanalyzing everything he did. It would drive her mad.

CHAPTER 11

Lincoln was in deep shit. No denying it.

Sasha had only flinched for a moment, and that was when he asked her to take off her clothes and put on the barely existent dress, leaving her nude underneath.

He had no idea what possessed him to insist on such a thing. It was so unlike him. He didn't ordinarily care what his subs wore or didn't wear. As long as they reacted appropriately to his cane or the palm of his hand, he didn't need them to be in any particular state of dress.

Until Sasha. She was different.

He was growing more and more aware that her needs were sexual in nature. She was strongly affected by exposure. Taking away her clothing—even partially—put her in a different mind frame. He hadn't stopped to consider that before. It wasn't his domain ordinarily. Subs came to him needing release through flogging or any number of apparatus. Often they chose whether or not they wanted to be naked or partially clothed. He didn't harp on that issue.

The moment Sasha stepped out of that bathroom, wearing

nothing but the thin material of her dress, he knew he'd been right. Removing some of the layers of barrier between her and her Dom automatically put her in a sort of subspace. He was itching to find out how she would react when he told her to take the dress off altogether. And his reasons were not altruistic at all.

Damn, but he wanted to see her naked. He didn't dare, but the next best thing was almost naked. He lied to himself when he decided it would be no big deal to have her change into this flimsy, see-through material. He'd told himself no one would notice. That had been a mistake on his part because he hadn't anticipated his own reaction to her public exposure. He'd held his breath all the way to the car, realizing the folly of his decision and knowing in a heartbeat he would never display her in public again.

It wasn't as if she was naked, but he hated worrying about other people possibly seeing what was his.

His? Fuck.

He should have known what his reaction would be based on how the hairs on the back of his neck had stood on end when Master Colin had lifted her skirt a scant inch or two. He had thought his body stiffened over *her* reaction to that last straw. Apparently he'd been wrong.

Granted *her* reaction was important also. She clearly didn't like it last Friday or today on the way out of her building. She was nervous and fidgety and never glanced around. It bothered her to be exposed.

He hesitated at that thought. It bothered her to be exposed to Colin, to other people at the club, or even random people they might have encountered on the way to his car this morning. But alone with him?

She wasn't concerned about being exposed to *him*. No way was he reading this incorrectly.

She was not an exhibitionist, but that was something else

entirely. And it worked out well since he wasn't inclined to ever share an inch of her skin again.

Possessive much?

He really needed a head adjustment. He owned a BDSM club for God's sake. He'd been surrounded by scantily clad women for years. It had never made him flinch.

But Sasha wasn't joining those ranks. Ever.

He inhaled slowly as he shook himself back to the present. He had no say in her life. He had no say at all in her future. She could pick any Dom she wanted and do whatever that man bid her to do, including strip naked in public.

He stared down at her sexy body and held his breath. Her nipples called to him. They were begging to be pinched or clamped or suckled. He could smell her pussy from several feet away. She was wet. If her squirming was any indication, her arousal was leaking down her thighs.

Fuck me.

Again, since when did he care about such things? What he needed to do was grab his toy bag and ensure she didn't like what he pulled out.

But the idea made him cringe. He wasn't going to do any such thing. She wasn't ready. He needed to ease her into the lifestyle. At the very least, he needed to maintain a level of professionalism fitting of the owner of a fetish club who offered to train a newbie. Anything less would be indecorous and morally disgraceful.

Fool.

His cock had been so hard from the moment she opened the front door that he'd had to adjust it several times.

He was treading in uncharted territory, and it both unnerved him and intrigued him. Maybe he could learn something about himself during this arrangement too. He didn't have any hope it would apply to Sasha, but he might be able to take something away that would benefit future submissives.

He had every intention of focusing on discipline and

obedience. Instead, his mind kept wandering to sex and gratification. Hers. Of course. Hers.

She clearly needed a Dom who would make her body hum. He had to step up to the plate since he'd been the one to propose this farce. It was his fault and on his shoulders now.

It would be easy to put any lingering doubt about how she would react to her nudity to bed. He would bet his last dollar her awkward nervousness did not extend to him. He was both dying to know the answer to that question and afraid to find out.

Disassociate, man. You can do it. This is for her. Her training. Her experience. Get your head out of your ass and teach her.

"Knees wider, sweetheart." Why the hell would he ask her to do that, and why would he call her that nickname?

He ran a hand through his hair from behind her.

She trembled, her legs parting farther, her shoulders thrusting back more.

Her nipples called to him. He was going straight to hell. Rowen was going to escort him to the gate.

Honestly, he couldn't remember when he'd ever been this turned on by a woman. He seriously needed to cool it before he hurt her. He could take things too far. He wouldn't fuck her, of course. That was out of the question, but he could take her places she might enjoy too much and then associate them with him. That would be detrimental.

His cock told him to strip her naked and make her hum. His brain told him to use his big head instead and take things slow.

The reality was he needed to nudge her in several different directions to prove his theory. It was against his normal procedure to assume. Maybe he was wrong about her. Maybe she needed a good caning in order to release pent-up frustration.

He nearly chuckled. As if he or anyone else would ever cane the beautiful unmarred skin of Sasha Easton.

Damn. He was doing it again. *Focus.* Time to get to work. "Tell me what you're feeling, Sasha."

She flinched. "What... I'm feeling, Sir?"

"Yes. The best way for me to judge where you are in your training is to stop and take your pulse often. If you're not honest with me, you'll slow down the process. When I ask you to tell me what you're feeling, I need you to do so without holding back."

"Okay... Sir."

"I know we're just getting started, but a lot has happened this morning already. You're now in an unfamiliar environment with a man you hardly know on your knees wearing very little clothing. How does that make you feel?"

She hesitated and then whispered, "Aroused, Sir."

Yep. He did not need her to tell him that. Had he done it for *her* or for him? Making her verbalize her arousal changed nothing.

"Is that hard for you to admit?"

"Yes."

He set a hand on her shoulder and squeezed. He hadn't meant to make direct contact with her yet, but he couldn't resist, and he also hoped she would take a cue from his firm squeeze that she'd displeased him.

She lifted her gaze and turned her head to look at him. "Sorry, Sir. I'm trying. I keep forgetting."

He smiled down at her indulgently. *Indulgently?* Fuck.

"Would you like me to call you Master Lincoln or just Master?"

He shook his head, releasing her and rounding her body to lower himself onto the sofa a few feet in front of her face. "No. I'm not your Master. Call me Sir." He was a complete idiot. Where did that come from? Almost everyone who came to the club called him Master Lincoln. It was normal. Obviously Sasha should do the same. His brain cells weren't firing properly.

"Okay, Sir." Did she look deflated?

He leaned back, aiming for nonchalant which had never been a problem for him in the past. After crossing his legs, he studied her.

She was still looking at him, which he should point out, but he needed to see into her eyes. They hid nothing. She was scared. She was nervous. She was also aroused. He let his gaze roam down her body intentionally, pausing at her chest for long moments so she would know he was admiring her.

Eventually, she shuddered.

He lifted his gaze to hers. "Does it embarrass you for me to look at your body?"

"No, Sir. It's… unnerving."

"Good girl. Always answer me truthfully. Would you say you have high self-esteem in general?"

"Yes, Sir. I mean, I guess so. Do you mean with regard to my body?"

"Yes. How do you feel when you're naked with a man?" He deliberately baited her with that question. She was twenty-two years old. Logically, she'd been with a man, probably more than one. But damn. His racing heart was praying she had not.

She lowered her gaze back to the position he had required in the first place. Hiding? "I'm not sure."

"You don't know how you felt when your partners looked at you? Aroused? Confident? Self-conscious? Embarrassed?" It seemed prudent to force this issue because until she told him how experienced she was, they would be walking on eggshells.

She swallowed, her thick, wavy curls falling around her face.

He needed to pull her hair back and clip it at the base of her neck so she couldn't hide behind it. Or perhaps he was telling himself that so he could get his hands on all those luxurious curls.

"Self-conscious, I guess. Sir." She sounded hesitant, and her words surprised him. They insinuated she *had* been naked with men. Why didn't he believe her? Wishful thinking perhaps.

"You guess?"

She didn't respond. Instead, she bit her lower lip and held it, though he had to dip his head to catch her reaction.

The hair had to go. "Don't move." He stood and stepped from the room, aiming for the guest room. He set her suitcase on the bed, opened it, and grabbed her toiletry bag. He hadn't gone through the small bag when he repacked for her earlier, and he hoped he wasn't violating her privacy by doing so now, but he needed a hairband, and that wasn't something he kept in his home.

Bingo. He grabbed the band, set her toiletry bag in the attached bathroom, and returned her suitcase to the floor.

When he was once again standing behind her, he reached for her hair. "Tip your head back, sweetheart."

She did as he instructed, which made it much easier to gather the thick curls at her nape and thread the entire mass through the hairband. "There. Now I can see your face."

He returned to sit in front of her, pleased with the way she resumed her position, face toward the floor. "Thank you, Sir."

"Hope you don't mind that I went through your stuff to find the hairband. I'm glad you had a package of them."

Her brow furrowed. She opened her mouth. Then she closed it.

"What were you going to say, little one?"

"I was, uh, wondering why you don't have any hairbands in your home. Surprised me is all. Sir." The way she repeatedly tacked the address to the end of her statements as an afterthought made him chuckle inside.

"I don't have enough hair to warrant them," he teased. "They don't exactly complete my look."

Her eyes widened. "I didn't mean... I mean, I've seen you use them at the club. On your subs, I mean. I just thought... Sir..."

Where was she going with this? "Yes. I do like to pin my subs' hair back during a scene. It helps me judge where they are emotionally if I can see their faces. It also prevents the possibility of injury. For some scenes, hair can get in the way and be a hazard."

He watched her closely. She was still confused. She bit the corner of her bottom lip between her teeth, her gaze fixed on the floor again. "So, you, uh, only use them at the club. Not at the house? Sir?"

Ahhhh. Now it was clear. "Sasha, look at me." The timing sucked. He didn't intend to tell her this yet. It might give her the wrong idea. But he also wouldn't lie to her, and he'd backed himself into this corner, so now he would have to deal.

She lifted her face, blinking.

"I don't bring subs to my home."

"Ever?" She swayed forward a bit as if she'd lost her balance and then righted herself.

"No. Never. You're the first."

"Oh." Her face turned a lovely shade of pink. He was glad to see it since he'd made her remove all that makeup she'd had on when he arrived at her place. She didn't need makeup. She was stunning without it. Pure. Innocent. The things that attracted him to her.

"I've worked with submissives many times over the years, usually in the club on designated nights. Sometimes in their homes. Never here."

Her mouth rounded further. "Why did you bring *me* here, Sir?"

"I didn't see any other choice. You needed a Dom to train you, and I was available."

She licked her lips. "You could have gotten someone else." She winced. She wouldn't have taken this challenge with any other Dom. He knew that. Nor would he have permitted her to do so. Nor would Rowen—if he could get his head out of his ass long enough to consider the options.

"There wasn't someone else." He managed to sound like a complete ass when he spoke. And then, frustrated with himself, he made matters worse by dragging the last topic back to the forefront. "Let's get back to my original question."

She tipped her face back down, a habit he recognized as her way of keeping him from seeing her expressions while pretending she was doing so in the name of proper positioning.

"How many men have seen you naked, Sasha?"

She swallowed and then muttered, "None."

His heart stopped. He'd pushed and pushed to get what he wanted, and now he couldn't breathe. The sexiest woman he'd ever met was a virgin.

He was so fucking happy he nearly pumped his fist in the air.

He was also scared out of his mind about how he would proceed with that important detail behind them. It was one thing to train a new sub to enjoy a flogging. It was another thing entirely to work with a sexual submissive. But taking on a virgin was out of the stratosphere.

No way in hell could he touch her. How was this going to work exactly?

She was trembling, making him realize he hadn't responded to her admission. "You misled me before. Intentionally."

"Yes, Sir." Her voice shook.

"Why would you do that?" He was being an ass.

"I didn't want you to think I was a baby, Sir. It's... embarrassing."

He flinched. "I most certainly don't think you're a baby, Sasha. Super aware of your age. And you shouldn't be embarrassed about being a virgin. Be proud of that. Hold it tight. Not many women your age can claim to have held on to their virtue." He had no idea who was using his body to speak through him, but whoever it was sure sounded eloquent.

She didn't move a muscle. He wasn't sure she believed him.

"Did you catch the part where I said I wouldn't tolerate lying?"

Her voice was barely audible now. "Yes, Sir."

"I will have to punish you. You know that, right?"

"Yes, Sir." This time she gulped. She also squirmed, pulling her legs together subtlety. The idea turned her on. She tucked her elbows toward her torso tighter.

He could see the faint outline of the disks of her nipples through the thin dress. He wondered if she'd ever worn the scrap of fabric even with a bra and panties. It wouldn't be suitable. Not on her. Not for any occasion. "When was the last time you wore that dress, Sasha?"

Another shiver shook her. "Um, maybe last year. To the beach, Sir."

"Ah." That made more sense. "Well, don't wear it outside of my house from now on." Oh, he was so in over his head. He needed to get control of his tongue before he totally confused her. And himself.

"Yes, Sir." This new voice was wobbly.

"I'll choose what you wear for as long as you're training under me. Understood?"

"Yes, Sir."

"On that note, I find I'm rather tired of that dress. Please take it off." Yep, straight to hell. He might as well call Rowen and ask him to send a driver. Instead, he shook thoughts of her brother from his head and pushed himself to standing. He had a sub to train. And he was completely clear on what her needs were.

All he had to do was keep his dick in check and follow her lead.

With renewed determination, he set out to do what he'd intended all along. He needed to prove to Sasha that she couldn't hack it in the D/s world. Originally he had thought that would entail pushing her masochistic boundaries. But that wasn't the case at all.

What Sasha needed was to have her sexual boundaries pushed. The fact that she had no experience would work in his favor. She would feel uncomfortable enough with his requests that she would eventually call uncle.

Everyone would win.

Rowen wouldn't have to worry all the time about his sister being involved in BDSM.

Sasha could find a nice vanilla man to buy her a white picket fence.

And Lincoln would go on with his life knowing she could never be the type of submissive he needed.

Win. Win. Win.

CHAPTER 12

Sasha was shaking. She'd been shaking for hours. Or perhaps days. This was what she wanted. She wanted Lincoln to see her as a woman. Hell, she wanted Lincoln to *see* her, period.

There was no better way to achieve that goal than to strip naked for him. She was already so close to naked that she was hiding nothing. His demand that she not wear her current dress in public was strange and confusing. He'd insisted she wear it in public just an hour ago. Against her better judgment. *She* was the one who thought it was too revealing.

She decided not to point that out to him. His growly command had heightened her arousal at the same time it confused her.

Nevertheless, she needed to remove the thin fabric. Now. He was waiting. Did he realize this was a huge pivotal moment in her life? Of course he did. She'd just told him moments ago that no man had ever seen her naked.

"Sasha…" he warned. "Don't hesitate when I tell you to do something."

"Yes, Sir." She released her hands from behind her back and fisted the hem of the dress at her thighs to pull it over her head. Goosebumps rushed over her skin. Her nipples—which had already been stiff—stood totally erect. She'd never felt them so tight. She might come if she touched one.

She lowered her face and forced herself to re-clasp her hands at her lower back.

"Good girl." He stepped closer, slowly circling her. "Shoulders back. Even when your gaze is directed to the floor, I expect your shoulders to be pulled back. It forces your chest higher, puts your tits on display. Any Dom you work with will want you to present yourself in the same fashion."

She did as he said, his crass words making her hotter instead of lessening the need growing in the pit of her stomach. It was like an ache by now. It had grown all week until fully blossoming this morning the moment he stepped into her apartment, all serious and demanding.

She got the impression he intended to keep her at arm's length, boss her around as if he were angry, and push her too far. He was sadly mistaken if he thought she would crack under the pressure.

After all, she had her own agenda. And top on that list was proving to Lincoln she could be the submissive he needed. No matter what he asked of her, she was resolved to deliver. She would do anything. Anything it took to get him to see she was good enough for him. Submissive enough.

She would consent to whatever he suggested. If she didn't like it, she would find a way to learn to like it. He wasn't a mind reader.

It helped that in her soul she knew he would never hurt her. He wasn't that kind of man. Not with any of his subs. Especially not with her.

Hell, she'd be lucky if she got him to touch her. She would, however, do her damnedest to try to convince him.

Yes, she was mortified to be naked at his feet. Not because she had a poor body image, but because she didn't know how Lincoln saw her.

As if sensing she needed affirmation, he positioned himself in front of her, crouched so they were at eye level, and touched the bottom of her chin with one finger. "Look at me, baby."

She nearly choked when he called her *baby*. For a second she considered smirking and crossing her arms, but then she saw his eyes. He most certainly didn't mean to imply she was an infant. There was smoldering heat in his eyes.

Nope. He'd adopted a new nickname for her. He'd moved from *sweetheart* to *baby*. And his words confirmed the sincerity in his eyes. "You're an extremely sexy woman. Perfection. Your curves make men's jaws drop. Your ass is the sort that will bring a Dom to his knees. Your tits are just the right size for a man to grasp. High and gorgeous. The pink of your areolas complements your skin tone."

The breath whooshed from her lungs. "Thank you, Sir." Her voice was husky.

He wasn't finished. "Do not ever demean yourself in my presence. Understood?"

Had she insinuated otherwise? "Yes, Sir. I didn't—"

He cut her off. "I know you didn't. I'm just preemptively warning you I will spank your bottom until you can't sit for a week if I ever hear you put yourself down. I don't tolerate that from any submissive. You won't be an exception. Every female body is perfect and deserves to be worshipped. But yours is particularly exceptional. Just a warning."

"Yes, Sir." He thought her body was exceptional.

He released her chin and stood. "I want you to stay in that position for a while. Get used to being naked in front of me. You might have wondered what I packed in that suitcase. It wasn't much." He walked away from her but not out of sight. He stepped into the kitchen area.

In a few moments she realized he was pulling things out of the refrigerator and working at the island. Was he cooking?

She was surprised he didn't insist she do the cooking. She'd read about domestic submissives, ones who derived pleasure from serving their Masters. Wasn't that an avenue he would explore with her? He'd intimated there were different kinds of submissives, and he intended to help guide her to figure out which kind she was. Although he made it clear his real goal was to prove she wasn't any kind.

She was naked. In Lincoln's family room. On her knees.

She ignored whatever he was doing and concentrated on that fact. He wanted her to get used to it. In fact, he'd bluntly told her he intended to keep her naked often.

She had mixed feelings. On the one hand, it felt strange, especially if he intended to keep all his clothes on. But on the other hand, she was oddly unconcerned. He'd complimented every single aspect of her body, painting the picture of a goddess. If that's truly how he saw her, then it would work in her favor to take advantage of those assets and tempt him into taking things further.

Lincoln left her there for so long her knees started to hurt. The carpet was plush and thick, but any surface would become uncomfortable eventually. Just when she thought she would need to shift her weight around, he called for her. "Come, Sasha. Lunch is ready."

She struggled to climb to her feet, trying to look graceful and failing miserably on shaky legs. He didn't comment or notice, however, so she took a deep breath and headed toward the kitchen.

There was only one plate on the table. It was piled high with food. She hoped he didn't expect her to eat all of it. Sandwiches cut in triangles. Grapes. Apple slices. Cheese cubes. Carrots. She realized she was starving.

She stood next to the table, unsure what he wanted her to do next. Finally, he answered that question as he tossed a thick pillow on the floor. "Kneel, baby. You can sit back on your heels if you'd like. Put your hands on your thighs, but keep your legs open for me."

Another rush of arousal pressed against her vaginal walls at his nonchalant demand that she keep her legs open. It unnerved her for him to specifically look at her there. She would get over it, but so far it still concerned her. It was one thing for him to openly ogle and admire her breasts. It was another thing altogether for him to scrutinize her sex. It was coming. She had no doubt.

She did as she was told, trying to relax.

A sense of déjà vu washed over her as she knelt next to him. A memory rushed to the surface from several years ago. She'd been at Rowen's for a staff BBQ. Lincoln had manned the grill. Burgers and hotdogs.

Sasha wasn't fond of either, but it was a BBQ. While everyone else was filling their plates with food, Lincoln had waved her toward the grill. Without a word, he slid a chicken breast onto a plate already filled with a variety of sides. When he handed it to her, she nearly choked. "You made me a chicken breast?"

He scowled at her. "You wouldn't have eaten otherwise. Go. Sit." He'd pointed at a blanket on the grass as he turned back to the grill. Demanding. Bossy. Confusing.

She hadn't been able to process the gesture at the time. Nor had she thought about it afterward. But now…

"Comfortable?" he asked, yanking her back to the present.

"Yes, Sir. Thank you."

"Keep your hands on your lap. I'll decide what you eat and when."

She nodded. "Yes, Sir." She should have been prepared for a scene like this. She'd read about it often enough. She was quickly learning that reading and experiencing were entirely different things.

"Did you see anything on this plate you don't care for?"

"No, Sir."

He grasped her chin and forced her gaze to his. "You're sure? I'm not interested in making you eat foods you don't like. Tell me now."

"I'm not a picky eater, Sir."

He smiled and released her. After sampling a few bites of sandwich himself, he tore off a bite and held it to her lips. "Open."

She did as told again, feeling like a baby bird. He followed the sandwich with a grape and then a carrot. When he lifted a glass of water to her lips next, he wrapped his fingers behind her head to steady her.

She felt cherished. It was a strange feeling having someone do everything for her. Especially since her expectation had been that he would require her to do everything for him. The turn of the table was intriguing.

He continued to feed her in silence until she was stuffed.

"More?" he asked.

"No, Sir. Thank you. I'm full."

"Good girl." He patted her head and then slid his hand around to cup her face and frame her chin again. Every time he did that he looked into her eyes, piercing them with his odd ability to see her soul and read her thoughts. "I'm going to be very demanding this afternoon. I need you to trust me to take my cues from you and make the right decisions. I expect you to trust me to know when to stop and when to keep going."

"Yes, Sir."

"We talked about a safeword in our emails. Did you decide on one?"

"Red is fine, Sir."

"Good. I don't expect you to need it. If you do, I'll have done a poor job of reading you. But never enter into any D/s relationship with anyone without establishing a safeword. That rule applies to everyone. Even married couples have safewords."

"Okay, Sir."

He stood from the table, took the dish to the sink, and returned, holding his hand out to her. "Come, little sub. Let's find out what makes you hum."

She gulped at his words. Hum?

He led her right back to the couch where she'd kneeled all morning and resumed sitting in the spot he'd occupied earlier. He still held her hand. "You owe me a punishment for lying to me earlier, and I'm going to collect on that now."

She swallowed, nodding. "Okay, Sir." How would he punish her?

He slid his hand to her wrist and guided her to stand next to his right thigh. His right hand landed on the back of her leg, slid up over her butt, and stopped on her lower back.

She shuddered at the contact and the way his gentle touch soothed and aroused her. His fingers had been so close to her sex.

"Later this week, I'm going to want to spank you for the purpose of making you come. When we do that sort of scene, I'll strap you to a bench or the bed or the ottoman or whatever surface I choose. That kind of spanking is meant to run straight to your pussy and clit until you want to orgasm so badly you can taste it."

She stopped breathing. At his words, the tightness in her belly doubled. Arousal leaked from her channel, and her clit literally pulsed in a mini orgasm. She hadn't thought she would enjoy being spanked after what happened last Friday night. Apparently she was wrong.

He grinned. "You like the idea. Huh. Maybe I won't wait until the middle of the week then. We'll see."

She swallowed. *How about you do it right now?*

"The point is that I want you to understand the difference between a punishment spanking and one designed for pleasure." He paused, maybe trying to read her.

She couldn't give him anything because she didn't know how she was feeling herself, and he still hadn't described what a punishment spanking entailed. As far as she was concerned, any spanking he gave her would probably make her come on contact.

"When I spank you with the intent of correcting misbehavior, I'll always take you over my knee. I will strike you harder, aim higher on your bottom, and do so rapidly. You won't have time to get aroused, and your mind will focus on the discomfort."

"Yes, Sir." Her voice wobbled again. She wasn't sure how she felt about what he was telling her, but she wanted to please him.

"Not every Dom handles spanking the same, but I like my subs to be perfectly clear about the difference. You won't like it. You aren't supposed to like it. But you'll think twice about lying to me later." He lifted a brow.

"Yes, Sir."

"I'm not going to drag this out any longer. Let's get it over with so we can get back to the more appealing parts of D/s." Without saying more or waiting for a response, he slid his hand higher up her back and pressed her forward until she had to bend at the waist.

She landed unceremoniously over his knees, feeling ridiculously like a small child. Could she do this?

She had to. For him. To prove to herself she could. To please him. But she didn't like it. She reminded herself he wouldn't hurt her. Not in any long-lasting manner at least.

He tucked her wrist behind her back and grabbed the other to join it, holding them both at the small of her back with his left hand. The position left her unsteady, but he had a strong enough grip not to allow her to fall.

Her ponytail fell over her right shoulder, and her breasts hung loose along his thigh. Humiliation sent a flush up her body.

"Spread your legs, Sasha." Not *baby*. Not *sweetheart*. Sasha. An unwelcome tear came to her eye. It was awkward, but she opened her thighs.

Without another word and no warning, he set his hand on her butt, lifted it, and swatted her. Hard.

She cried out. It hurt.

He did it again.

She was more prepared the second time and emitted more of a squeal. The third swat forced out a muffled sob. Several more spanks landed hard in the same spot. And just as fast as he'd started, he was done. He righted her immediately, standing her next to him with one hand on her waist.

Tears escaped. She couldn't stop them.

He took her chin. Damn him. "What are you feeling?"

She sobbed when she tried to speak.

"Don't think about it. Tell me," he demanded.

She blurted out the first things she could think of. "Shamed. Humiliated. It hurt."

He nodded. "That's the goal. And I appreciate your honesty. Are you going to lie to me again?"

"No, Sir."

"I didn't think so. See?"

"See what, Sir?" she choked out, reaching up to wipe the tears from her eyes. She tried hard to gather her composure. Half of her wanted to slap him. It took a lot of energy to keep herself in check.

"Punishment spankings are effective. Tell me why you felt shamed."

She sucked in a breath, hiccupping. "I felt like a child, Sir. I'm not a child."

"Then don't act like one."

She nodded. In a way he made sense. She was a grown woman, however. Why would she permit anyone to spank her like that?

"This is part of submission, baby." His voice was soothing now. He pulled her around to face him, holding both her wrists. "You wanted to experience it. I'm not going to go easy on you just because you're my business partner's sister."

She winced. "I never asked you to."

"In fact, I'm going to be harder on you than I would someone else. Partly because you've known me for years so we don't have to dance around trust issues. Partly because I want you to be absolutely certain this lifestyle is for you. If I half-ass this, you won't be prepared for another Dom, and I won't have done my job. I warned you throughout the week this was going to be hard. I'm demanding. Any Dom worth his salt is unwavering about his rules. Lying is on the top of my list. Cussing, in your case, is up there too."

Damn. That made sense too.

"Some submissives get off on the consequences of intentional disobedience. We refer to them as brats. Have you come upon that in your research?"

"Yes, Sir." She shuddered. She was not a brat.

"Brats represent a specific niche group of submissives. They're usually easily identified in the lifestyle. Did you enjoy having my hand spanking your bottom hard and fast?"

"No, Sir." She shook her head vehemently.

"Did you get aroused?"

"Definitely not, Sir."

He smiled. "Then it's safe to say you're probably not a brat. In addition, I wouldn't expect me or any other Dom in your future to have to dole out punishments to you often. You're more of a pleaser. If you don't like having your ass red and burning, you won't misbehave frequently and certainly not intentionally. It's simple. Do you have any questions?"

She squirmed. "Yes, Sir. If you know I wouldn't intentionally do anything to get myself punished, then why would you be so hard on me when I accidentally mess up?"

He smiled. "That's a great question." He shook her wrists in his excitement. "Because, sweetheart, as a submissive, you'll be held to a higher standard. Any Dom will expect you to pay close attention to details and think before you speak. It's one of your jobs. Attention to details. When you're disobedient, intentionally or accidentally, the correction will encourage you to pay closer attention the next time. It will help you be a better submissive. You'll find yourself improving in the role and you'll need to be disciplined with less frequency."

She nodded. "Okay, Sir."

He squeezed her wrists again. "Does your bottom burn?"

"Yes, Sir." It stung like tiny needles were poking at her.

"Will you lie to me again today?"

"No, Sir."

He smiled again. "Good girl. Now, I want you to go into your bedroom, lie on the bed, and spread your legs wide. Before we do anything else, I want to shave your pussy."

The blood drained from her face.

He lifted a brow. "What are you waiting for?"

She swallowed for the millionth time. "Sir…" *Shave my pussy?* There were so many things she'd researched and been prepared for. That was not one of them. It hadn't factored in on the short list or the long list. She wasn't sure she could go through with something that intimate. He would put his hands there and look closely and smell her and… Oh, God. She couldn't do it.

She wasn't overly attached to her genital hair or anything, but having someone shave her? Her heart rate sped up. "I… I can do it myself, Sir."

"I'm sure you can. But I didn't ask you to, did I?"

Shit.

"Sasha, your hesitation tells me I didn't make my point clear enough with my palm on your bottom."

She jerked back to the present. "No. I mean, Sir. Yes. You made yourself clear. Sorry, Sir." She turned and padded from the room hastily. Flames licked up her chest and cheeks. She wasn't at all sure she could go through with this, but she needed to get away from him in order to think.

When she reached the bedroom, she wasn't sure what to do, so she pulled back the comforter, climbed onto the mattress, and eased onto her back. Her ass hurt. Luckily the sheets were cool and expensive. They didn't add to her plight. For a moment she held her breath until the pain of pressing her ass into the bed subsided and then she panted through the worst of it and tried to relax.

She did not, however, have enough time to think about the upcoming shaving scene. Before she had gathered enough brain cells to shift her concentration from her sore ass to her next plight, Lincoln wandered into the room with a tub of items in his hand.

Yes. This was going to happen. It wasn't the end of the world. It wouldn't hurt. It would simply be emotionally draining. She needed renewed commitment to this submissive training.

Lincoln had warned her several times he wouldn't go easy on her. He'd made a point of indicating he would in fact be harder on her. Like a test. A test he didn't think she could pass.

He was wrong.

CHAPTER 13

Lincoln set the tub of shaving items on the bed next to his sweet submissive. She was frazzled. No doubt about it. She hadn't fully wrapped her mind around the spanking scene before he threw this next test at her.

Was he moving too fast? Going too hard on her?

He had to think not. For one thing, that was the goal. For another thing, if for some reason she continued to show truly submissive tendencies, then she would be that much more prepared for her next Dom.

He stiffened at the thought. There would be no next Dom. *Fuck.*

He had two choices, convince her not to enter the lifestyle or keep her for himself. Since option number two was out of the question, he needed to stay focused on the first goal.

Eight swats to her ass wasn't going to kill her. He knew it had to burn, especially now that she was lying on her back, but submissives endured far more intense spankings than that one. She only thought it was horrifying because it was her first.

Frankly, he was shocked by how well she'd endured it. She hadn't even tried to escape his palm. She'd cried out, but otherwise, she'd been brave. Quite the accomplishment after running from Master Colin's mere suggestion of swatting her bare bottom last week. He now knew that was different, though. She hadn't liked the public exposure. She hadn't known Colin. Master Colin was not Lincoln.

Lincoln took a breath. She would blossom for him. *She will do it for me. No one else.*

Looking at her now, spread open for him. Naked. Exposed. Laid completely bare a few hours into her training. He was undone.

Damn, she was gorgeous laid out for him like she was now. Shivering, teeth almost chattering, but sexy as hell. "I want you to reach under your knees for me and hold your legs open."

She turned her head to one side, pursing her lips, but she did as she was told.

His heart raced. He let his gaze roam down her body from her tight nipples to her pussy. He set his hands on her inner thighs and stroked the tender skin, helping her open farther while soaking in the sight of her tight pubic hair and the treasure it attempted to hide.

He vowed not to dwell on her pussy or its promises until after he'd bared her to his scrutiny. Instead, he reached for the towel in his tub and tapped the side of her butt. "Lift your bottom, sweetheart. I need to slide this under you."

She used her heels as leverage and did as instructed. As she settled back onto the towel, Lincoln couldn't stop himself from gently stroking through her pubic hair. He needed to feel it, feel her. It was soft. His cock stiffened. The small head was being tortured today. After he shaved his sub's sweet mound, he really needed to escape for a bit into his own bathroom and relieve the pressure before he exploded.

Never in his life had he gotten hard during a scene. Granted, this was far more than a scene. It was a full-time arrangement. But he still shouldn't be this fucking hard all the time.

A soft moan from Sasha reminded him he was stroking her fucking pussy. He pulled his hand away and reached for the shaving cream. Forcing himself to disassociate, he spread the white foam around her pussy all the way back to her tiny hole.

His reason for shaving her had nothing to do with his aversion to a woman's genital hair. He found women sexy with and without the barrier. But for this week, he wanted to keep Sasha totally exposed. It would make her feel that much more vulnerable without the added protection.

Women had a thing about having their pussy shaved. He found most of them had a different head space when they were bare to his view. They also inevitably got more pleasure from having their naked lips stroked and their clit exposed to the air. And hell, this knowledge came from having sex with women, nothing to do with BDSM. He really did keep the two separate in his mind.

Until Sasha.

He also knew it was unnerving to have a Dom shave a woman himself. Totally different from instructing the sub to do it.

Yeah, he was pushing her limits. But she was yielding them just as quickly. A fact that made him harder. *Dammit.*

When he set his left hand on her lower belly to hold her steady and pull her skin tight, she whimpered. "Deep breaths, baby. It won't hurt. Most women find it soothing."

He half expected her to ask how many times he'd done this, but she didn't. She was stiff and distracted. The truth wasn't very interesting. The few times he'd had a sexual relationship with a woman that lasted longer than a few dates or trips to the club, he usually asked them to let him shave them.

He didn't question what his obsession was. He just knew he liked the way they submitted to him when he did it. The idea jolted him while he continued to rub the foam into her mons. It didn't need further attention, but it mesmerized him, and she was panting through the attention so deliciously.

He tried to grab on to his last thought. It never occurred to him that shaving a woman like this was indeed a sign that he enjoyed a bit of sexual kink alongside his sadism. Huh.

He removed his fingers, wiped them on a smaller hand towel, and grabbed the razor next. "Stay still for me, baby. I don't want to cut you."

She was holding her breath. Too stiff.

"Sasha, look at me."

Her throat moved up and down and finally she lowered her gaze. Her mouth was still pursed tight. Her eyes blinked.

"Trust me?"

She nodded. He wouldn't ask for a verbal this time. She was totally unaware of her indiscretion.

"It's just hair," he pointed out. "If you hate it, it will grow back."

She let her lips part. "I know, Sir. I'm ready."

He smiled warmly at her. "Good girl." And then he bent to the task, slowly dragging the razor over the curls above her clit first and then working his way down to her pussy. He had to grit his teeth to keep from moaning as he so intimately parted her lower lips and bared them to his view with long, drawn-out drags of the razor.

He concentrated. Hard. Forcing himself to get the task done before he would allow himself to stop and admire her sweet, sweet pussy. He was the first man to ever see her spread open like this. The first man who would carefully bare her. The first man who would watch her come undone, witness the swell of her lower lips, watch the throbbing of her clit when she came, taste her essence.

He was so fucked. No way in hell did her brother intend for Lincoln to so thoroughly defile her like this. Sure, he'd emphatically insisted on no sex, but where was the line? Lincoln knew he had crossed it about three hours ago, if not from direct contact then at least from his carnal thoughts.

He quickly continued down to her tight hole and then gently

pushed her labia from side to side to make sure he didn't miss a spot. And then he was done.

She exhaled a long breath as he used the hand towel to wipe the remaining shaving cream away. She was probably relieved to have that small measure of cover.

But it was short-lived. Lincoln tossed the razor and towel back in the tub and set his hands on her thighs, pressing them wider. He needed to see, soak in this moment. So pink. So damn sexy.

When he gave a pull on her skin, her labia parted for him, exposing her wetness. He slid his hands closer, using his index fingers to draw the hood off her clit.

Damn. Damn damn damn. The bundle of nerves was swollen and red and tight. It pulsed while he stared at it.

Hell loomed up behind him, beckoning him to lean backward into the heat so it could swallow him whole.

The willpower it took not to more thoroughly violate her right that second was intense, and the only way he figured he would actually be able to hold back from touching her clit or pushing a finger into her pussy would be if someone else did it for him so he could watch. *Sasha.*

"Let go of your legs, baby," he whispered. "I've got you."

She released her thighs. He held her open. He inhaled her scent. Musky. Arousal filled the air. She was panting. Desperate. "Sir…" The word trailed off on a moan.

He wasn't even touching her directly. "Touch yourself."

She flinched, her hands fisting at her sides. "Sir?"

"Baby, stroke your pussy for me. Use your fingers."

She hesitated, her torso arching. *Fuck me.* She moaned. "Don't ask me to do that, Sir. Please…"

He lifted his gaze and waited for her to look at him. "Did you masturbate this past week?"

"No, Sir."

"Then you must be really needy right about now."

She swallowed. Her eyes were wide.

"Under my care you will never be permitted to touch your nipples or your pussy without permission. I'm giving you that permission right now. I want you to stroke yourself to completion. Show me how you bring yourself pleasure when you're alone."

She panted, still staring at him.

Fuck me. If she doesn't even masturbate, I'll die right now. "Sasha... You do masturbate, right?"

She flinched. "Of course."

He lifted a brow. "By that do you mean you have done so once or twice? Or often?"

"Often, Sir." Her voice was barely audible.

Thank Christ. "Show me, baby."

She inhaled sharply, shaking her head. "I don't. I mean, I don't usually use my fingers."

He took a deep breath, his eyes sliding shut for a moment while he processed visions of her fucking her pussy with a dildo or a vibrator. "What do you use to make yourself come, baby?"

"A, uh, a little vibrator usually. It, uh, it's like a butterfly." Her face was dark red.

"Thank you for being honest. I don't think you'll need a vibrator this time, though. Do you?"

"No, Sir. But..."

"You going to use your safeword?" he pushed. Admittedly he held his breath, praying she would not back out now.

That was the intention, asshole. The goal is to get her to give up this notion of submission. Eye on the prize.

He didn't want her to fail, though. He couldn't begin to know what that meant, but he knew he was counting on her success. "Touch yourself, Sasha," he ordered. "Do it. Don't think about it. Close your eyes and slide your fingers through your folds."

She hesitated for one more second, and then she slid her uneasy fingers between her legs. Her eyes closed. Her head tipped back. Her mouth fell open. She was in the moment before she even touched herself.

He yanked his attention to her tiny fingers, mesmerized as she stroked two of them slowly through her folds, gathering the moisture and spreading it up to her clit. When she flicked those fingers over the swollen nub, she moaned.

Fuck yes. Doesn't usually masturbate with her fingers, my ass…

She rapidly flicked her clit, her breaths coming in shallow pants. Shocking the hell out of him, she let her other hand slide to her nipple and pinch the tip. Holy mother… The bud grew tighter as she worked it. And then she switched to the other one, her hand smoothing gracefully between her mounds.

The entire time she was working her clit, her fingers flat on the nub now, pressing, rubbing. Her heels dug into the mattress, making her thighs stiffen in his grip. "That's it, baby. You're so damn sexy. Come for me, Sasha. Let me see you shatter."

Suddenly, her hand flew down from her breast to join the first one between her legs, and she shocked him again when she worked her clit with both hands, rolling it between her forefingers.

She cried out, so involved in the scene that she probably didn't know it. And then she gave an incoherent scream. It was short, but it correlated with the exact moment her entire body went rigid.

He could swear he actually saw her clit pulse with the force of the orgasm. Her body jerked with every wave of release. Over and over. So many he lost count.

When she was done, her hands slid to her sides and her body went slack.

And Lincoln's world tipped on its axis.

The little minx had lied to him again. No way in hell had she not done this before. The woman regularly got off with her fingers. She may own a vibrator. He had no doubt she did. But she knew her way around her body, and she was skilled without electronics.

He wasn't going to call her out on this, however. She was sated and relaxed. He didn't want to ruin that by embarrassing her. Because he had no doubt the reason she hadn't been completely honest was because she was mortified at the idea of having an audience.

He'd let it slide.

For now.

CHAPTER 14

Sasha was sated. So calm and relaxed that she didn't even care what she'd just done while Lincoln watched. It felt fucking amazing. So much more intense with his gaze nailed to her than any prior orgasm.

She'd been wound up so tight by the time he ordered her to masturbate, she would have done nearly anything in the world to get relief. And she had.

Lincoln released her thighs slowly, easing them closer together.

She winced at the stiffness in her muscles from being held open for so long. But he knew that, and he took care to make it as tolerable as possible. And then she felt the dip in the bed as he climbed onto it, straddling her with his knees. He leaned forward, propping himself above her with hands to the sides of her head.

All of this she knew without opening her eyes.

"Look at me, baby." His voice was hoarse. Strained.

She blinked up at him.

His expression was pained. Odd. His brows drawn together. He licked his lips. "Thank you, Sasha. I'll never forget that gift. It was the most beautiful thing I'll ever have the pleasure of seeing if I live to be two hundred years old."

She smiled. It was involuntary. "You're welcome, Sir." The pride spilled out. She'd pleased him. Immensely. There was no lie in his eyes. He was totally serious.

He lowered the rest of the way over her and kissed her forehead. And then he pulled back, slid from the bed, and gently scooted her body until she lay with her head resting on a soft down pillow and curled onto her side.

He tugged the comforter over her, kissed her forehead again, and gave her shoulder a squeeze. "Sleep, baby." He padded across the room, closed the blinds, and then he was gone.

The room was bathed in the dim light coming from the window.

Sasha was a wild mix of emotions. Half of her was still relaxed and completely sated from the amazing orgasm. She wanted to listen to that side of her brain, sigh, snuggle under the covers, and slide into oblivion.

But it wasn't that simple. The other half of her was disappointed and deeply saddened. He'd said such nice things, but he'd given her nothing. Even the two kisses on her forehead only served to remind her she wasn't his. Not in a permanent way. If he truly felt the strong emotions of the moment that she had, he would have slammed his mouth over hers and kissed her senseless.

He did not.

He detached himself and left her.

A tear slid down her face. She fought to keep them at bay so she wouldn't slip into a loud ugly cry. It wasn't warranted.

Lincoln hadn't brought her to his house to make her his. He'd brought her there to train her to be someone else's submissive.

Not his.

Not his.

Not his.

It hurt. The pain squeezed her chest, making her curl up tighter. She drew in a deep breath. And another. And another. Until she calmed her nerves.

This was just a small hurdle. It was the first day. It hadn't even been a full day yet. It was only afternoon. She had so much time. She would convince him. It would be crazy to give up.

She'd seen the look in his eyes before he closed them, schooled his expression, and then changed his tune. She'd brought him to his knees.

She could still convince him she belonged to him. She simply needed more time. This was just one inning. She had eight more to go. And if it was necessary, she was prepared to go into extra innings.

She forced herself to smile and wipe away the pain. She had this. Lincoln was hers.

Lincoln paced the house while she slept. He was bungling this entire arrangement. He rubbed his temples with his thumb and middle finger, trying to ease the tension. He'd lost his mind. What the hell was he thinking? He was clearly short on brain cells.

The entire day had led him down an unexpected path. Every command he made, she followed. She'd surprised him over and over, stripping for him, letting him spank her, holding her legs open for him to shave her, stroking herself to orgasm while he watched...

You're an idiot.

He'd picked her up from her apartment that morning with a far different picture in his mind of how this would go down. It certainly didn't include an entirely naked Sasha spread open for him, fingering her clit to orgasm.

Jesus, Lincoln.

The words he'd spoken to Rowen haunted him. *"I gave you my word I wouldn't sleep with her."* He'd just fucking splayed her open and watched her masturbate. The very definition of sex was in serious jeopardy.

He'd ensured his best friend he would push her to drop this insane desire to explore BDSM. His motives were much further reaching than anything Rowen had in mind. Lincoln needed Sasha to give up the lifestyle for his own self-preservation.

Instead, he'd spent the day proving she was unbelievably submissive while his cock got stiffer and his mind became befuddled. She had a freaking spell cast over him. He was mesmerized by her every move.

He wanted her so badly he could taste her on his tongue. Hell, he'd had his face so close to her pussy, her scent alone told him exactly what he was missing. It had taken great willpower to keep from closing the gap and sucking her clit into his mouth.

Lincoln ran both hands through his hair, tugging it hard. Maybe the slight pain would jar him back to sanity.

He had to get this train wreck back on track. Force her to cry uncle. He should have seen this coming. He'd had a week of texts and emails to remind him over and over that she might be right about her tendencies.

Nevertheless, in his wildest imagination, he had never expected her to be able to take things this far. *She's fucking naked in my house.*

How hard was she working to submit to him? He worried—not for the first time—that her submission was for him only. He had his doubts about whether or not she could submit to another Dom. If Carter was right and she had a crush on him that had lasted five years, it was possible she was doing all this to force his hand.

Was there anything wrong with that? Not really. Except she didn't understand the kind of cards he'd been dealt. He didn't play in a friendly game of poker. He played in the big leagues. She had no idea what the rules were, and she never would.

This had to end. Even if he hurt her.

He wandered into the spare bedroom silently. She was sound asleep, her lips slightly parted, tendrils of her gorgeous curls begging him to brush them off her face. For a long time he stared down at her, watching her chest rise and fall under the sheet.

He wanted her.

She's not yours.

She can never be yours.

You're a sadist.

She's not a masochist.

She can't give you what you need.

He had to let her go. He had to get her to see reason. He needed to push her so hard that she screamed her safeword. Why had it not occurred to him that this experiment would end so badly?

He'd pictured an hour or two or a day of him directing her and her fighting against him. He'd visualized her laughing at his orders and throwing her hands in the air and accepting defeat.

But no. Of course not. She was not going to go down without a fight.

And the fucking worst part about the entire thing? He didn't want her to go down. She was perfect just the way she was. Perfectly submissive. She could make another Dom's dreams come true.

But he was not that man. He was far too dark for her.

He needed more time. And being the greedy bastard that he was, he decided to pamper her before he fucked with her head again. Pretend she was his for a while longer.

Something was touching her arm.

Something warm. Firm.

She was so deep in sleep it was hard to fight her way out.

A voice called to her. "Sasha. Baby. Wake up."

She knew that voice.

Lincoln.

Her memory flooded back. She was in his house. Training to be his submissive. No. Training to be someone else's submissive.

She opened her eyes.

He was smiling down at her. "I didn't want to let you sleep too long. You'll never be able to sleep tonight if you don't get up."

He was right. "What time is it?"

"Five. I drew you a bath."

She lifted her brows. *He drew me a bath?*

"Come." He pulled the blankets back.

She wasn't fully alive, let alone awake. She curled up into a ball, the chill of the air hitting her bare skin.

Lincoln's hand slid over her hip and then her waist until he cupped her breast.

She started to moan into his touch, but suddenly his fingers found her nipple and he pinched. Hard. So hard she screamed, her body uncurling to flatten on the bed and push at his hand. Her eyes flew open wide.

He held on tight though, anticipating her reaction.

When she stopped fighting him and searched his eyes, having difficulty inhaling, she found him staring at her with one brow raised.

She was no longer half asleep. "I'm sorry, Sir."

He released her nipple and then surprised her by bending over and reverently kissing the tip before flicking it with his tongue. Just as fast, he stood and walked away. "Come."

She scrambled off the bed, her hand automatically reaching for her nipple to rub the throbbing tip.

Lincoln was leaning over the tub, testing the water, when he spoke again without glancing at her. "Did I give you permission to touch your tits?"

She jerked her hand down. "No, Sir."

He turned around, met her gaze, and reached out a hand.

She came to him. Naked. Tired. Adrenaline pumping. Nipple on fire. Ass still stinging from the earlier spanking.

He turned her around so that her back was to him and then worked her hair free of the band. His lips landed on her ear, and she shuddered when he whispered, "Get in, baby."

Her legs were wobbly. So many things had happened in the last fifteen seconds that she couldn't gather her thoughts. As she stepped into the water, she sighed. The temperature was perfect. She gladly lowered her body into the water.

Lincoln kneeled beside her, cupped the back of her head, and set his other hand over her face. "Close your eyes."

She closed her eyes, her hands reflexively reaching up to grab his forearm as he lowered the back of her head into the water. Her face never got wet. He was being cautious. But she couldn't figure out why he felt the need to dip her hair into the water. She could have done it herself. In a while. After she had a chance to find her brain cells and enjoy the warm water.

"Sit up, baby."

She wanted to lean back. In fact, she'd already started to do so when he spoke. Instead, she sat up straight.

He reached for a bottle of shampoo next to the tub and poured a generous amount in his hand. He was going to wash her? "Tip your head down." His words were tranquil.

She relaxed into his care as his strong fingers worked a lather into her hair. It wasn't her normal shampoo. He obviously hadn't unpacked her toiletry bag when he riffled through it to find a hairband. The shampoo smelled good, though. Vanilla. She hoped he realized she would need half a bottle of conditioner to tame the curls.

After massaging her scalp far longer than necessary, long enough to lull her into a state of bliss, he set a hand over her face again and tipped her back. With one hand, he held the back of her head. With the other, he worked the shampoo out of her hair. And then he righted her again.

He grabbed a wash cloth, poured bath soap on it, and lifted her arm. Gentle, slow strokes, up and down her arm. And then the other.

She watched his face as he worked. It was like a ritual, as if he derived comfort from reverently caring for her. She felt cherished.

He continued, meticulously washing her entire body, spending equal amounts of time on her breasts as he did her back and her legs and her feet. He then nudged her legs apart and ran the washcloth over her sex.

She sucked in a sharp breath at the contact, a tiny noise escaping her before she could stop it. She was turned on.

Shit.

He froze, the wash cloth pausing over her clit.

That was when she realized she'd spoken that last word out loud.

He lifted a brow as he set the cloth aside and reach for the conditioner. "Your bottom doesn't hurt?" She thought he was fighting a smirk.

She pursed her lips. *Shit. Shit shit shit.*

"It does, Sir. I'm sorry. It slipped out. I didn't mean to cuss." Would he punish her?

He kissed her forehead, his head shaking as he threaded his fingers in her hair, gave a slight tug, and then angled her face once again toward her lap.

She closed her eyes, a memory flooding her system. He'd done that before. She remembered it well. Right after her high school graduation. They were at the beach. About six employees from Zodiac had gone. And Sasha.

She'd been eighteen by then, though she'd only seen Lincoln a handful of times since that fateful day more than a year earlier.

The only words he'd spoken to her had been clipped, and he never made eye contact.

She hadn't known what possessed her, but she'd decided to pretend she was some other woman that afternoon. One who was bold and confident. So, she'd intentionally tugged off her cover-up two feet from him, stretching her arms to pull her long hair into a bun at the top of her head.

He'd shocked her when he spoke. "I hope you're wearing sunblock."

She'd slowly turned to smile. "Thanks for the tip, Dad."

He'd scowled. "I'm definitely not your father. But you're gonna burn if you insist on being stubborn. Put the damn sunblock on."

Still possessed by a far more outgoing and flirtatious vixen than she'd ever be, she had responded with, "Okay, but you'll have to get my back." And then she'd handed him the sunscreen.

He'd tugged her hair and then dipped her head toward the ground the same way he'd done moments ago. She remembered him quickly rubbing the lotion into her shoulders and back before he turned and walked away without a word.

She'd been left standing there, not breathing. Shaking. Stunned. Her body on fire for him for the second time since she'd met him at her seventeenth birthday party. His dominance had been palpable. She'd stared down at her mostly bare skin for long moments.

And she did so again now, eyes on her naked body, her nipples hard peaks, her mound shaved, her lower lips swollen from masturbating earlier. She subtly pulled her knees closer together, the throbbing need equal to what she'd felt that day at the beach.

Only this time, Lincoln hadn't walked away. He was right beside her, his hands still on her hair, rubbing the conditioner in thoroughly. He lowered one hand and grabbed her closest thigh. "Legs parted."

She bit her lip, fighting the urge to moan as she spread them open again.

After repeating the earlier routine to rinse the conditioner out of her hair, he stood and reached for her hand.

He wanted her to get out? Already? So fast? She wanted to rest. Relax. Think. Be left alone. "Sir, the water is so warm. Can I—"

"Sasha. Don't argue." He shook his outstretched hand.

With a deep breath, she took his hand and shivered as he helped her from the tub. She folded her arms across her chest when he turned to take a few steps across the room.

He opened a small closet and grabbed a towel. "Don't cover your tits. Drop your hands," he said as he returned. "Stand still."

She lowered them, but she was losing ground. The soothing bath was over. His face slid from peaceful and reverent to something unreadable.

Lincoln took a deep controlled breath as he patted her skin dry. He was totally out of his element, and he knew it. He never should have given her a bath. He should have shut the door and left her alone to soak in the water. Instead, he'd started down a path that had no return.

Every inch of her body was so sexy he couldn't resist the urge to touch her, and he'd hidden behind the bath as an excuse to do so. He'd never bathed a woman before. It was so intimate.

Every second he fell deeper under her spell. Each tiny noise she made... The way her skin pinkened... Her nipples sharp points above the water... How she fought to keep her legs spread... The bare skin of her swollen pussy...

He was mesmerized by her. He couldn't get enough.

What he wanted to do was cradle her in his arms, carry her to the bed, and fuck the daylight out of her. That's how slippery the slope was. Tempting. So totally not in the plan.

He gritted his teeth as he leaned down to pat her legs dry, tapping one to get her to spread them wider. His face was inches from her pussy. So close he could smell the sweet scent of her arousal.

He needed to rein in his physical attraction to her and regain the upper hand. His job was to train her. His goal was to get her to see the light and run from this life. He reminded himself that the objective was pushing her to use her safeword. ASAP. It's what he'd told Rowen he would accomplish. It's what he'd told *himself* he would do.

Instead of following his instinct by wrapping her in his arms and kissing her senseless, he stiffened his spine. He'd given himself this time with her. Or perhaps he should say he'd "taken" this time *from* her. This bath. This opportunity to enjoy every inch of her skin. Listen to her sighs of pleasure. Stare at her nipples as they puckered.

Selfish.

It was time to stop this charade. *Convince her to run.* From the look on her face, she was a little off-balance at the moment. Perfect time. And she'd presented him with the perfect segue when she tried to convince him to let her stay in the tub.

He stood and stepped back to lean against the vanity. His heart was racing.

She didn't move. How long could she hold off before speaking again?

Fuck. She was submissive. He hadn't anticipated her being able to go this far. She went out of her way to please him. Including right now. He could see she was on an emotional precipice. Her small body shook. She was cold. Frustrated. Her fingers were stretched toward the floor—fighting the urge to fist them?

He wanted her. Fuck, but he wanted her. Her body. Her mind. Her submission.

You can't have her. She's too sweet for you. She needs a Dom who can guide her to serve him sexually, not someone who's more comfortable with a crop or a whip than cuffs and feathers.

She had good form even now, her face toward the floor, her

legs spread, her shoulders back. It was costing her. But she did it. For him.

He waited, testing her patience, hoping she would break form. It was a dirty move. He was not this guy. Breaking her was not in the plan. Wait. Wasn't it though?

Now what? Somehow he had to get her to bail on this arrangement without hurting her. He didn't think it was possible. He was going to hate himself when this was over. He couldn't see any other way.

He had to push her. But with what leverage? He could make a big deal out of her cussing or touching her nipple or rolling over in bed when he instructed her to get up, but punishing her severely for any of those infractions seemed irrational.

Suddenly, she flinched and lifted her gaze. "Sir?"

He lifted a brow.

She licked her lips. "Sorry, Sir."

"Stand still. Head bowed. Feet wider. I didn't give you permission to move."

She lowered her gaze again, her body shaking. She reached behind her back to clasp her hands. She inched her feet out farther.

He could do this. Wait her out. Why did his stomach clench? This was the right thing to do. Push her. Make her see reason.

She couldn't stand there forever. She was itching to move. Speak.

Maybe he didn't need to rely on those minor prior infractions to push her over the edge. Maybe he could simply insist she stand still in the bathroom, damp, naked, exposed, cold until she couldn't take it anymore.

I'm a total ass.

CHAPTER 15

Goosebumps rose on Sasha's skin. Tears welled in her eyes. Emotional overload. She didn't want to cry in front of him and appear weak. She needed a few minutes alone.

She was cold. Frustrated. Grasping for sanity. Confused. It wasn't that he'd done anything to specifically cause her to feel so unbalanced. It had snuck up on her.

Suddenly, she felt the tight rein she had on her emotions begin to reach a breaking point. She wanted to rush into his space, scream, demand he say something. Anything. She needed him to hold her.

Exhaustion set in even though she'd taken a long nap and then been bathed without lifting a finger. Mental exhaustion from trying so hard to please Lincoln and feeling the weight of failure. Was he mad because she'd spoken out of line, cussed, touched her nipple? He didn't look mad. He was just… waiting.

He knew she had no experiences like this—not just with a Dom but with any man. He was the first to see her naked, and he'd bared her to the point that she felt more exposed than just naked. As if he'd also removed her skin. She'd given him everything, leaving herself raw.

She wanted to speak, ask questions, sob out loud.

Maybe he was disappointed in her. The idea made her chest tighten since all she wanted to do was please him. His silence was poignant though.

She decided to try again. "Sir, I—"

"Sasha," he warned, her name sharp on his tongue.

She started to fidget. Knowing he was staring at her threatened her sanity. Her breasts were high and swollen, her nipples sharp points from the cold and the stress. Even her sex was exposed.

She was not aroused. She was annoyed. Whatever he was doing, it was starting to piss her off.

"You're shaking with frustration," he pointed out. At least he spoke.

"Yes, sir." She kept her head bowed.

"Being submissive sometimes means following orders without explanation." He pushed off the edge of the vanity and sauntered closer, circling her. Stalking her. Annoying her.

Seconds ticked by. Maybe minutes. She shifted her weight from one foot to the other.

He stood behind her for a long time, making so little noise she considered the possibility he'd slid into another dimension. As her body adjusted to the temperature and the moisture on her skin dried, she was no longer freezing, but her anger grew by the second.

What the fuck is the point of this?

Was he waiting for her to do something?

It was like a standoff. And she was losing. Finally, she couldn't take another second and she dropped her form entirely, spun around, and faced him. "What the hell do you want, Lincoln?" Her chest was pounding. If he was testing her, he won.

He lifted a brow. "Safeword?"

She shook her head. "You wish."

Without a word, he set his hand on her shoulder and ran it

down her arm until he held her wrist. He guided her from the bathroom and out of the bedroom. She hadn't been able to read his expression at all.

At least they were leaving the bathroom. She had been close to losing her mind standing there. She wished he would say something. Anything. There was a total disconnect that unnerved her.

She was shivering again. Her hair hung in long wet ringlets down her back, not helping matters. The house probably wasn't that cold, but the chill she felt was more from frustration than from temperature.

They entered the family room. The sun was still out, but it had moved across the sky to the other side of the house, leaving the backyard in a glow of evening colors. It was beautiful. She could stare at it for hours.

But apparently not right now. Her breaths were coming in short sporadic bursts as she worried about what his next move would be. Would he make her leave even though she hadn't used her safeword? Maybe she had blown this entire arrangement with her outburst and he would take her home and declare her unfit to be submissive.

Shit, maybe he was right. At this point, she wanted to haul off and slap him. She was no longer about to cry. She was furious.

Lincoln led her to the opposite side of the room next to the entertainment system. He kept walking until they were standing in the corner with no place to go. She couldn't imagine what he wanted to do there. Nothing was nearby. Not even furniture.

She took several deep breaths, forcing her hands to remain at her sides to avoid taking a swing at him. She pursed her lips to keep from yelling at him and making things worse. She needed to regroup and think before she spoke again.

When he released her hand and stepped behind her to set his palms on her shoulders, she began to worry. And rightfully so. He angled her toward the corner. "Hands clasped behind your back." His voice was matter of fact. Soft. Giving nothing away.

She grabbed one wrist with the opposite hand at her lower back. And then he guided her the rest of the way into the corner. *Oh God. Oh God.*

One hand slid from her shoulder to the back of her head. He angled her face toward the floor. "Lean on your forehead. Nipples to the wall. Feet wider." He stuck a knee between her thighs and nudged them open.

She couldn't breathe. Her body went limp, totally flattened to the wall in the awkward position. There was no way to balance, so she gave in and pressed her breasts and even her belly into the corner.

His lips came closer to her ear. "Wider, Sasha. I want your pussy open and exposed so you have something to think about while you stand here."

She whimpered involuntarily while she spread her legs wider. Obscenely wider. *Oh my God.*

"That's a good girl." He released her. "Perfect form. Don't move. Thirty minutes."

And then he was gone.

She tried to inhale, but only managed to sob. A time out? Is that what this was? A time out?

So matter of fact. Not a single mention of her outburst. She hadn't managed to get him to break from his dominant stance. Nope. Instead, she'd earned herself a time out.

Shit. Shit shit shit.

She really needed to stop thinking that word at all. Obviously she was unable to keep it from slipping past her lips. And why did he care if she—a grown woman—occasionally used that simple four-letter word? It wasn't like she cussed like a sailor. It was one small word. She never said *fuck*. Or even *damn* usually. Just *shit*. Was it that bad?

Jesus, Sasha, who cares about your damn cussing?

She was cold. Apparently he didn't care. It was probably part of his plan.

This was too much. She hadn't signed up for this kind of treatment. It was abasing. She didn't want to stand in this corner. She also didn't have to. She could use her safeword. Turn around, face him head on, and say *red*. And then she could flee the room, find something in her suitcase to wear, and get the hell out of his house.

No. She mentally shook her head. *Don't move. Don't move a single muscle.* She was not going to give up. She came here to prove something to herself and to Lincoln. That she could submit to him. He wasn't hurting her. He hadn't hurt her at all physically. The last half hour had been emotionally challenging. Nothing else. Maybe even intentional.

Had he pushed her to get her to break form so he could punish her?

She realized the two of them had conflicting goals. She wanted to prove she could be his. He wanted to prove she wasn't submissive and get her to use her safeword. She would not give him that satisfaction. She was stronger.

She'd come to his home to learn to be submissive. For *him*.

That wasn't his aim, of course—at least not verbally. He insisted he was training her to prepare her for another Dom. Not him. That infuriated her every time he reminded her.

Why? Why couldn't he see that she wanted *him*? Not someone else.

Maybe he doesn't see you that way, Sasha. Did you ever think of that?

She shook the annoying thought from her head. No. He wasn't just a firm and angry Dom. He had other sides to him. He was also kind and caring.

She inhaled deeply several times to calm her nerves.

It was humiliating standing in this corner like a naughty child. *Isn't that what you are, though?*

She had let him down. She had let herself down. She had misbehaved. Tested him. Even sparring with him verbally when he told her not to. He'd warned her he would be firm and strict if she didn't follow the rules. He hadn't minced words.

He had told her to obey his commands immediately without question. And yet, she'd lost her patience and blatantly disobeyed him.

She was pissed. Half at herself for letting him treat her like this and half at... well, herself again for doing the things that earned her this time out. *Shit. I mean, darn.*

How long had she been here? Two minutes? Twenty? She had no idea.

He was throwing everything at her at once. So many things in one day. Why? She knew why. He wanted her to safeword. She would not. She might have lost it there for a while after her bath, but she was pulling herself back together.

Noises behind her told her Lincoln was in the kitchen. Maybe cooking. When the smell of red sauce hit her nose, she sighed. Something Italian. Her stomach growled.

Again she wondered if he intended to do all the cooking while she did nothing but look pretty? This wasn't how she pictured D/s. She'd read about submissives servicing their Doms. Wasn't that what he would expect?

The clock kept ticking. Surprisingly she wasn't uncomfortable. She wouldn't want to stand like this for hours, but putting the majority of her weight on her forehead, chest, and belly made it tolerable. Her sex was exposed, making it difficult for her to ignore its existence. And her butt still burned from earlier.

As time wore on, she calmed herself. In a way, this was a blessing. It gave her a chance to remind herself of her goal. She could do this. He wasn't hurting her. He would never hurt her. He'd promised. And besides, she knew better. Injury wasn't a concern in her mind.

It was just a time out. It hurt her heart because she hated

disappointing him. But *had* she disappointed him? He'd gotten weird on her after the bath. Switched his mood to quiet brooding. She got the impression he was pulling out all the stops to get her to safeword. What would he do next? Chain her to the wall in a dark room?

Deep breaths. The time out was humiliating. But no harm was done. And she had to admit she'd learned a lesson, even if that lesson was simply to never put herself in a position to warrant a time out.

She could do better. She could do this. For him. For herself. He wouldn't break her. No matter how hard he tried. And she now had no doubt his main goal was to get her to break and give up the idea of being submissive. It was possible her brother had even put him up to it.

She would not give up. She would win.

CHAPTER 16

Lincoln had forced himself to get dinner in the oven, and then padded silently back into the family room and leaned heavily against the back of the couch, staring at Sasha's back.

He was so completely out of his comfort zone that he struggled to follow his own internal monologue. From the moment he woke her up, he'd been ad-libbing. For the last week, he'd pictured training her about postures and different positions and keeping her gaze lowered and kneeling at her Master's feet. He'd incorrectly assumed she wouldn't be able to go through with any of that.

She'd proven him wrong, knocking him off his foundation. Time and again. Sure, she'd had minor infractions but nothing any ordinary Dom wouldn't deal with even from a seasoned submissive.

So, he'd pushed her. Hard. Forced her hand. It was a dick move. He knew it. And dammit, she had not used her safeword. He'd had to think fast. Plan B. A time out.

He watched her closely, his heart at war. The battle raging inside him would not be won. No matter what, he would lose.

Either she found herself pushed too far and used her safeword or she found a way to weather the storm. He honestly hadn't been sure which way she would go as he arranged her naked body in the corner.

She'd given no obvious signs to indicate which way she was leaning—telling him to fuck himself or submitting to his discipline.

Half of his heart rooted for team Sasha. He wanted her to succeed. He wanted her to push through the punishment and come out on the other side stronger.

The other half of his heart rooted for team... What was the other team? Team Broken Sasha? The one where she shoved off the wall, used her safeword, and left the house while glaring at him for being a total dick?

Team Broken Sasha would be better in the long run. Safer. At least she would stop pressuring everyone to let her join Zodiac. She could move on with her life and put this nonsense about submitting behind her. Right about now, she should be feeling the pressure to do just that.

And yet, she stood perfectly still right where he'd left her.

Why did he want to pump his fist?

He was an ass. No Dom should handle a new sub the way he'd handled her all day. Especially with the silent treatment he'd subjected her to since he'd helped her out of the tub.

He could have spent the evening wearing her out with the mundane aspects of D/s. He probably should have. It would have been safer. Easier. It would *not* have pushed her away, however. The goal. *Eye on the goal.*

At this point, he'd crossed so many lines, they were a blur of blackness. As if he needed reminding, he pictured her once again masturbating for him after he spanked her ass and shaved her pussy. His cock had gotten harder as the day wore on with every test to his willpower.

He was playing with fire, and it would bite him in the ass if he didn't rein it in and get control of his physical responses to her.

He continued to watch her standing there, her fantastic body displayed for him. So brave. So obedient. His cock stiffened further, infuriating him. And then he paced, running a hand through his hair, angry with himself for treating her so coldly. It was uncalled for. And it had backfired. She'd proven she was up to any task, even if he was a total fuck about it.

She was not going to use her safeword.

She was strong. He was so proud of her. Dammit.

She deserved better.

At this point his goals were foggy. The lines he intended to draw were blurring, and he'd only had her one day. Not even a day. Eight hours.

He'd gotten so far off track he didn't even know what success looked like. He had a foot in two worlds. He was playing a game, but he was the only player on both teams. Every point scored was a win and a loss.

This tennis match had to stop soon, or Lincoln was going to need a straitjacket. Back and forth.

He wasn't right for her.

She wasn't right for him.

The sooner he got that through his thick skull, the sooner he could get on with her training and let her go.

He wanted her to succeed in her training, he realized. He wanted to watch her blossom under his tutelage. He wanted her to blossom and grow as a submissive. And she was hanging in there even though he'd thrown too much at her in eight short hours. He'd taken her places he wouldn't recommend a Dom take his sub in a week.

He'd asked her to do things she wasn't ready for. And she'd done them. All of them. It was time to admit she was indeed submissive, she was also strong enough not to allow failure, and he was a total dick.

He'd pushed her to do so many things outside her comfort zone. She'd gotten naked for him first thing that morning. He knew that was hard for her, and yet she'd stripped down to her soul for him. It humbled him and made his cock rock hard at the time and every time he thought about it since.

He couldn't shake the vision of her pulling that flimsy piece of cotton over her head. The first moment he saw her rosy nipples, the swell of her sweet breasts, the dip of her stomach, the flare of her hips, the curls between her legs. She'd been so brave, clasping her hands above her bottom and pulling her shoulders back to lift her tits.

His cock couldn't take the visions anymore. He shook them from his head and glanced at his watch. Her time was up. His previous intentions to pressure her into using her safeword vanished. She'd proven herself. She deserved praise and aftercare.

She was not going to back down. Ever. What did that leave Lincoln with? He'd made her a promise to train her to be the best submissive she could be. Regardless of the fact that his intentions had been completely different, she had proven herself worthy all day. He'd be a total dick not to acknowledge that, regroup, and figure out what the fuck he was going to do next.

He approached her, schooling his voice. "It's over, baby," he soothed.

She wobbled as she pushed off the wall.

He reached out a hand to steady her and wrapped a blanket around her shoulders. When she sighed, her shoulders falling, he leaned down and picked her up. The breath whooshed from her lungs, unmanning him.

He carried her to the sofa and sat, settling her across his lap. "I'm so proud of you, baby." He tucked the blanket around her and inhaled slowly. She'd been through a lot since he'd yanked her awake. He couldn't imagine everything that had gone through her mind in the last hour.

She was calm. A bit stiff. But calm. So he held her and decided to let her be in silence for a while longer.

He closed his eyes and thought about her pinkened bottom. So fucking sexy. She'd taken the punishment like a seasoned sub, not a newbie. Not someone on their first day. She'd endured it without stopping him or trying to get away. And then he'd had to stare at that still-pink ass while she stood in the corner.

He took long breaths, hoping she wouldn't notice he was out of sorts. The tables had turned. He needed to figure out a new game plan. Pushing her to safeword was no longer a viable option. He held her tight as she relaxed into him, snuggling closer.

Could he actually train her and then let her go? Turn her over to another man? Risk having to watch her blossom and grow under someone else's care? He had no choice. He knew in his soul he couldn't have her.

Before today he had truly believed she was too innocent for BDSM. Too pure. But then why was she doing this? Why push herself to endure everything he doled out when it didn't suit her?

He couldn't ignore the possibility that niggled in the back of his mind over and over.

What if it was *him*?

What if she was doing all this to please *him*? What if she really did have a childhood crush on him that caused her to irrationally leave her body and do everything in her power to win him over?

Fuck. She had no idea who he was or what he was. She couldn't understand that he was a sadist. He needed to top women in ways she couldn't imagine. He enjoyed the endorphin release from flogging or caning a woman as much as they needed to receive the release. He'd been that way for years. Since he could remember. He didn't permanently harm them. Ever. He simply gave them what they needed. What they begged him for.

He'd been underage when he'd first realized he had a need and the accompanying gift. He'd gone with his older brother, Alex, to an underground private club. It had been seedy and dark and a little trashy, but he'd stayed there all night. Watching. Learning. Craving.

He'd gone again without his brother. Several times, and then every weekend. Eventually he'd gotten lucky when he caught the eye of the seasoned Dom who happened to be a sadist and noticed him studying his work.

That was when he met Master Christopher.

He'd changed Lincoln's life. He taught Lincoln everything he knew about how to turn every implement in his arsenal into an appendage, at one with its owner. He'd helped Lincoln select and purchase his first flogger, his first whip, his first crop.

All of this happened before Lincoln even turned eighteen. Nearly a year's worth of tutelage before he enlisted in the army.

When he was home on leave, he spent as much time as he could in the club with Master Christopher. It rejuvenated him, made him feel alive in the face of so much death overseas.

He was twenty-one when he returned to the underground club on a more regular basis. Master Christopher took him as an apprentice of sorts, claiming he knew Lincoln had the special gift most aspiring sadists never quite achieved. The rest was history.

Lincoln jerked himself back to the present. How long had he been holding Sasha in his lap?

She sighed and squirmed her bottom on his thighs. He stilled her with a squeeze of his hand over her hip. She tipped her head back to look at him.

His heart melted.

So much trust and devotion in those gorgeous green orbs. Questions loomed deep inside, but she held them back. *Good girl.*

He needed to come back to the present, get on track, discuss what she'd endured. He brushed a long curl from her forehead and tucked it behind her ear. "Do you know why I put you in time out?"

"Yes, Sir."

"Did you enjoy it?"

"No, Sir."

"I've pushed you hard today. Probably too hard."

She nodded.

"You wanted to know what it was like to be someone's submissive."

"Yes, Sir. I do." That last word, so poignantly stated in the present tense made his heart sing. It shouldn't have. That wasn't his goal. What he needed to hear was the word *red* and a request to take her home.

But Sasha was a fighter. She was not going to give up.

And he was growing more and more proud of her by the hour.

"You have questions," he stated. "Go ahead."

She licked her full pink lips. "Why are you holding me so caringly in your lap if you're mad at me, Sir?"

He cupped her face, holding her chin steady so she couldn't look away. "Oh, baby, I was never mad at you. That's not an emotion I will ever have when it comes to you." He was getting too personal. *Keep it neutral, Walsh.*

She stared at him wide-eyed.

He continued, staying firm, "When a submissive is disobedient, it's important for his or her Master to correct the infraction as soon as reasonably possible. Not out of anger, but in order to teach the sub discipline. In this case, when I'm training you twenty-four seven, we're living in an artificial environment derived to give you a taste of what the lifestyle is like.

"You might not understand this, but I'm taking my cues from you. I have been all day. For the last week actually. In fact, your reactions to what I do and your behaviors are continually altering my responses. This isn't how I pictured the evening starting out."

She nodded. Damn, she was so open, batting her eyes, soaking in his words.

He adjusted his hand so that it curled around the top of her thigh instead of her bottom. The blanket had been between his palm and her butt cheek. Now his fingers gripped her bare thigh.

She settled into the touch. So open. Willing. Eager.

"In a normal D/s arrangement, like the ones you might experience with a more permanent Dom later, you'd negotiate terms. Perhaps you'd designate certain hours in the evenings or weekends to get into the roles." A stab of pain jabbed his chest as he implied repeatedly she would one day have another Dom.

"I've read that, Sir."

"This arrangement is not something I ordinarily do. I don't train subs like you." *Never.* "I'm doing this because I didn't want you to fall into the wrong hands. An inexperienced Dom could cause serious psychological damage to a newbie sub." These things were true. All of them. But Lincoln choked out the words nevertheless when what he wanted to say was: *You're mine. I will never let another man, Dom or vanilla, touch you.*

Without moving a muscle, her eyes changed. A sadness filled the green depths. He did that to her. And it hurt him dearly. But he had no choice.

Her eyes confirmed what he suspected. She wanted this to end with them together. His words were hurting her. Deeply.

Fuck.

He kept talking, needing to stay on track. "Every Dom is different. Most would not get too bent out of shape about small incidences of misbehavior. A stern look or a verbal warning might be sufficient. But you didn't come here to half-ass this experience. You came here to get the full picture of what it means to submit to a Dom at the deepest level. So I'm going to give you worst-case scenario."

"I understand, Sir." Her voice was stronger, but still sad. Disappointed.

He had to keep this strictly business.

He needed to get her sexy body off his lap first and then feed her. The separation would help him regroup so they could resume her training for the evening.

She stared at him. She needed more. She held his gaze. "You needled me on purpose tonight, didn't you? You wanted me to use my safeword." Her voice was strong, but a tear slid down her cheek.

"Yes." He would not lie to her.

"It was your goal all day," she deadpanned.

"Yes." He held her gaze, not backing down.

"Why?"

He licked his lips. No way was he going to go into the details, but he owed her an explanation. "I didn't think you belonged in this world. I was trying to help you see that sooner rather than later. It was a shit move. I should have known better. I owe you an apology."

She blinked. "Have I proven you wrong? Are you done testing me?"

"Yes. I'm sorry I pushed you so hard. It was inexcusable. You're definitely submissive." *At least with me.*

"You'll keep working with me?" Her eyes were hopeful.

He didn't have the willpower to turn her down. He was damned either way. If he made her leave, she would never forgive him, and he would worry about whoever dominated her next. If he let her stay, he needed an abundance of self-control. In both scenarios it was going to devastate him to turn her over to someone else. "Yes."

Was he seriously going to continue to fucking train her?

He slid his hand into the hair at the back of her neck, keeping her head steady. It occurred to him that he used that tactic with all the subs he played with. It was a trademark of his. When he wanted a sub's attention, he insisted on it, not giving them the opportunity to look away. It was domineering. It worked.

So, no, he was no longer gripping her chin, physically forcing her to look at him, but he now had his fingers on her neck, doing the same thing. "I've learned things about you." He needed to get them back on track.

"Like what, Sir?"

"You don't like to be punished."

"No, Sir." She might have attempted to shake her head in the negative, but he held her neck firmly.

"You didn't get off on having your bottom spanked, nor did you get off on being ignored in a time out."

"No, Sir," she repeated softly. "Isn't that the point?"

"Yes." He smiled. "But it doesn't work for everyone. I told you about brats, earlier."

"Yes, Sir."

"Brats and other types of submissives enjoy being punished. They crave it. They intentionally disobey their Masters in order to get punished. They get off on it."

"Wouldn't that be annoying, Sir?"

He chuckled. "Yes. Very. To me anyway. Some Doms love it. For every type of sub, there's a Dom waiting somewhere in the shadows to complement him or her."

"I see." She shivered. "Well, I don't like to be spanked or ignored in a corner."

He winked at her. "Then I won't have to worry about you deliberately disobeying me, will I?"

"No, Sir. And I've learned those two lessens well. You don't need to repeat them either." She grinned, more like half grinned. Testing him. *Topping* him.

He narrowed his gaze. "You need to learn another lesson about submission before you speak again."

The color drained from her face.

"Never suggest to a Dom what he should or shouldn't do. It won't go well for you. You're the one training here. Not me. It's a Dom's job to take care of his sub, not the sub's job to offer suggestions. I've been a Dom for many years. I'll decide what punishments to dole out and when. Are we clear?"

"Yes, Sir." The words were weak. Nervous.

But she needed to understand. Learn. "When you tell a Dom what to do, it's called topping from the bottom. It puts you in charge and spins the table so the roles are reversed. Any Dom worth his salt won't stand for it. If he does, he's not a Dom at all. It's the worst kind of disobedience. You're likely to find yourself severely punished in a way that would make spanking and time outs seem like a trip to the amusement park."

She swallowed. "I'm sorry, Sir." A tear came to her eye.

He eased his thumb up and swiped it away. "Don't even attempt something like that again."

"Yes, Sir." She was going to cry if he didn't pull her out of it. Not that he had a problem with submissives crying. It happened. He dealt with it. But he'd given her a stern warning, and she'd learned her lesson.

She'd also had a long stressful day, enduring two forms of punishment she was not used to receiving. She was mentally drained. He had lofty goals of pushing her too far, but he would never do something he didn't think she could emotionally handle.

"We need to eat. You need your energy for later."

She nodded. "Okay, Sir."

He slowly stood, set her on her feet, and tugged the blanket free. "Are you warm enough? I turned the air up earlier to make you uncomfortable during your time out. It should be warmer in here by now."

She flinched. "You made it colder?"

"Yes."

"I was freezing... Sir."

"I know." He grinned. "There's a vent over that spot."

"You're devious, Sir."

"Never forget it."

CHAPTER 17

Sasha was surprised that Lincoln let her feed herself. He didn't let her sit at the table. But he did let her sit fully on the thick pillow on the floor on her butt, and he handed her a plate with her own fork. Small blessing.

He was an amazing cook. She hoped he didn't ask her to cook in the near future. He would be disappointed.

The pasta casserole filled her quickly, but she ate every bite, including the salad, assuming he wouldn't appreciate it if she didn't clean her plate.

When he took her dirty dish from her, she told him how she felt. "That was delicious, Sir. You're a great cook."

"Thank you, baby."

"May I clean up, Sir?"

He set their plates in the sink and turned back to her. "Not tonight. Maybe another time. Let's leave the dishes for now."

"Okay, Sir."

He took her hand and helped her stand, and then he shocked her by leading her out the sliding glass doors to the backyard. The temperature was perfect. The usual humidity known to Miami was lower now that it was dark.

Lincoln took a seat in one of the large, cushioned lounge chairs, spreading his legs and patting the space between them. "Sit, baby."

She crawled up between his knees, facing the pool. Strategically placed lights made the inviting water cycle through a rainbow of glowing colors.

Lincoln wrapped an arm around her waist, holding her against him beneath her breasts. He leaned back against the chair, taking her with him.

She was surprised by her ability to relax. For one thing, it hadn't escaped her notice that she'd been naked all day. And Lincoln was fully clothed. At some point it stopped bothering her. It was still super weird, but she was no longer freaking out over it. After all, by now the man knew every inch of her body. The only place he hadn't touched was the inside of her pussy.

Not to say he wasn't intimately acquainted with every inch of her sex. He'd watched her up close and personal, including when she thrust her own finger inside her.

She shuddered at the visual of him between her legs, his face so close he could have tasted her.

Lincoln drew a lazy circle on her arm with the hand not holding her. "What was that, sweetheart?"

Shit. "Nothing, Sir."

A soft chuckle vibrated both their bodies. She loved it when he laughed. She loved to watch the lines on his face that spread from the corners of his eyes when he smiled.

"Baby, you're a horrible liar."

She said nothing. If he thought she was lying, would he punish her again? Probably, and she was so comfortable. Was omission considered lying? Digging into her brain wasn't a skill he had.

His hand trailed from her arm to her breast, one finger swirling around her nipple.

It jumped to attention. So did she. Wetness pooled between her legs. She squeezed her thighs together.

"It's so easy to read you, baby." His words were a soft whisper so close to her ear that she could feel his breath where her head lay below his against his shoulder. "You were thinking something, and it disturbed you enough to jump. Now tell me."

She couldn't imagine what she would say, but certainly not what she had been thinking. "I was just admiring the pool."

He chuckled again. "And?"

She needed to give him something more believable than that. "And thinking about how I've been naked all day and you have not."

"And?"

What the hell was he, a mind reader? "That's all, Sir."

"That is most definitely not all." He flicked his finger over her distended nipple and swirled it around the tip some more. "Try again."

She sighed. Maybe if she answered his question with a question. "Is it weird that it doesn't feel strange to me anymore? Being naked, I mean."

"No. It's normal. You're desensitized for the moment."

For the moment? Would it feel odd again later? Tomorrow?

He continued. "It will never have the same impact in the future that it did the first time—stripping for me—but every time you're dressed and I ask you to remove your clothes, you'll feel the rise of self-consciousness and arousal. It's who you are." His voice dipped to a soft whisper. "It's who you are with me. It's who I want you to be. And it's sexy as hell."

She stopped breathing. He gave her whiplash with the way he switched back and forth between talking about her future in the subjective as if she would be with any number of other Doms and never see him again and then switching to a more present tense that implied he owned her.

She liked the latter better, but every time she allowed herself to hope, he turned on her.

He kissed her ear and then ran his tongue along the lobe.

"Now, it didn't escape my notice that you still haven't answered my question."

She held her breath, memorizing this moment. She'd never been so turned on. The sexiest man she'd ever known—the only man she would ever love—was holding her naked body on a lounge chair on a perfect Miami evening. His hand held her so close it was impossible to misinterpret his feelings. Fingers danced around her nipple to drive her mad with need. She closed her eyes to burn the image into her mind for later.

She wanted him to talk to her. She wanted to have a normal conversation like two people dating would have. Was it possible? While they were simply lying outside, lounging in the night air, maybe he would let his need to control everything down for a few minutes.

"May I ask you some questions, Sir?"

"Of course. Go ahead."

"Personal questions, I mean."

"Hmm. I suppose."

"You were in the army, right?"

"Yes. Four years." He continued to draw circles around her nipple while they spoke.

"Why did you leave?" She held her breath. Would he tell her?

For long moments he said nothing while her hope dissipated. His fingers trailed away from her breast to stroke her arm lazily. Finally, he surprised her. "I enlisted right out of high school, same as your brother and Carter, though two years after them. My brother Alex was twenty. He talked me into joining with him."

"You have a brother?" Would he care that she didn't address him as Sir while they were having this personal discussion? He didn't say anything.

"*Had.* He was killed in action a few months after we were deployed."

She winced. "I'm so sorry." She could hear the depth of pain that still lingered in Lincoln's voice.

"Yeah, me too. We were close. When he enlisted, I couldn't let him go alone. I thought I would look weak, so I followed in his footsteps.

"It wasn't a difficult decision. Our parents were hard-working, middle class. They hadn't saved for a college education. It was my ticket. When he was killed, I knew I had to work twice as hard to stay alive, for my parents. A shrink would probably say I buried my sorrow by redoubling my efforts."

Sasha set her hands on Lincoln's thighs and gripped his muscles in silent support.

"I'm not sorry. My service made me into the man I am today."

She pushed for more. "Is that why you only served one term?"

"No. Not directly. My father got sick. Liver cancer. He didn't have much time. My mother needed me, perhaps more emotionally than anything else. She always looked at me with fear in her eyes when I was home on leave. Her son had died and her husband wasn't going to live much longer. I couldn't blame her. She was so worried about me that she was losing weight. Her hands were always shaking. I knew she wasn't sleeping. So I came home."

Wow. She'd never known all this. Rowen didn't speak about it. "Is your mother still living?"

"Yep. About five miles from here. I have lunch with her as often as I can."

She smiled. She was glad he had a good relationship with his mother, especially since she would never know an adult relationship with either of her parents.

He gave her a squeeze. "She's an amazing woman. Even as a grown adult, I lived with her for three years after I left the service. I wasn't home much between working and going to college, but I know she appreciated having me around. Maybe you'd like to meet her someday."

"I'd like that." She pursed her lips, fighting back unbidden tears. Why was she so emotional? Perhaps because he'd just implied she might meet his mother. That wasn't something someone said casually to a woman they didn't see a future with.

Hope.

"When did you start practicing BDSM?"

He stiffened. And then he chuckled. "You'll kill me for admitting this, but I was seventeen."

She jerked in his arms and twisted her face toward his. "Please tell me you're kidding?"

He was grinning, a twinkle in his eye. "Nope."

She rolled her eyes, knowing he hated it, but it was warranted in this case. "Hypocrite."

"Yep."

"You aren't even apologetic about it."

"Nope." He squeezed her chest tighter, his fingers finding and pinching her nipple, making her yelp.

She was surprised he would admit something like that to her, of all people.

Suddenly, his chest stopped jiggling with mirth and he sobered, his hand trailing from her nipple to her chin. He held her steady. "I know I was an ass that day, and I'm sorry."

"You've already apologized." Her face closed up a bit at his admission. She hadn't expected him to ever take responsibility for hurting her feelings that day. And now he had twice.

"I know, but what I did was unnecessary and uncalled for. It has bothered me for all these years."

Wow.

He smoothed stray hairs off her forehead. "You didn't deserve my outburst. I embarrassed you in front of everyone at the club. You weren't responsible for John's decision to allow you to spend your evenings in his office. You were only twelve years old when the arrangement was made. I didn't know all the facts that day. I acted hastily. And I'm truly sorry. When I later learned what your situation had been—what Rowen's situation had been—I felt like a total ass."

She stopped breathing.

He cleared his throat.

She waited, not moving an inch. Knowing whatever it was, it was important.

"That's not all."

"Okay."

He shifted his weight under her. Nervous? "The truth is that I saw you from across the room and thought you were hot. You exuded the perfect combination of innocence and confidence. My heart skipped a beat. I thought I'd struck gold. I tried to pretend I hadn't seen you as I made my way around the room, shaking hands and making nice. But my mind was focused on one goal— meeting Rowen's bewitching sister."

Oh. My. God.

"I knew he had a sister. I knew it had to be you. I knew it was your birthday. What I assumed was that you were twenty-five. No one had mentioned a word yet about your mother dying and Rowen raising you. I was blindsided, and I acted like an idiot to save face. I felt like a fool lusting after an underage kid. I was embarrassed and pissed with myself and John and Rowen, so I turned that around and put it on you. It wasn't fair. And I've kicked myself ever since."

Now she thought her heart was going to stop. She tried to soak in everything he'd said, especially the part where he'd thought she was hot. Did he still? And why did he keep up the charade for five years, acting like she was a pariah?

He gave her another squeeze, his hand trailing back to cup her breast. He spoke again, cutting off her opportunity to ask him that last question. "Okay, that's done. Too much deep conversation. It was years ago. I was young. You were… way younger. In a way, it was a blessing."

"Why's that?"

"Because I'm totally not right for you. If you'd been twenty-five, I would have swept you off your feet and then hurt you when it didn't work out. I didn't always make the best decisions at that age. Obviously. So, my rudeness saved me hurting you in the long run. That and your age."

Totally not right for me? She had no idea what he was talking about, but the hope that had bubbled up inside her at his admission that he'd been attracted to her snuffed out in an instant. Her heart went from stopping to beating erratically to stopping again.

For several minutes they sat in silence. Sasha's mind waded through everything he'd said, confused and a little hurt. An odd mix of emotions after such a heartfelt apology.

Lincoln's fingers landed on her breast again, languidly drawing circles on her tender skin.

She tried to relax and concentrate on the feel of his touch. Perhaps it had been a mistake to take them out of the scene. She wanted to get back where they were before she'd led them on this detour.

"Relax, Sasha." His words were soft. Gentle. His fingertip trailing to her nipple again. "Let your mind rest. Stop thinking so hard."

She took several deep breaths, wanting to do that for him.

"Get back in the role, sweetheart." His words were whispered in her ear.

"Yes, Sir."

More silence. Nothing but his easy breathing so close to her ear that she found herself falling in sync with it.

Finally, he spoke again, his next word deeper, hoarse. "Baby…"

"Yes, Sir?" She knew nothing but the feel of his lips on her ear and his finger circling her nipple without touching her where she needed it most.

"Spread your legs. Drape them over mine."

She hesitated a moment, knowing how vulnerable that made her. Even though he'd held her open earlier and shaved her with his face so close to her pussy, she still felt the twinge of self-consciousness the exposure produced. They were outside. Yes, it was dark. Yes, there was a high fence around his property. Yes, it was quiet enough to indicate the neighbors on both sides of him were not outside this evening. But still.

"Don't make me repeat myself, Sasha. Open your pussy."

She pursed her lips as she obeyed his command, lifting her feet to set them on the outsides of his thighs. Instantly she felt vulnerable. Exposed. Open.

"Good girl." He slid his finger over her nipple as if it were a reward for her obedience. "Tell me how that makes you feel. I sense the hesitation. Your body got stiff."

"Exposed, Sir."

"I've seen your pussy before."

She nodded against his chest.

His lips found her ear again. "It's a lovely pussy. Any Dom would be proud to own it."

And there it was again, his shift from being the one to own her himself to implying someone else would. She also wasn't sure how she felt about being owned. To keep her mind off her disappointment over his choice of words, she asked. "Own, Sir? Someone can't really own another person."

"Ah, but you're wrong. In the D/s world it's common. Accepted. It's a term that implies one person has given themselves to another. No, it wouldn't hold up in court or anything. But it's symbolic. A submissive is often owned by her Dom. She may even wear a symbol of that ownership that tells others in the lifestyle he or she belongs to someone."

"I see," she murmured, forcing her body not to react to his words. He made it sound so romantic that she wished she could be owned. By him.

Lincoln released his hold across her belly and slid his palm down to her outer thigh, stroking the sensitive skin so close to her pussy. "When you open to me like this, it shows me that I own you, however temporary it may be. This pussy is mine." He tapped it with two fingers.

She gasped, her hips lifting off the chair as arousal flooded her system. Blood raced to her sex.

The finger still circling her nipple flicked over the tip again. "I love how your tits respond to my touch."

Was she expected to respond? Because there was no way she could.

His tongue hit her ear again. "Sasha…"

She moaned, falling under the spell he created. At no point in the last week of research had she imagined a scene like this. She'd pictured kneeling and worshiping him. She'd envisioned taking his cock into her mouth—which both worried her and aroused her.

She had not visualized lying on a lounge chair in the dark, being teased to the edge of sanity. Was this part of her training? Or had he abandoned the plan because he wanted to fuck her? Please, God. Door number two. If she somehow managed to get him inside her less than twelve hours after arriving—score.

He teased the sensitive skin inches from her pussy. Miles from where she wanted his fingers. "Sasha," he repeated. "Tell me what made you flinch before."

Shit. He still hadn't forgotten that?

"Warning. If you cuss at me in your mind, it will sometimes accidentally leak out of your mouth."

She twisted her face to look at him. "You're annoying."

He smiled. "You're stalling."

"Do you have to know every intimate thought I have? Can't a girl have some secrets, Sir?"

"I'm sure you've had dozens of secret thoughts today. More than I can count. I just want that one. The one that made you shudder before you relaxed into my body."

She faced the sky, blinking at the stars. *Oh, who cares?* "I was thinking about how you've seen my entire body and I'm no longer as embarrassed now."

"You said that part."

She swallowed. "And… I was thinking that there is one part of me you have not touched."

Did he inhale sharper than normal? "Ah, inside you. Inside your pussy." He smoothed the hand on her breast down her body to press it against her opposite thigh, and then he used both sets of fingers to pull her lips apart.

She moaned. No way to stop it. She didn't even cut it short. Her hands gripped his thighs at her hips, and she dug her nails into them. Her butt lifted off the chair.

"Set your bottom down, baby."

She eased it back to the cushion, but the tension had a firm grip on her.

His fingers stroked her thighs, inches from her pussy. So close. Again. If he kept that up, she would come without direct contact. It wouldn't be as satisfying, but it would happen.

"You want me to touch your pussy, Sasha?"

"Yes," she breathed out.

"Sasha," he clipped.

She startled and then realized her mistake. "Sir. Please, Sir. Yes."

"If you can't remember to speak respectfully, I will walk away and leave you sorry I ever touched you anywhere. Understood?"

"Yes, Sir."

"Good. Addressing your Dom with respect is never optional. No matter how aroused you get or how badly you need to come, you will not ask for it. You will not slip out of the role. You do not have permission to get so lost in your lust that you lose sight of your place. For as long as you're in my home, you're my submissive. You'll do as I say. You won't stray from that for any reason. Am I clear?"

"Yes, Sir." Her belly dipped. Her arousal should have fallen into the cold water of the pool at his chastisement. She hated when he had to reprimand her. When he spanked her, her sex had gone into hiding, shriveling away. Same with the time out.

But now she was squirming, her mind focusing on three words —*you're my submissive.*

"Let's get something else straight, while we're at it."

"Okay, Sir." Her legs were stiff across his knees. When had they seized up like that?

He still held her thighs apart this entire time. "I know you're aroused. I know your heart rate picks up when I place demands on you." His fingers teased the sensitive skin so close to her sex. His voice dipped, his lips on her ear again. "Obeying me makes you horny. It's normal. It's expected. It's precisely why I also know you're truly submissive by nature, baby."

She jerked on his body. He knew that? Now? Already? Wasn't the entire point of this experiment meant to prove her wrong?

"Don't freak out on me. We still have a lot of work to do. Ground to cover. Just because I've recognized your submissive tendencies doesn't mean you fully grasp what that means or what belonging to another person would entail. It doesn't mean you definitely belong in this lifestyle. Many people can get off on some level of dominance. I'd go so far as to say most. That doesn't mean they have what it takes to turn themselves over to another's care for an extended period of time."

She was confused. "Sir?"

He slid his fingers closer to her opening. "Enough talking for now. Grab the arms of the chair with both hands, hold on, and don't move them."

She released the grip she didn't realize she had on his thighs and reached for the wooden spindles at the outside of Lincoln's hips.

"Good girl. If you want to come, you'll listen closely. If you think I'm kidding, try me. If you think I won't make you go to bed horny, try me. If you lose so much of yourself while I'm touching you that you address me disrespectfully or can't control your mouth, you'll be left so horny it will physically hurt."

She sucked in a sharp breath, so focused it was hard to do anything except concentrate on all the things she was supposed to be doing. Hands on the spindles. Legs open. Mouth shut.

"Now, I'm going to bring you to orgasm because you've been an amazing submissive today and you deserve it. It's going to blow your mind. But I decide when and how. Not you. Do not try to manipulate me by lifting your bottom off the cushions or pulling your legs together, or verbally begging me. Do not speak unless I ask you a question. You may moan, whimper, scream, cry. Whatever you want, but no words. Understood?"

God, she hoped so. "Yes, Sir."

Several seconds went by, her heart pounding so hard she could feel it in her ears. He had not dipped a finger inside her yet and she had never wanted anything so badly in her life. What this man could do to her with nothing more than words should be illegal.

Finally, his fingers moved. He started by stroking her outer pussy lips so gently it was hard to discern. The pressure increased gradually until he used his forefingers and thumbs to pull her lips open wide again.

She tipped her head back against his shoulder, her mouth falling open. If she could just concentrate on the moment, she would be in heaven. But she had to also focus on her hands, her thighs, and her mouth—keeping it shut.

He dipped a finger through her wetness next.

She nearly came off the chair. Thank goodness she held the urge to buck into him at bay. She would never be able to survive this test at this rate.

His finger trailed up to her clit next to circle the swollen nub begging for attention without words.

She willed him to touch it.

He did not. Instead, he eased that damn finger back to her

opening and slowly pushed it into her pussy. "Jesus, Sasha. You're so fucking tight."

That was enough to make her come. But he pulled his finger out immediately and returned it to her clit. His other hand spread up that way also, holding the hood back while he tapped the nub lightly. Not enough pressure. Not nearly enough of anything.

Which he knew.

After teasing her clit for an eternity, he slid his fingers back to her opening. That one pointer pressed inside, but only an inch. "What's been in here, baby? Tell me."

What?

"What have you masturbated with?"

"Uh…"

"Be careful."

She licked her lips. He wanted to have a chat about her nonexistent sex life again? Now?

His lips teased her earlobe again. His breath hit her to make her shiver. Or maybe that was from the embarrassment. "You're very tight, baby. Not just virginal tight. But I don't believe you haven't experimented. Not someone as passionate as you."

Passionate? Was she? *Shit.* "I have toys, Sir."

"You've mentioned that before. What toys?"

"A vibrator, Sir." *More like a butterfly, but it's got batteries. Same thing, right?*

"Really? You're so tight. How often do you use it inside you?" His voice told her he was seriously confused.

She turned her face away. It wasn't as if he could see her expression, but she was mortified again. If he knew the real reason, what would he think of her? He curved his finger up to press against the inner wall of her channel. Her G-spot?

She lit on fire. If he kept that up, she would come in seconds.

"Answer me, baby. I'm trying to figure you out. You're making no sense."

She couldn't tell him what he wanted to hear. Not a chance in hell. He had stripped her bare and shaved her and bathed her and punished her and made her masturbate for him. But he couldn't have that. It was hers. It was embarrassing and not up for discussion.

His fingers moved away, retreating to her thighs, holding her lips open, but no longer touching them.

She moaned, desperate. Her teeth clamped down. Could someone die from orgasm denial? It felt likely.

"You have a secret, Sasha."

"Please, Sir. Don't make me say it."

"I fail to understand what could possibly be so embarrassing about how you masturbate. There's nothing to be ashamed of. Everyone does it. It's normal. I'm just asking what you use inside you. It must be narrow for you to be this tight at twenty-two. So, I assume it's some other object. Do you have a wand?"

"A wand, Sir?"

"Okay, so not a wand. What?"

She was stuck on whatever a wand was.

"I'll tell you about wands later, baby. What goes into this tight pussy?" He slid a finger in again.

She moaned. It felt so amazing.

His finger came back out. He dragged it through her folds, over and over. "We can do this all night, Sasha."

"Nothing," she blurted out, a whoosh of oxygen leaving her lungs. "Nothing goes into me, Sir."

He stilled for a moment, his finger hovering against that elusive spot, driving her impatience through the ceiling. "Nothing," he murmured. "Though that makes sense, it also doesn't. I know you masturbate. You have told me so, and you demonstrated your ability earlier."

He released her pussy with the hand not currently inside her and slid it up her body. Before she had an idea of his intentions, he pinched her nipple. Hard. Not as hard as earlier, but he got her attention. "Tell me what you're holding back or I stop."

She whimpered. Was it worth this battle? Not if he followed through on his threat. "I saved penetration, Sir." *For you.* "I come easily from touching my clit, especially if I use the butterfly. Really easily. So, I saved it."

He stilled, his finger languidly resting against the inside of her channel. "You're telling me you haven't experimented with even a dildo?"

"Right, Sir." She was mortified. Who did that? Masturbated. Daily. Religiously. Without allowing herself penetration. To visions of the unobtainable boss at her brother's fetish club.

She swore she could feel his smile against her cheek. "And this embarrasses you?"

"Yes, Sir," she whispered. It was humiliating.

"Well, I don't see why. It makes my cock so hard, I'm going to come in my jeans. That's the single sexiest thing I've ever heard."

She pursed her lips. His response seemed strange.

Besides, she wished he would at the very least remove said jeans. Damn him.

He inhaled slowly, his finger still lodged inside her, making her want to scream. Sure, she could come easily and with frequency. But he was torturing her. When she did it, she knew exactly where to focus her attention with what pressure and how long. He kept flitting away from the place she most needed his attention just before she came.

Maddening.

"How often?"

"Pardon. Sir?"

"How often do you masturbate?"

No. No no no no no.

He chuckled. "Don't answer that."

Thank you, God.

"I have never met a woman like you."

Like me how? Freakishly weird about her obsessive need to

come while denying herself the feeling of having even an object inside her?

"You're so damn sexy. You don't know it. And you're filled with surprises that would bring any man to his knees. We'll be discussing this again another time. But for now, I'm going to assume that my little sub needs to come so badly she's about to explode."

He was not wrong.

He added a second finger to the first, thrust them inside her, and fucked her so fast and hard the breath left her body.

She didn't need it. Breathing was highly overrated. She simply prayed she could follow all his rules while he drove into her. If not, she would die. It was no longer questionable.

She arched her neck, gripped the arms of the chair, and held her breath.

"Come for me, baby."

At his command, she shattered around his fingers, her channel gripping them with every pulse. It was even better than her earlier orgasm when he watched her masturbate.

It was the first time she'd ever come at someone else's hand.

It was Lincoln's hand.

It was exquisite.

It was perfection.

CHAPTER 18

Lincoln stood in front of the glass door that led from his bedroom to the backyard. He'd intentionally had the builder add that feature so he could walk right out into the night and take a dip in the pool.

Tonight he didn't even see the pool. Maybe it was still there. Maybe it wasn't. He was facing the night, but all he saw was the running reel of Saturday's events as they rushed through his mind.

It was so late now, it could no longer be considered Saturday.

After making his little sub come harder than he'd ever seen a woman give it up for him, he'd carried her limp body into her room, ensured she could stand to use the bathroom, and then tucked her into bed when she returned.

She hadn't spoken. Every sound she'd made was unintelligible.

She'd been in subspace. From coming around his fingers. He'd climbed onto the bed and held her back against his front, carefully staying on top of the blankets. He'd smoothed his fingers over her temple until she fell into a deep sleep.

It had taken every ounce of his willpower not to strip off his jeans and fuck the life out of her.

As it was, he was struggling to see how that wouldn't happen in the end no matter what.

He set his forehead against the cool glass of the door and groaned. He hadn't even taken his cock in hand after leaving her. In his warped mind, his punishment for even thinking of fucking her was to deny himself release.

Rowen was going to kill him. That had been established several times. This was day one for fuck's sake.

Sasha was his. *His.*

The thought of her with another man made him fist his hands. His blood boiled. No one else would ever touch her.

But fuck. That was not the plan. Not even close. Fuck it all. He was in so deep he couldn't see straight. What was he supposed to do?

He couldn't keep her. She was not his. She was his and she was not his.

He was an ass for thinking that he wouldn't have her but no one else would either. She deserved more. She deserved the world.

He could not give her the world. Even if he somehow lived through her brother filling him with holes, he still couldn't have her. She was not a masochist. His life had revolved around taking women to subspace through sadism. Years of carefully and artfully arranging women to get emotional release from whatever form they needed. It was ingrained in him. People counted on him to take care of them. They arranged scenes with him weeks in advance.

He enjoyed it. It gave him a sense of peace. It was in his blood. He owned the club for fuck's sake. It was his life.

Sasha would be horrified if she knew who he was and what he did. He groaned again. He pictured the look on her face if she ever saw him beating another woman until she cried. Because that's how it would appear to Sasha. She wouldn't understand. He would look like a monster to her, or at the very least an abuser.

He knew better. He knew he was a master at his work—literally. He could read a sub so well that no one had ever needed to use their safeword with him. That wasn't to say he'd never drawn blood. Occasionally that's what a sub requested. If Sasha knew that...

Fuck.

Frustration ate a hole in him. He was stuck. Damned no matter what.

He had to let her go. Go where? He had no idea. He needed to talk to Carter. Figure something out. Today was the one and only day he could have her. It had been the best day of his life. Perfect in every way. Beautiful.

But he would only make things worse the longer he kept up this farce.

Training her? What a joke. If he admitted it to himself, he'd known what would happen the entire time. He'd taken a risk. He'd been selfish. He never should have been the one to follow her last Friday to Breeze. He shouldn't have offered to train her. He should have recused himself later and turned her over to Carter. Anyone else. Not him. Not a sadist. Not someone who could never be who she thought he was.

He knew she had a thing for him. He'd known that before last week. He'd seen the way she looked at him over the years. When he caught her, her face would flush a deep pretty red and she would look away.

It made his cock hard every time. He could deny it. But he would be lying.

At first it had been plain sick and wrong. She'd been seventeen and he'd been twenty-five. Illegal. Thank God she had avoided both him and the club for the entire next year. At least the next time he set eyes on her, she wasn't jailbait.

He should have turned around that day too. Run. She'd been too young even then. Too innocent. Hell, she still was.

Or had been.

Until he fucking touched her today.

He'd taken a piece of her a few hours ago, a piece he never should have stolen. It wasn't his to take. He'd been selfish, his decision making clouded with lust. He'd thought of nothing except ensuring *he* was the first man who had the privilege of bringing her to orgasm. He could still taste her sweet essence on his lips. Had she even been coherent enough to notice when he sucked her juices from his fingers?

He'd held himself together for over an hour reclining on that lounge chair with her sexy, pert, naked body plastered to his chest. He'd even given her a piece of himself—because she'd asked it of him. He'd told her things he'd never discussed with anyone. Freely. Without hesitation.

He'd been in control.

And then from one beat to the next, he'd lost all control when he realized how fucking sexual his little sub was. So sexual that he knew from her words and the look on her face that she fucking masturbated every day, at least once. Probably more often, though he hadn't forced her to admit that out loud.

And she'd saved herself. He couldn't stop thinking about the beauty of knowing she hadn't simply been a virgin. She'd literally saved herself entirely.

For him?

His chest hurt. *God.*

No one would ever suspect what lay beneath the innocent-looking exterior that was Sasha Easton.

A Dom could use that to his advantage, especially when working with a sexual submissive. One so needy that she required frequent release. Thoughts of keeping her on edge for long periods of time slammed into his imagination. Restraining her so that she had no choice but to endure that sweet edge. Making her go without for entire days. Forcing her to come so many times in a row that she lost her mind.

The possibilities were endless with someone as responsive as her.

For someone else, you ass. She's not yours.

But he couldn't stop the mental assault that tortured him, tempting him with what he could not have.

He groaned against the window at the memory of the moment he'd internalized how greedy her sweet body was. She clearly had an enormous sexual appetite most men wouldn't be able to compete with.

His damn stiff cock grew harder. Again. He needed to stop this trip down memory lane. Stop picturing the way she so wantonly blossomed for him. The way her mouth hung open in raw ecstasy. The way her eyes glazed over after she gave it all up. *For me.*

He was a total ass. He never should have taken that from her.

And Rowen. He groaned again. The man was like a brother. They had a bond. Same with Carter. All three of them had a special connection from serving in the army before coincidentally making their way to the same BDSM club and discovering this mutual background when Lincoln bought Club Zodiac five years ago. He loved those guys. They were brothers.

And he was about to fuck that up so royally it would never be repaired.

All because he couldn't keep his dick in his pants.

Well, technically, it had never come out of his jeans, not even when he was alone today. But in the past five years it had been out. Lots of times. More than he could count. With her image in his mind.

He'd had other women. Several of them. But he'd never let them inside his shell. He'd done what was socially appropriate by taking them to dinner before he'd fucked them, but he never felt a connection.

And the women he dominated? He'd never felt sexual while working. It was more like a job. It filled a craving. Not a sexual one. Sadism was an outlet. Ingrained in him. Part of what made

Lincoln who he was. It had blossomed from a young age and matured over time until it became his primary focus after he got out of the service.

For a long time, he led a double life, living with his mom, working, and attending college by day while learning everything he could from Master Christopher as his apprentice by night. The day he finally graduated with his business degree was the one and only time he ever saw Master Christopher outside of the underground club.

The mentor and friend he'd come to love had attended his graduation, shocking Lincoln and humbling him. Afterward, he had given Lincoln a gift, a crudely wrapped package that made Lincoln smile trying to picture the older man wrangling wrapping paper and tape.

Master Christopher showed Lincoln more emotion in that moment than he'd seen in all the years he'd known him. "I'm proud of you. Open this in private, son," was all he said.

Lincoln had nodded and watched as his mentor walked slowly away, swallowed up by the crowd. Lincoln had soon been swept into his mother's embrace and had waited until later that night in the privacy of his room to open the gift. There were two things inside—an intricately crafted soft leather whip that Lincoln was certain Master Christopher had made himself and an envelope.

He admired the craftsmanship of the whip for several minutes before setting it back in the box and taking out the envelope. Carefully tearing the end, he extracted the single trifold page. When he opened it, something else fell into Lincoln's lap. A check. Shocked and unwilling to look at the dollar amount, he leaned back to read his mentor's words.

Dear Master Lincoln,

I can call you that. You have more than earned the title. I want you to know how proud I am of everything you've accomplished. If I'd had a son, I would have wanted him to be exactly like you. Strong. Confident. Intelligent. And a Dominant in every sense of the word.

You have persevered through hard times, fighting for our country and then putting yourself through school while taking care of your mother and burying your father. I've watched you grow into the finest young man I know.

I know you are destined for great things in life. The world is your oyster. But I also know your passion will always lead you back to BDSM. You are a true Master Sadist. They are rare and precious in the community. Any masochist, male or female, would be privileged to submit to you.

Years ago, in my youth, I had the lofty idea that I would open my own club. I spent my adult life saving to make that a reality. I never had the guts to go through with it, always finding excuses. The truth is I didn't have the business sense to manage a club.

I'm an old man now, ready to retire my flogger and my whip. My hands are no longer as steady as they once were. I won't be returning to the club anymore. I'm leaving this evening to join my daughter and her family in Colorado. They've invited me to move in with them. I've missed seeing her as often as I should, and I want to watch my grandchildren grow up.

I saved a bit of a nest egg over the years, and I want you to have a piece of it. Open a club of your own and fulfill my dreams. You have the strength, the education, the youth, and the skills to be the best club owner in Miami.

Take this check. Do as I've said. It's time for me to leave the sadism to the younger crowd. I'll be watching for your name and smile with pride when I see your success and prosperity.

It's been a pleasure having you as my apprentice. I hope it has meant as much to you as it has to me.

Good luck. Make me proud. Follow your passion. Trust me when I say you are a true sadist. You are ready. Go. Grab your dreams. Don't let the years slip away like I did. Nothing will make me prouder than to watch you making my wish a reality from a distance.

Peace,
Master Christopher

For a long time that day Lincoln sat there, holding the single piece of paper and fighting his emotions. The thought of Master Christopher moving across the country dug deep and left a hole in his chest. Lincoln had grown accustomed to seeing his mentor at least once a week. When he finally managed to pick up the check that had fluttered to his lap, he was stunned.

The next day, Lincoln had set out to make Christopher's dream—and Lincoln's too—a reality. Two months later, he'd met John Gilbert and knew that fate had brought him to Club Zodiac.

Lincoln opened his eyes, jerking back to the present. His mind had wandered for so long he didn't even know what time it was. He righted himself and stared out into the night once again. He wasn't perfect. Far from it. But he knew several things about himself.

Why the memory of that letter and all it represented filtered into his mind tonight of all nights, he would never know. But it jolted him back to reality. He was a sadist first and foremost. Not a lover. The two things didn't go together. He was resigned to the knowledge that he would never find the right sort of woman to permanently take to his bed.

Hell, he had not even taken Sasha to his bed or even his room.

No. He had to separate himself from her, get her out of his system. He was doing a disservice to Master Christopher by even thinking about taking on a sexual submissive and hanging up his whips.

Sure, he could try, but how much time would pass before he missed the thrill of sadism and grew to resent the woman who kept him from it? In the end, he would only hurt her more.

This had to end now.

He needed to explain to her that this wasn't working. It could never work. She was the wrong kind of sub for him. He was the wrong kind of Dom for her. She needed to understand that before this went one second further. Before she got hurt. Before *he* got hurt. Because dragging this out any longer would be detrimental to both of them.

He needed to arrange for her to leave. He needed to make a call. He just hoped Carter wouldn't come over with a rifle when Lincoln woke him up this early on a Sunday morning.

CHAPTER 19

As Sasha slowly came awake, she sighed, burrowing deeper under the covers. Her pillow felt unusually soft, her sheets smelling odd as if she'd switched detergent. She was so tired. Not ready to get up. As she stretched from her balled-up position to roll onto her back, her nipples grazed the top sheet.

Her eyes bolted open. Why was she naked?

Shit.

She was not in her apartment. She was at Lincoln's house. She sucked in a breath as the memories of yesterday flooded back to her. She dragged one hand out from under the comforter and flung her forearm across her eyes.

The first thing that came to mind was that she needed to remain quiet so Lincoln wouldn't know she'd woken up. The man had several extra senses, and she needed a few minutes to regroup before he descended on her and started ordering her around.

She'd failed miserably the last time he'd woken her up. She didn't want to start today with a repeat performance. The half hour spent standing in that corner, lonely and cold, had been enough for a lifetime.

She would do better today. Show him she was the good girl he sometimes implied her to be. Make him call her *sweetheart*. Make him teach her to be what he wanted in a submissive. Make him take her virginity and claim her as his own.

Minutes ticked by. She was surprised he hadn't barged into the room and interrupted her internal pep talk. Finally, she decided to get up and start the day on her own. Maybe he wasn't a morning person, though he'd sure shown up at her place yesterday rested, relaxed, and ready to start her training. He didn't strike her as the kind of man who required much sleep or slept very hard.

She smiled at the thought as she eased from the bed and padded to the attached bathroom. One look in the mirror told her she was a hot mess. Her hair was unruly and all over the place. Her face was pale. Her eyes puffy.

It seemed prudent to at least shower before she presented herself to Lincoln, so she flipped on the water and waited for it to heat while she pulled her long messy curls up on top of her head and wrapped a hairband around them two times.

It surprised her that even after turning on the shower, Lincoln still didn't surface. She expected him to fling the door open at any moment. He had to hear the water running.

Making quick work, she washed her body, toweled dry, and brushed her teeth. She looked marginally more alive. It would have to do.

Padding back into the bedroom, she looked around for her suitcase. It was nowhere to be found. She smiled and rolled her eyes. It was so like him to leave her with nothing to wear.

Fine. She didn't need clothes anyway. She hadn't had any on in twenty-four hours. Hopefully, if she walked out to the main rooms, demure and naked with her head bowed and her body presented, he would be proud of her and their day wouldn't start off with a punishment, the likes of which made her shudder to consider.

With a deep breath, she left the room and made her way down the hallway. She found Lincoln easily enough, standing by the wall of windows looking out at the backyard. He made her mouth water with his torso and feet bare, the only article of clothing on him a pair of loose navy flannel pants. He hadn't taken his shirt off yesterday. The view from behind was spectacular. All muscles and firm, hard skin.

She hated to let the moment end. "Sir?"

He turned around quickly as if she'd startled him out of a deep thought. His face was all wrong. His expression serious and difficult to read. Had she already displeased him this morning?

"You're up," he pointed out, as if she weren't aware. And how the hell had he not known that?

"Yes, Sir." She heard the wobble in her voice. Something was wrong. Something was terribly wrong. Her heart raced. Her hands grew sweaty as she clasped them tighter at her back.

His gaze moved away from her. "I've gathered your belongings. Carter is picking you up shortly."

"What?" The word flew out of her mouth without any filter or the addition of his appropriate title. He would probably spank her later for not addressing him respectfully. Except, no. He wouldn't, because she wouldn't be here later.

He said nothing but turned back to the window, putting his back to her.

She inched forward. "Sir? Why? Why are you sending me away? I thought you were going to train me. I thought…" She didn't know what she thought. So much sorrow filled her, she choked on her words. No. This couldn't be happening. She hadn't had a chance to win him over. To make him see.

"You should get some coffee if you want. There's a full pot. He'll be here soon."

Her body started shaking. What was happening? He was going to brush her off and toss her away like yesterday never happened without even an explanation.

Fuck no. Fuck. No.

She drew in several deep breaths, gathering strength. She

would not go without a fight. "Why are you doing this? Why send me away when we're just getting started?"

He didn't move.

"What's wrong with me, Sir?" she added, her voice more hesitant.

He spun around to face her. "You? My God, baby. Nothing's wrong with you. You're exactly perfect. Pure and innocent and eager and so many things. Things I am not, Sasha. You need a man who can take care of you the way you deserve."

A man? She paused. "Don't you mean a Dom, Sir?"

He said nothing, his gaze settling on something across the room, avoiding hers.

"Look at me, Lincoln. At least have the balls to look me in the eyes while you lie to me," she shouted. The time for respectful titles was past. Desperation took over.

He jerked his gaze to her and shot her a glare. "Watch it, Sasha. You're still under my roof. Don't try to top me."

"Fuck you." She stood taller, fisting her hands at her sides. Her voice was raised. "Don't you dare stand there and order me around while you're planning how to get rid of me as quickly as possible. It's hypocritical. You can't tell me I'm perfect out of one side of your mouth while instructing me to get out of your house from the other. Obviously I'm not quite perfect enough. At least not for you." Unbidden tears ran down her face without her permission. She left them.

His body jerked. He lurched forward and then stopped himself as if he might self-combust if he got too close.

Fuck him.

"Do not put yourself down in my house, Sasha."

"Why? So many rules. *Do this, sweetheart. Don't do that, baby.* I'd need a ladder to reach high enough to list all your rules. But it doesn't matter if I follow them because no matter how many you pile on..." she sucked in oxygen, forcing herself to continue, "...no matter how many I learn, it's never going to be good enough for you. *I'm* not good enough for you.

"So yes. Fuck your rules. You only put them there as roadblocks to ensure I would fail your tests. You can't stand it that I passed with flying colors because now you don't know what to do with me. You're right. I *am* perfect. It's you who isn't. I don't know what it takes to break down your walls and get inside, but whoever manages to do it better come with explosives because that stubborn wall is high and thick."

Something snapped. He rushed forward until he was in her space. And then he grabbed her biceps. Squeezing almost too hard. At least he was showing signs of being human. She'd rather take his wrath over his complete lack of emotion any day. "You're right. I'm not perfect. This has nothing to do with you," he shouted. "Can't you see that? This is about *me*. Yes. I have walls. They are there to protect you from what's inside, not keep you out."

What was he talking about?

She wished she were the kind of person who could stop tears from falling. But she couldn't. And the fact that they slid down her face made her even angrier with herself for her weakness. She squared her shoulders and looked him in the eye. "Have I ever asked you to protect me from what's inside? No. I'm a strong woman, Lincoln. I don't need that kind of protection."

"Sasha…"

"If you just give me a chance. I need a man who's willing to take a chance and let those walls down. I need a man who isn't so closed off from me that he can't see me."

He jerked, shaking her with the reflex reaction. "Woman, I can see you fine. Every single inch of you. Even the parts that make you blush. All of them perfection. Surely if you learned nothing else from me, you leave here with at least enough self-esteem to know you're so fucking beautiful it hurts to look at you. You make my cock so hard, I can't see straight."

"That's complete shit," she hissed.

He flinched again. "Why would you say that? What have I done to make you distrust and disvalue the way I and everyone else you meet sees you?"

"For all the reasons you listed, Lincoln. If I was so damn perfect that I took your breath away, then you wouldn't be standing in front of me—me, naked and exposed—unwilling to put aside whatever is holding you back and creating a thick wall around you. Unwilling to claim me as your own. Unwilling to continue training me." She sucked in a sharp breath. "Unwilling to fuck me."

He flinched again. His grip got tighter on her biceps.

She continued. "You heard me. You say I'm strong, but you can't trust me to handle a good hard fuck. I've done everything." Her voice rose an octave. "Everything you demanded. Even things you didn't think I could handle.

"I let you spank me and stick me in the corner like a child without a word. I let you shave me and watch me masturbate and bathe me and rock my world with your fingers. I've seen the look in your eyes when you think I don't. I've seen it for a lot longer than you think. I'm good enough for you. You just refuse to see it for some unknown reason."

"Sasha. Stop. That's enough."

She ignored him. "Flashes of your lust for me wash across your expression, and then you snuff them out. So don't tell me I'm enough. If I were enough, you wouldn't be standing there holding me at arm's length, telling me how hard I make your cock. Instead, your cock would be buried inside me."

Something cracked. His expression changed to one she couldn't read. She recognized the moment she'd gone too far, but it was too late. Or maybe it was exactly right.

One second he was staring at her like she had two heads. The next second he was picking her up and slamming her back against the wall. His huge hard body flattened against her. He threaded his hands in her hair and slammed his mouth down over hers. It was demanding. Hot. Scary. Amazing. She couldn't breathe. But he wasn't done. He pushed a knee between her legs to hold her up, stuffed a hand between their bodies, found her pussy, and thrust two fingers into her. She screamed out her instant arousal into his mouth.

His fingers disappeared just as fast as they'd filled her, and he wiggled against her. His hips moved back and forth. It took her a moment to realize he'd yanked his sleep pants down. His cock was suddenly hot and hard against her belly.

He broke the kiss and separated their faces a few inches, holding her by the shoulder against the wall with one hand as he leaned back. He stroked his cock hard against her with the other hand. "Look at me," he demanded. She jerked her gaze back to his face. "No, Sasha, look at my cock."

She did. It was huge and angry. Come dripped from the tip. "You want this, baby? Is this what you want?" His tone was all wrong. But she didn't care.

"Yes." She breathed out the word. She'd never wanted anything more in her life. "Yes, Sir. That's what I want."

And then she was no longer flattened against the wall with her pussy pressed into his thigh where he still held her up with one knee between her legs. No. She was higher up the wall, her back flattened hard against it. Instinct made her wrap her legs around his waist. His cock was at her entrance. And then it wasn't... because he thrust it up inside her.

For a moment she couldn't breathe or even think. Searing, white-hot pain exploded inside her as if he'd ripped her in two. Before she could process this, his cock was gone. Almost out of her. And then it was back. Deeper. Harder. Rougher. It hurt. She bit her lip against the pain of his second thrust. But this time the pain had a different edge to it. He did it again. Less pain. More edge. Again. Holy shit. So much edge.

Again. Stars. Her vision blurred. Euphoric pleasure replaced the pain until she thought she might split in two from the amazing sensations prickling her skin. It took her breath away. She tried to look at him. See his expression. But he held it away from her, smashing his face into her neck. She thought she saw a look of anger or frustration on his pinched face but she couldn't be sure, and she was too consumed by her own lust to care.

He thrust again. She reached for his shoulders and dug her nails into them. Holding on. On the next pass—she'd lost count of how many thrusts of pure pleasure she'd withstood—she reached some sort of precipice. And just as fast, she fell from that precarious peak and crashed all around like broken glass.

The orgasm that shook her body was so powerful and consuming she stopped being Sasha and instead turned into a sex goddess. Nothing could have prepared her for how amazing it felt to have Lincoln inside her. Consuming her. Taking. Giving. Destroying. The waves of sexual gratification didn't subside. They morphed into more as one orgasm became two while he continued to fuck her. So good. So perfect. So much more than she ever imagined.

And then he was moving faster. Thrusting harder. Deeper. Angling his hips so that his cock hit a new spot. She gasped. Her mouth fell open. Her breath whooshed out. His thick length slammed against that elusive spot inside her.

Just when she thought she couldn't possibly come any more, she was on the edge again. A different edge this time. A deeper level. It frightened her with its intensity. But she couldn't escape it. Escape *him*. It was happening. There was no way to stop it. More white-hot pleasure. Blinding heat.

She came again, this time from somewhere deeper. Her entire body participated in this new kind of orgasm. Shaking. She was losing the ability to remain upright. But Lincoln held her. He finally lifted his head and stared down at her face. One hand moved to her jaw, cupping her neck and the base of her head possessively, his thumb stroking her bottom lip hard.

She fought to focus on him through the haze of the aftermath of whatever just happened. He looked… surprised? And then his expression turned to something else. It softened for the briefest second. Then it grew harder. His eyes rolled back and he thrust one more time and held himself steady inside her.

She could feel the pulse of his cock as streams of his orgasm filled her. It lasted longer than she expected. But maybe time stood still. He was so beautiful. His defenses gone for those precious moments. His face slack. Nothing but joy as his mouth curled slightly at the edges and his eyes softened—still closed but not squeezed tight. He grunted finally. Spent. Sexy. Larger than life.

She would have to remember that moment forever because it passed so quickly. One second he was inside her, holding her, enjoying everything she gave him. The next second his gaze pinned her to the wall. He blinked and seemed to come back into his body from another place. His eyes widened. He licked his lips. And then he pulled out of her, lowered her to her feet, and jumped back as if she had the plague. His chest heaved. He ran a hand through his hair. His face hardened with pure anger.

She had never before been scared of him, but she was now. Frightened out of her mind. She didn't know this man in front of her. He was not her Lincoln.

She jumped when he shouted out one word. "Fuck." He spun around and padded away. "Get the rest of your stuff together and get dressed. Carter will be here to get you in a few minutes." And then he was gone. *Gone*. She didn't move or breathe until she flinched when the door to the master bedroom slammed shut. She heard a visceral scream of anger. And then nothing.

CHAPTER 20

Sasha was numb. There was no other way to describe it.

She floated out of her body at the slam of Lincoln's bedroom door and stood there, dazed, confused. Wetness between her legs made her lower her face to see pink streaks running down her thighs.

She wasn't even angry yet. That emotion didn't come for a long time.

There was a knock at the front door eventually, but she didn't move. She was still facing the hallway where she'd last seen Lincoln's enormous frame.

A key turned in the lock, and then it opened. "Sasha?" She heard Carter's voice, but she still didn't move.

Out of her peripheral vision, she saw him grab a blanket off the couch and rush forward to wrap it around her. He angled her toward the couch and sat her down, kneeling in front of her. "Where's Lincoln, honey?"

She didn't speak. She couldn't. Words were illusive—totally out of reach. She looked right through him.

"Sasha?" He prompted again. "Honey, talk to me."

She couldn't. What would she say?

"Sasha, did he force you?"

She blinked at Carter. What?

He narrowed his gaze, squeezing her thighs. "Did he hurt you, honey?"

She shook her head. "No. God, no." Not like that. Not like Carter meant.

Finally, he stood. "Don't move." He rushed away from her and headed down the hallway.

She heard him knock on Lincoln's door and then open it. His voice floated into her, but not the words. They were loud enough, but she blocked them, not wanting to hear anything either man said.

She had no idea how much time went by before Carter returned, but suddenly he was there, right in front of her again, his phone to his ear. "Yeah, that's right... Can you come?... If I knew anyone else to call, I would... Thanks... Yes. Soon." He ended the call.

Why she heard that part and not the previous shouting she would never know.

Carter grabbed her suitcase from the front door and set it on the sofa next to her. He opened it, took something out, and handed it to her. "You need to get dressed, honey. Can you do it yourself?"

She finally blinked at him. *Focus, Sasha.* What did he say?

He held a sundress in front of her, shaking it gently.

Clothes. She needed clothes. Right. Of course.

She reached out a hand that wasn't attached to her body and took the dark blue fabric from him.

He spun around to face away from her, and she realized she was meant to put the dress on while he wasn't looking. She managed to shrug into it and tug it down. No panties. No bra. Who the fuck cared.

As she shoved the blanket to the floor, she stood.

He must have sensed her signal because he was once again

facing her, closing her suitcase, picking it up, taking her hand. He led her to the front door, stopping to grab her purse on the way.

And then she was outside. The sun was warm against her arms. Why would she notice something like that?

She followed him, barefoot. Again, who cared? He helped her into the passenger side of his sports car, stowed her suitcase in the trunk, and jogged around the hood to the driver's side. And then they were gone, pulling away from Lincoln's home.

She'd been there for one full day. A lifetime.

She closed her eyes, startled when he touched her arm again moments later. "You're home, honey."

Already? She opened her eyes to find someone standing outside her door. Whoever it was opened it. "Oh, Sasha." The voice was familiar. Her gaze rose to see Rayne standing there, her expression pained. She bit her lip. "Let's get you inside."

Sasha let Rayne help her from the car. Rayne grabbed her things from the backseat and then shut the door. Carter never exited the car. In fact, the moment Rayne shut the door, he peeled away from the curb.

The next several hours passed in a flurry of movement around her that seemed to occur without her participation. A slideshow of events filtered into her mind like photographs, seemingly blinding her with the flash.

She didn't remember entering her apartment or climbing into bed, but she knew Rayne had pulled her through the motions. She'd even suggested Sasha take a bath first.

Sasha had shaken her head adamantly, not quite cognizant of her reasons.

Rayne gave her a pill and a glass of water.

Sasha dozed.

When she woke up, the sun was high in the sky, its rays filtering across the room through the closed blinds. She was alone, but movement in the rest of her apartment told her someone was in the kitchen or living room.

Her body hurt, and she tried to take stock of what muscles didn't want to participate. She stretched out her legs, wincing at the pull of skin on her thighs. She fought back her tears as she remembered she was coated in her own blood and dry come. Lincoln's come. Proof that she had not imagined what had happened to her.

"Sasha?" Rayne stood in the doorway, her brow furrowed in concern. She held a steaming mug. "I brought you some tea. Can you sit up? You need fluids."

She winced again as she pushed her body to sitting and leaned against the headboard.

The scent of herbal tea soothed her as it hit her nose. She took a sip and then another, her strength returning slowly.

Rayne sat on the edge of the bed, a hand on Sasha's thigh. "You want to talk about it?"

Lincoln sat at his kitchen table, head bowed, hands clasped on the table, all feeling gone from his existence. He deserved whatever his partners flung at him and more.

Things had not gone even close to his plan this morning. He'd meant to tell her they weren't compatible. Point out that she wasn't the kind of submissive he needed. That he wasn't the kind of Dom who could fulfill her. Instead, he'd gotten tongue-tied and then… He couldn't even bring himself to think about what he'd done next.

Rowen was pacing. He hadn't spoken a single word since Carter let him in. Or if he had, Lincoln hadn't heard him.

Lincoln vaguely realized that Carter had taken Sasha home and then returned in less than half an hour. He'd silently handed Lincoln jeans and a T-shirt. His expression—the few times Lincoln had dared look at his face—was tight, his lips pursed, his brows furrowed. He was disappointed.

He'd dragged Lincoln to the kitchen table and handed him a cup of coffee. The untouched mug still sat in front of him.

Suddenly Rowen stopped pacing across the table from Lincoln, threw his hands in the air, and screamed, "You fucked her. I asked you not to fuck her. You promised you wouldn't fuck her. And you fucked her."

Lincoln's head dipped lower, his chin practically touching his chest. There was nothing he could say. Rowen was right.

Rowen started again. "I asked you to do one thing. One goddamn thing, and you couldn't manage to keep your fucking dick in your pants. Not even for one *fucking* day?"

Carter interrupted. "Calm down. We don't know the details here."

Rowen exploded. "Don't tell me to calm down. Fuck." He turned around and slammed his fist through the drywall. "*Fuck,*" he screamed again.

Lincoln doubted the man could even feel pain. He knew he wouldn't if he were in Rowen's shoes.

"Talk to us, Lincoln," Carter said, his voice significantly less violent. He had always been the most level-headed out of the three of them. It was ironic since he was their bouncer and he exuded force and strength. Outwardly he was a beast, but he was not hot-headed, and it made him perfect for the role he played in the club.

Lincoln lifted his hands and ran them through his hair. He needed to stop being a pansy and own up to his mistakes. "I fucked up."

"You think?" Rowen shouted. "She's my fucking *sister*, asshole."

"You think I don't know that?" Lincoln straightened his spine. "It's like a goddamn mantra constantly running through my head. It has been for years. I. Fucked. Up."

Rowen flinched. "Years? What the hell are you talking about?"

Carter turned his attention to Rowen. "Oh, come on. Don't tell me you didn't know Lincoln has been hot for Sasha from the moment he met her."

Rowen flinched. His eyes went large.

Lincoln jerked his gaze to Carter. He knew that?

Carter continued, still staring at Rowen. "Sasha too. That woman can't even pull together complete sentences in his presence. Five years, Rowen. She's lusted after him for so long I don't know how it hasn't come to a head before now."

"Sasha?" Rowen stepped back a pace as if someone shoved him in the chest.

"Yes, Sasha. Jesus, you're blind. Both of you." Carter jerked his gaze to Lincoln. "I can't even imagine how she would have reacted to the opportunity to spend unlimited time trying to convince Lincoln to claim her." Carter continued to stare at Lincoln, even though his words were spoken to Rowen.

"My sister," Rowen deadpanned. "You're saying my sister would throw herself at Lincoln because she's had some kind of crush on him?"

"That's what I'm suggesting," Carter said, switching his gaze to Rowen. "Although now might be a good time for you to recognize she's a grown woman, not a girl with a crush. There were two grown adults in this house. They have to take equal responsibility for whatever happened between them. Nobody forced her to take this risk."

Rowen flinched again, shaking his head. "No. Not buying it. Lincoln knew better. He should have been professional. I don't care if she draped her naked body over him and begged, he should have kept his dick in his pants."

Lincoln winced. Rowen had no idea how accurate his description was. But that didn't change the facts. He finally spoke. "Rowen's right. I fucked up. I'm an asshole. I knew better. I take full responsibility. She was under my domination. I have no excuses. It was my job to guide her. I never should have let my personal feelings get in the way. I never should have taken on her training in the first place. I knew better."

"You *knew* better?" Rowen grabbed the back of the chair in front of him. "You knew this might happen, and you brought her to your home anyway?"

Lincoln nodded.

Rowen shoved off the chair, stepping back again. "What the absolute fuck? Have I fallen into another dimension?"

Carter squared off with Lincoln, ignoring Rowen. "I'll admit I could see the writing on the wall. I was hoping the two of you would stop dancing around each other and work something out. I thought if you spent some time together, you might actually be able to break down whatever wall was between you and forge a relationship. What happened?"

Lincoln's eyes went wider as he stared up at Carter. "You knew this might happen? Why would you do that? Why didn't you stop me?"

"Because she's in love with you. I thought it was obvious. I thought you realized that. The woman hasn't dated a single man in her entire life because the first man she fell for at seventeen stole her heart. How the hell am I the only one who noticed this?" His gaze darted back and forth between his partners.

Rowen's face was pale, his mouth hanging open. He didn't blink.

Lincoln exploded, shoving from the table so hard his chair fell over backward and slid across the floor to crash into the kitchen island. "Why didn't you say something? You know I'm not right for her. Why would you encourage her to foolishly pursue me?"

"What the fuck are you talking about? Why the hell can't you be right for her? You've been equally as enamored with her as she has with you. You follow her around a room with your eyes as if she hangs the fucking moon. You watch over her like you own her already. Like you're her Dom. Why would you think you're not right for her?"

Flames climbed up Lincoln's face. His head pounded behind his eyes. "I'm a fucking *sadist*, you asshole. Did you forget that detail?" He was shouting so loud the neighbors could hear.

Carter rolled his eyes. "So? Who cares? Doesn't mean you can't have a relationship with someone."

Lincoln flinched again. "Sasha? Have you met her? She's the poster girl for innocence and sweetness. She's not a masochist. She probably wouldn't even be able to tolerate a gentle pat on the ass while wearing jeans." *Except she has...*

"Oh, come on, Lincoln," Carter broke in. "No one is that averse to play."

"At least I know you didn't beat her to the breaking point," Rowen mumbled.

Lincoln shot him a glare. "Don't be a fucking moron. I wouldn't hurt her if my life depended on it. Give me a break."

"Except somehow you did," Rowen pointed out.

Carter lifted both palms out toward his friends to stop them. "Cut it out. Both of you."

Rowen was right. Lincoln could shoot himself. He'd hurt her in the worst possible way. Far worse than if he'd taken a cat o' nines to her entire body and splayed it open.

Carter lowered his hands. "This is Sasha we're talking about. I don't care how freaking inexperienced she is or how conservatively she dresses, she's been around the club for ten years. Even though she doesn't have a membership and hasn't spent many hours in the actual playroom, doesn't mean she isn't super clear what happens inside."

"Just because she isn't judgmental of others doesn't mean she has the capability to practice the lifestyle herself, and you know it," Lincoln shot back, lying to both himself and his friends.

Carter cocked his head to one side. "Except she's made it clear that she is interested. Over and over again. What's the deal with you? Why would you dictate how Sasha needs to live? Are you suddenly ashamed of the lifestyle?"

Lincoln's body stiffened. "What? Fuck no. Obviously not. I own the damn club. But, I don't own *her*. So, I'm selfish. I don't want someone else to fucking own her either." He blurted all that without thinking. With no filter.

Rowen gasped.

Carter groaned in frustration. "So claim her yourself, Lincoln. Why do you feel the need to martyr yourself in this way?"

Lincoln's blood was boiling. He shouted, "She's not a fucking masochist. Are you listening to me?"

"So? Who cares? What difference does it make? She doesn't have to be a masochist for you to make a life with her. It's not a requirement. She doesn't even have to be submissive. All that matters is that you negotiate what works between you two. Nothing else."

Lincoln spun around and paced away, trying to figure out how to get Carter to see reason. "I can't just turn off who I am and ignore it to set up house with a pretty girl, no matter how badly I'd like to. It would bite me in the ass eventually. It wouldn't be fair to her. I would climb out of my skin from denying who I am, and eventually she would resent me if I didn't resent her first."

"Who said you have to have one or the other?" Carter asked, his eyes wide in shock. "My God. You know better. The majority of our members don't live twenty-four seven lifestyles. They come in, play, get what they need, and leave.

"Even married couples go their separate ways inside the club. How many masochists do we have on our roll who get what they need from you while their partners either watch or participate in something else at the same time? Dozens, I'd bet. Just because someone is a masochist doesn't mean their partner is a sadist. They negotiate. Work it out. You know it isn't sexual. You've pointed that out so many times it's beaten into people's heads."

Lincoln understood what Carter was saying, but he still would argue the table didn't spin the other way. "That's not the same thing."

"Why not?" Carter asked.

At least Rowen had stopped shouting or interrupting. He seemed resigned to listen to the volley, taking it all in.

"I'm the sadist in this equation. I have an inherent need to dominate submissives in the darkest of arrangements. I would never ask Sasha to try submitting to something like that, let alone watch me do it to someone else."

"Who says Sasha has to participate?"

"It's who I am," Lincoln reminded them. "I've known for years I would never have a permanent woman in my life. There's no way to mesh my need to wield a whip with my sexual desires on the side. That sort of sub doesn't exist."

Carter chuckled. "Dude, your head is so far up your ass you can't see straight."

"Fuck you."

"Hear me out. Jesus. Under your premise, your perfect woman needs you to whip and crop her body into subspace with no sexual overtures and then turn around afterward and flip a switch to become a sweet, doting sexual submissive."

"Finally he gets it." Lincoln sighed. "You see? There isn't such a thing. So give it up."

"Lincoln, you're dumber than a fucking rock. I'm sorry, but I don't know how else to say it. The woman who warms your bed doesn't need to also be strapped to your cross. They are mutually exclusive. In fact, even if she did exist, it would never work because you would feel the need to dominate other masochists too. So lose the ridiculous obsession with fitting one woman into that tidy package. You're right. She doesn't exist."

Rowen suddenly broke in. "He's right, dude. You're being a complete imbecile. There's no reason you can't have both. And— goddamn I hope I don't regret saying this—even with Sasha. So what that she's not a masochist? Who cares if she's even submissive? You do your thing at the club. She does whatever thing interests her in or out of the club, and then you go home to each other."

Lincoln blinked. Both men were starting to make sense. Still... "I can't ask that of her."

Rowen groaned. "How do you know? Have you tried?"

Lincoln shook his head. "Of course not." Hell, he hadn't even told her why he'd sent her away, let alone gave her a choice.

"You think that's fair?" Rowen asked. "You think she doesn't get a say in what she's willing to tolerate? She's not fragile. You've said so yourself. She's not even uneducated in the key points of the lifestyle. At the very least, she's probably flexible enough to be game for a lot of things vanilla women wouldn't entertain"—he held up a hand—"though please spare me the details."

Lincoln swallowed. No way he'd ever discuss his relationship with Sasha with her brother.

Rowen took a deep breath. "All I'm suggesting is that you let *her* decide. Give her the choice. You're a total asshole with a double standard if you think you're so high and mighty that you'd turn her away and let her slip out of your fingers because you were too busy being all macho with your chest pumped out to even give her the option to turn you down.

"Perhaps you need to attend some of the BDSM 101 seminars we offer. They might help you with your negotiation skills. Get yourself over the notion that you need to protect my sister from the world. If I can get over it, surely you can too." Rowen planted his feet wide, hands on his hips, brow furrowed.

No one said another word.

Lincoln stared at Rowen for a long time. Finally, he took a breath. "I really fucked up."

"I see that. Maybe you should fix it," Rowen suggested.

"I'm in love with her," Lincoln added.

"I know, brother. Maybe you should tell her that instead of me." His expression softened, and then he winced as he flexed his fingers.

Lincoln glanced at the hole in his kitchen wall behind Rowen. "You broke my wall."

"You broke my sister."

Lincoln nodded and then he rushed from the room to go find his shoes. He ignored the two men still standing in his kitchen as he grabbed his keys and headed for the door.

"Lincoln," Rowen called after him.

Lincoln turned around to face his best friend, his hand on the doorframe. "Yeah?"

"You better fucking do right by my sister."

Lincoln swallowed the lump in his throat. What if it was too late?

"Just make her happy," Rowen added.

"She hasn't agreed to anything yet."

"It's called negotiation. You really should look into those classes." Rowen shrugged. "Just sayin'."

Lincoln rolled his eyes. He started to push off the doorframe when Rowen took a step toward him.

"One last thing: If she does accept your sorry ass, promise me you won't play with her at the club when I'm on the floor. My level of acceptance doesn't reach that far."

Lincoln smirked. "Done." He shuddered as he headed for his car. What Rowen didn't know was that Lincoln would never expose an inch of Sasha's skin to *anyone*, especially not her brother.

CHAPTER 21

It was dark out the next time Sasha woke up. A soft glow of light came from the partially open bathroom door. She inhaled slowly and closed her eyes again. It was cruel that every time she woke up the world was still spinning.

Voices coming from the living room caught her attention. That must have been what woke her. She couldn't identify who was out there, but the hushed tones sounded angry. Probably Rowen. If Rayne was still in her apartment, Rowen would have eventually shown up.

The last person Sasha wanted to face today was her brother. She didn't need his disapproval or his condemnation. She had her own.

Rayne had been a godsend. She had kicked off her shoes, climbed onto the bed, and held Sasha's head against her shoulder, rocking her gently as she cried a river. She hadn't pried her for information or judged her in any way.

If Rayne hadn't been there, Sasha had no idea how she would have managed. She supposed she would have lain in bed until she got dehydrated.

The voices were getting closer.

Shit.

If Rowen thought now was a good time to lecture her—

The door opened, and Sasha was shocked to find not Rowen but Lincoln standing in the frame, larger than life, his expression filled with so much concern she thought he might have actually been crying.

She rolled onto her side, putting her back to him. "I'm not in the mood to submit to you tonight, Lincoln. Go find someone else to confuse."

He came in anyway, of course. After all, the man might have sent her about ten thousand mixed signals, but he'd done so without ever lowering his shield of dominance.

He sat on the edge of the bed, his weight making her rock toward him a few inches.

Shit.

"Sasha…"

She bit her lip, forcing herself not to make a sound while a new wave of tears fell. On second thought, maybe dehydration would have been preferable because now she wouldn't be forced to show any more emotion.

He didn't touch her, which was good. If he had so much as set a hand on her thigh, even with the comforter protecting her skin from him, she still might have swung around and punched him.

"There's no excuse for what I did this morning. Hell, there's no excuse for anything I did for the last two days or even the last week. Or fuck, let's go back five years. I've been an ass for five years."

She stiffened. What the hell?

"I spent the day with Rowen and Carter in my face."

Good. I hope you mean literally. Like their fists in your face. Asshole.

"Apparently I've had my head so far up my ass—Carter's eloquent words—that I haven't had a sane thought since I bought the club."

She didn't move. She didn't dare breathe.

"According to Rowen, I need to enroll in some of our beginner seminars so I can learn some negotiation skills."

Was he chuckling?

A rustling sound accompanied by two soft thuds told her he'd kicked off his shoes. And then he had the audacity to climb onto the bed next to her and prop himself against the headboard, making himself at home.

"I'm pretty sure both of them are right. I've been making stupid choices for years, ever since I walked into my own club one evening and saw the prettiest girl I've ever seen laughing nervously with my new employees across the room."

Sasha fisted the sheets under her chin, grateful he couldn't see her face and that she had curled into herself. Her hair fell over her cheek to block her completely.

"She was wearing these obscenely short white shorts and a silky yellow shirt with tiny spaghetti straps. She took my breath away with her innocence and purity."

Sasha continued to lie perfectly still. Stunned. *He knows what I was wearing the day we met?* He was going to ruin her perfectly good mad. She could already tell. And that pissed her off.

"I was a stupid fool that day, and somehow fell into the role of jackass that I wore like a cloak from then on. I hurt her. Badly. But I was so damn self-righteous that I convinced myself over and over again that I wasn't good enough for her anyway."

Sasha sucked in a breath. *Not good enough for me?*

He kept going. "I had a thick head. I owned a BDSM club, and I had dark tendencies when it came to the lifestyle. I knew she did not and never would. So I shunned her every chance I got, pretending she was a nuisance. My partner's kid sister.

"She didn't go away, however. She didn't find a nice vanilla guy and get married. She kept getting prettier and sexier as she turned into an amazing woman. I had to keep her at arm's length to avoid the possibility that I might fall for her."

Sasha had no idea what he was referring to, and she hoped he would eventually spit it out. Nevertheless, his words kept her tears falling silently onto the pillow.

"Apparently, I wasn't the only one with a crush. That sweet, sexy woman was into me. She was shy about it. She didn't flaunt it or approach me, but she didn't hide it well either."

"I had hoped she would move on so I could too. It was a catch-22. On the one hand, I knew I would be happy for her if she found a nice man and settled down in a vanilla life with a white picket fence and everything he could offer her that I knew I couldn't. On the other hand, I knew it would hurt. I would never recover from her. I would never find another woman like her."

More tears. Sasha hiccupped. She leaned farther into the pillow.

Lincoln slid down the bed, rolled onto his side behind her, and leaned on one elbow. He set a hand on her hip. His next words were closer to her ear. Gentle. "Somewhere along the way I knew she was mine. I knew it, and still I denied it. I convinced myself I was wrong for her. It wasn't fair to her. And it wasn't fair to me."

She inhaled sharply. Damn him.

His hand smoothed down to her thigh and then back to rest on her hip again. "I didn't have the right to decide what she could and couldn't handle like some holier-than-thou, all-knowing God. I treated her like shit in an effort to get her to walk away from BDSM. To get her to walk away from me. It was selfish and unforgivable.

"I can't change who I am, but she deserves to make her own choices instead of me dictating them for her and acting like she isn't smart enough to think for herself. She deserves my honesty about who I am deep inside. She deserves to have all the information so she can make an informed decision. She deserves the world."

Sasha held her lip so hard between her teeth she thought she might draw blood. She wanted to roll over and face him, but she knew if she did, the ugly cry would turn into a fountain. And besides, he still hadn't told her what the mysterious secret was.

His hand slid up her arm to cup her shoulder, which was tucked deep under the covers like the rest of her. He didn't try to roll her his direction. Instead, he held her in place, encouraging her silently not to face him.

"So, here's the deal. No matter how you slice it, I still hurt you. Cruelly." He'd switched to speaking to her in first person. Interesting. The strange long story was over. "I don't deserve to even ask for your forgiveness after the way I treated you, not just today and yesterday but for years. However, I'm also clear now that forgiveness is your choice. Yours to give. I don't get to dictate who you should fall in love with, and I don't get to decide if you should forgive me for being a jackass."

She winced. Apparently he *did* get to decide *that* she was in love. She smiled inside, incongruent with her perfectly good sad that accompanied her totally legitimate mad.

"I don't want you to say anything. Not today. Not for a few days. I want you to spend some time thinking about what I've said and how you feel. I took things from you in the last two days that I had no right to claim. Inexcusable. I'll understand if you can't forgive me and want me to bow out and leave you alone.

"I also want you to know this had nothing to do with dominance and submission. My feelings for you are not related to the lifestyle at all. I don't care if you never want to practice any form of BDSM, decide to become a flashy, boisterous brat, or pick up your own whip and switch sides. It changes nothing. Those things are just details. We can always work through them later.

"What I want is to invite you to come to the club Wednesday night as my guest. I'd like the opportunity to show you who I am and what I do at Zodiac. I don't want you to make any definitive decisions between now and then. I won't contact you. You need time to think and breathe after what I put you through this weekend. It was intense."

He had that right. She'd never been so tired in her life. She might sleep clear until Wednesday.

He squeezed her shoulder when she started to roll backward, stopping her. "Don't, baby." His words were soft. "I don't deserve to meet your gaze right now, and to be honest, I don't think I could look into your eyes without crumbling. I'm feeling cowardly.

"And don't say anything either. I don't need an answer. Just think about it. If you want to take a chance on me, come on Wednesday. Carter will check you in. If not, I'll understand. I might not like it... Okay, I might actually freak out, but I'll learn to live with it." A slight hint of humor ended his words.

He leaned in, kissed the hair curtaining her forehead, and then his weight left the bed, and he was gone.

Sasha couldn't move for a long time. Rayne didn't come in either. She was grateful for the solitude.

CHAPTER 22

What the hell had he been thinking?

Lincoln was a nervous wreck by Wednesday night. He hadn't slept. He hadn't eaten. His hands were shaking and sweaty.

He'd been pacing his office so long the carpet was worn.

Sasha had taken his words to heart. Not only did she not try to contact him, but she hadn't spoken to *anyone*. Not Rowen or Carter or even Rayne. Lincoln got no information from any of his friends to tell him if she was leaning one way or the other.

He assumed it was possible some of them were lying, especially Rayne, but he couldn't do anything about it, so he stopped badgering them twenty-four hours ago.

His well-thought-out plan that had seemed brilliant Sunday afternoon before he spoke to her no longer seemed viable. How was he supposed to demonstrate his sadism in front of her if he couldn't steady his hands or concentrate on his submissive?

It wasn't safe. No one should dominate another person in this state of mind. He'd made a lot of poor choices over the years, but he wouldn't make this mistake tonight.

He hadn't canceled on anyone who'd scheduled a session with him for tonight yet—mostly because it hadn't occurred to him how totally incapable he was until a few minutes ago. He'd have to wait until they arrived or find another Dom to fill his slots.

Jesus.

He stopped pacing and turned to look out the window. Would she show up?

What if she didn't?

He'd told her he would respect her decision, but he wasn't at all sure he could go through with it. If she didn't come to the club tonight, he would undoubtedly head to her apartment and beg her to give him a chance.

He closed his eyes.

The door to his office opened. He waited for whoever it was to speak up. It was early, so it had to be either Rowen or Carter there to tear him another new asshole. He wasn't eager to find out who'd come to rip into him this time.

No one spoke. Had he imagined the sound of the door?

Nope. Because then the door closed with a soft snick.

He took a breath, bracing himself to face the latest firing squad, and then he turned around.

His breath hitched. Damn. It was Sasha. Right there. In the flesh. In his office. Wearing a sexy pale pink sundress and silver sandals.

His heart leaped. He didn't dare move. He didn't want to spook her by running across the room, slamming her into the door, and kissing the sense out of her, but that was his first inclination.

She looked nervous. Hesitant. She tucked an unruly curl behind her ear and cleared her throat. "I heard you had a thing for innocent-looking girls. Is that a fetish?" Her voice was teasing.

Thank you, God.

A smile split his face. "If we want it to be." *Control yourself. Stay calm. Let her determine the course.*

She stepped farther into the room, her fingers playing with the material of her dress at her sides.

Holy shit. His heart stopped. She wasn't wearing one of her regular sweet, innocent dresses. Not this time. This dress would make every man in the building turn to stare with their throats dry and their balls pulled up tight.

His eyes went wide as he let his gaze roam down her body, taking it all in. The dress—if you could call it that—was indeed pale pink. But that's about the only thing it had in common with her regular choices in clothing. It was short, almost too short— did it even cover her ass?

He swallowed a lump in his throat. He was afraid to find out.

The spaghetti straps were so thin he wasn't sure they would hold up the bodice, which was more of a corset. It made her breasts look amazing, lifting them so much she had the hint of cleavage. The skirt was loose... and again, so damn short. If she spun, it would flare out and everyone around would see... what? He was dying to know and he prayed he got that opportunity at some point.

But holy mother... she was not wearing dainty silver flat sandals either. She was wearing dainty silver heels that made her legs go on and on forever and gave her shapely calves enough definition to cause him to drool.

Realizing he'd done nothing but stare at her hot body, he jerked his gaze to her face to find her biting her lip. Should he compliment her? "Baby... you look amazing."

A slow smile. "I wasn't sure you'd like it."

He took a few steps forward. "Anything you wear looks amazing. And nothing." He hoped he sounded light and joking as opposed to suggestive.

She worried her bottom lip again and looked away, blushing. Yeah, this was his Sasha. His chest tightened just looking at her, and he knew he would take her any way he could get her. He would move heaven and earth for her.

He would even give up sadism and sell the club for her. That's how much he loved her.

He had intended to say nothing and let her watch him in

action. But that was before. Before he realized he wasn't in the right frame of mind to play tonight. Before she walked into his office wearing that damn outfit that made his cock hard and tied his tongue in knots.

He wasn't sure he wanted her to leave his office wearing it. In fact, he was concerned about who had seen her between her apartment and his office. Irrational jealousy reared its head. She would be pissed if he dictated what she could and couldn't wear in public.

Suddenly he knew what he needed to do, so he started talking. "I had a mentor," he began, taking a deep breath.

She startled. "You did?"

"Yeah. Master Christopher. I've never told anyone."

"Okay." She worried her fingers together. It was cute as fuck, and he had to glance away to keep his train of thought.

"I met him at an underground club when I was seventeen."

She smiled. "I met a man in a club when I was seventeen too. What a coincidence."

Lincoln smirked. "Don't remind me." He watched her drop her hands and wipe them on the sides of her skirt. She was nervous. And again, she pulled at his heartstrings. How and why had he denied himself this woman for so many years? "Master Christopher was a sadist."

She nodded. "Okay." Matter of fact. Huh.

"I found his work fascinating. He was brilliant. Watching him was like a form of art."

She held his gaze, giving nothing away.

"I was intrigued, and I soaked up everything he had to offer. He thought I had a gift, so he shared it with me." She still watched him, so he continued. "Apparently I was good at what I did. People booked time with me. Masochists, I mean."

She lifted a brow, her head tipping slightly.

"A masochist is someone who enjoys receiving pain."

"Yeah, I know what a masochist is. They booked time with you?"

He nodded. "Yes. They trusted me. I had a reputation. I still do."

She licked her lips, thinking. "So, you're saying people schedule a session with you? People who like to be flogged or whatever?"

"Yes."

"Okay." She nodded. "Go on."

Okay? That's it? He almost laughed. "You're making this too easy." He gave her a slight grin.

"What? Talking? You have trouble telling people about your past or something? I'm not sure I follow, Lincoln. I'm waiting for some big secret. That's not the end, is it? What did Master Christopher do?"

Lincoln chuckled. "That part's not important. Although I will tell you something I've never told a soul."

"What?"

"He gave me the money to buy Club Zodiac."

"Really? Your mentor?"

"Yes. He'd saved it all his life but never got around to following his dream. He wanted me to do it."

"That's so generous. I can't wait to meet him someday."

Lincoln sighed. "He died two years ago, unfortunately."

"I'm so sorry."

He took a second and then continued, "Anyway, without him, we wouldn't be standing here."

"So, that's it? The big secret you're stammering to get out is that you had a mentor and he gave you money? I don't think that's earth-shattering, Lincoln."

He tipped his head back and stared at the ceiling. "I don't deserve you."

"Okay. You said that repeatedly the other night. What'd I do now?"

Lincoln rushed forward until he was right in her space.

She didn't retreat.

"You… You're… Damn, Sasha. You're so fucking amazing. I kept that secret from you for years, worrying about what you'd think of me if you knew. And you're only interested in my mentor." He laughed. "I'm a fool."

"What secret? Lincoln, I'm not following you." She reached behind her back and grasped her hands together.

Fuck. Me.

"I'm a sadist, Sasha."

"Okay. So?"

He laughed again. "This doesn't bother you?"

"Should it?" Her head tipped to the side again, her brow furrowed. "I mean, you said you're good at it. You own the club. I assumed you were into some sort of pretty serious dominance. Did you think I would care?" Her eyes suddenly went wide and she took a step back, dropping her hands and swallowing hard. "Wait. Shit. Are you trying to tell me that the only way you can be with me is if I let you dominate me like that? Because Lincoln, I'm not sure, but I don't think I could be a masochist. It doesn't turn me on. A spanking is one thing, especially if it ends in my favor. But real pain for the sake of the adrenaline rush or something? I don't think that's for me. If it's a deal breaker, tell me now."

He jerked. "What? No. God, no. I don't think you're a masochist either. You'd know if you had a predilection for pain, whether or not you'd seen it in person before. I saw the way you recoiled when you watched some hardcore stuff at Breeze. That's my point. I would never expect you to do anything you weren't one hundred percent comfortable with. That's not what I'm saying at all."

He hesitated and shook his head to clear it. "Okay, no. I'm messing this up. Yes, at one point I did think we couldn't be together because I needed a masochist, but that was dumb. I see that now. I don't need a masochist.

"I was fixated on the fact that Master Christopher asked me to follow my passion. I twisted that and internalized it to mean he didn't want me to veer from my dream of being a sadist and opening a club. Somehow I thought I would disappoint him if I didn't continue to practice."

Her words were soft and her face filled with sorrow. "That's a heavy burden, Lincoln. I'm sure he never intended for you to take him so literally. Staying true to yourself can look like many things. People change. They evolve. They meet other people and are influenced by other ideas."

"I've never actually had a permanent sub who was mine. I top people who want to scene with me. It's not sexual for me. It's a mutual arrangement where I get a release from dominating them and they get what they need from submitting to me."

She nodded.

"Since being a sadist is a big part of who I am, I thought I needed a masochist as a life partner. But that was plain stupid. Couples in the lifestyle don't all practice the same form of BDSM. Sometimes their tastes run in different directions. They negotiate. Figure out what they can both live with. It's a give and take. They make it work. There's no law that says my life partner also has to be into the same kink as me. I got stuck on that and wouldn't let it go."

"Let me guess, you figured that last part out on Sunday."

He winced. "Yeah. Kinda. I mean, I was confused. Rowen and Carter helped set me straight. Or rather, they screamed at me until I saw reason. Some reason. I still have concerns. And Rowen might have broken his hand."

Her eyes went wide. "He hit you?"

"No, but there's a hole in my kitchen wall."

She tipped her head back and laughed. It was the most beautiful sound. And then she held out a hand. "Wait, did you say Rowen was trying to get us together?"

"Not initially. At first he came to my house to cut off my balls and feed them to me. I deserved that. I can't blame him. But Carter, ever the observant mediator, pointed out where both of us were wrong and patched things up."

"Isn't that nice?" she joked. "You boys had a get-together to decide who I'm allowed to sleep with and whether or not it would be prudent for me to join your club. What did y'all decide in the end? I mean, while I was bawling my eyes out on Rayne's shoulder because the man I love fucked me and then tossed me out the door without a word."

The blood rushed from Lincoln's face. *The man I love...* That line in the middle there stopped time. It was in present tense. He wanted to fist pump the air. Instead, he tried to gather his wits. After all, she had followed those three words with more important ones—*fucked me.*

She was not going to make this easy. He had to dig out of this hole. "No one made decisions for you. But we did agree you should be able to make them for yourself, including your decisions regarding submission."

"Should I be grateful?" More sarcasm.

"No." He blew out a breath, needing to get this train back on the tracks. "I'm totally butchering this, aren't I?"

"A little. But it's kinda cute." She tried not to smile. Total minx.

He narrowed his gaze at her. No matter what happened, he hoped she would at least be able to submit to him in some fashion, because at the moment he wanted nothing more than to take her over his knee and find out what she was wearing under that skimpy skirt before turning her bottom a delicious shade of dark pink. His cock stiffened.

Who knew he could react sexually or get aroused from dominating a sub? Until ten days ago, it hadn't happened with any sub. It didn't happen with other women. Not that he didn't have relationships and sleep with women. But he didn't do it at the club. He didn't get hard from sadism or even domination. Except how would he know? Sasha was the first woman he'd practiced another form of dominance with. And he most definitely got hard with her. Just looking at her. When he considered spanking her... *Fuck.*

"Go on. Keep digging." She pursed her lips.

"Baby..." he warned. He flexed his hand, the desire to spank her sweet ass growing. Inappropriate for the seriousness of this conversation.

Now she smiled. "No. Really. Don't stop. This is just getting good. You can *baby* me later. I want to hear the rest of what you have to say first."

His heart seized again. *You can baby me later...* There was a God. "What I was so ineloquently trying to say is that I didn't think *you'd* want to be with *me*, knowing where my tendencies lie. I thought you'd be disgusted. Mortified. Think less of me. Frankly, this is still my primary concern. Just because you have no interest in practicing masochism doesn't mean you can tolerate me doing it either."

She shivered. "Why not? Lincoln, I know I'm not a member and I haven't spent much time in the club, but I've known about the lifestyle for ten years. I've studied it thoroughly. You can't shock me. Not verbally anyway. Yes, I'm new when it comes to witnessing, and I begged you fools to let me join the club so I could get a feel for the different types of dominance, but I wouldn't judge anyone."

"You nearly fainted watching that sub get cropped at Breeze last weekend."

She rolled her eyes. It wasn't her best-laid plan even under the circumstances, but he would refrain from pointing it out. "Are you listening to me? Jeez, Lincoln. I haven't watched many scenes in person. Sometimes I'm going to be shocked or react negatively. Sometimes I'm going to get aroused and react positively. But I won't know which scenes turn me on and which ones make me cringe until I observe them. Thus the need for the *denied* membership," she pointed out again, her brows lifting high in a way that shouted *duh*.

"You really are interested in the lifestyle? You're not just trying to piss off your brother... or me?"

Her shoulders dropped with her chin as she shot him another look, this one said *seriously?* "Why would I go to all the trouble to visit Breeze last week if I wasn't interested in exploring my submission? It was stressful. I didn't know anyone. I've never been so nervous in my life.

"But you three gave me no choice. You wouldn't relent, so I found my bravery and explored elsewhere. I would much rather have been here with you or Rowen or Carter. People I know. People I'm comfortable with. But, nooooo." The sarcasm that oozed in that word was thick in the air. "God forbid sweet, innocent Sasha be treated like an adult. After all, she's just a kid. She can't possibly know what she likes and doesn't like. Let's choose for her and set her straight."

Lincoln winced. She was right. "We did that," he admitted.

"Yes. You did."

He schooled his face and his voice. "I'm sorry, sweetheart."

"Apology accepted."

That was easy.

She tipped her head again. "Are you sure you don't think I can be a masochist?"

He flinched again. That came out of nowhere. And then he saw her fighting a grin. "Watch it."

"So, what's your plan for tonight? You want me to watch you work so I can make an informed decision? You think it's important that I know exactly where your kink lies so there are no secrets between us?"

"Yes." She had it all figured out. "But now I'm too flustered to do any scenes, so it's not going to happen tonight."

Sasha blew out a breath and wandered toward the window.

The back of her "dress" was mouthwatering. The skirt was too short for public consumption, and although her long curls hung down her back to cover it completely, he could see that the majority of her back was bare.

Her voice had changed tone when she spoke, softly. Sadness filled the room. "You made me feel like I wasn't good enough, Lincoln."

His heart seized again. He slowly walked toward her back, but he needed to let her speak.

"I realize it was stupid of me to take you up on your offer to train me. It was childish. I did it to get your attention. I wanted you to see me. I thought if I could prove to you I was strong enough to submit to you no matter what you threw at me, I could make you love me."

He couldn't swallow. "I know. And I never should have made the offer. I thought if I pushed you hard enough, you would give up the notion you were submissive and run from me."

She turned to look into his eyes. "Why, Lincoln?"

"Because I didn't think you could love me if you knew who I really was, and it would hurt too bad to see you in my club with other Doms if you rejected me."

She stared at him.

He stared back.

"We were both stupid."

"Yes, but I had a responsibility as a Dom to protect you, and I failed you."

She took one step closer. "You didn't fail me. You're here now."

He lifted one hand tentatively and tucked a curl behind her ear.

She tipped her face into his touch. "So what do we do now?"

"Step back. Take it one day at a time. Get to know each other. Date. If you're willing, that is." It was too soon to say the things hanging on the tip of his tongue. *The truth is you never needed to work so hard to make me see you. To make me love you. I already did. I was just too stubborn to admit it.*

She shook her head at his suggestion.

His stomach dropped. His hand, still stroking her cheek, froze.

"I don't want to take a step back, Lincoln. I want to move forward. Why would we dance around each other and pretend we feel less than we do?"

Fuck me.

He nodded, a small smile forming. "You're in charge, baby. I'll do whatever you want. Lead the way."

CHAPTER 23

Sasha blinked up into her Dom's eyes.

He was her Dom. No doubt about it. Sure, he felt bad. His tail was currently between his legs. He was groveling. And well he should be. But that didn't change the fact that in the end, he was her Dom.

If she had walked into his office and found him surly and demanding she strip and stand in front of the window, she would have done it. He'd already won her heart over Sunday night. He'd already paid a hefty price for treating her with the same disrespect he insisted she not give him. He recognized the double standard. She could have easily turned over that night, faced him, and accepted his apology.

But she'd also recognized his need to extend a longer olive branch, and she'd granted him that play, even though she would bet her life her brother had figuratively beaten the living hell out of Lincoln until he'd suffered enough.

Today was today. A new day.

She let her gaze roam down his body. Did he know how much it turned her on every time she saw him dressed like he was tonight? It was his usual work attire, nothing special. Professional by club standards. But seeing him in those tight black jeans with that black cotton T-shirt stretched across his chest always lit her on fire.

With his black hair, dark eyes, and dark skin, he turned heads everywhere he went. Right now his brow was furrowed.

Lincoln had concerns. They needed to put those fires out before they could move forward. She was confident she could separate herself from his role as a sadist. She seriously doubted watching him perform was going to bother her as much as he feared.

He was right about one thing, she needed to see him in action. Was he truly able to separate sexually from the masochists who came to him? Because watching him or even knowing he was doing a scene when she wasn't around wasn't likely to bother her, but if she thought he had sexual interests outside of her relationship with him, that would be a deal breaker.

Trust was crucial. They couldn't move forward until she proved to both herself and Lincoln that his sadism wouldn't affect their relationship. "I need you to keep your schedule tonight," she told him.

He frowned. "Sasha, I don't think—"

"I know. I know. You don't think you're in the right frame of mind. So, what do we need to do to get you in the right frame of mind? This is important."

He nodded slowly and took a deep breath. "You really want to watch me work tonight?"

"Yes."

He glanced at his watch. "We have another two hours before my first appointment."

"Then I guess we better use our time wisely."

He lifted his brows again in question. "You know this isn't a deal breaker, baby. You don't have to prove anything to me. You don't *ever* have to prove anything to me. I realize that now. You're perfect the way you are. In every respect. If you don't like watching me, I won't perform in front of you. If you don't even like knowing I'm topping people, I'll stop altogether. At some point in the middle of this new self-awareness of mine I realized you mean more to me than anything else, even sadism."

Her chest seized. "I believe you. Now, I need you to believe it's not a deal breaker for me either. I need to witness you doing what you do for myself too. It will help me understand the dynamic."

He licked his lips. Nervous. So much so that he was willing to put it off just to enjoy one more day with her before she left him. She could see that in his eyes. He was leery.

She took a step closer and tipped her head back. "You're worried I won't be able to accept you for who you are. I get that. But you have to understand I have a far different concern you have not considered."

He flinched. "What's that?"

"Sex. You say sadism isn't about sex for you, while frankly I can't wrap my head around any aspect of BDSM not being about sex. It's going to take me some time and education to grasp that."

He nodded. "That's because you're a sexual submissive. For you everything in the lifestyle is about sex." He gave a half smile. "Thank God. It's what makes my cock so hard I can't think around you."

A flush rushed up her cheeks. How could he so thoroughly distract her in the middle of this important discussion? She shook her head to clear it. "Even if *you* don't get off dominating other people, you can't control whether or not *they* get aroused."

He nodded. "That's true. But does it matter? I disassociate from that aspect. Sometimes a submissive does get aroused, whether he or she intended to or not. I always make it clear I'm not interested in a sexual encounter. If they want to have sex with someone else after our scene, that's great. It's not going to happen with me."

She tried to absorb everything he was saying. It was complicated.

He held out a finger. "In fact, let me present this from another angle. The entire reason you and I are in this predicament is because in my twisted head I thought I needed to find a masochist for a life partner in order to be fulfilled. I not only turned my back on you for that reason, but I turned my back on all women before you. Since I didn't believe I could ever find a woman who could fulfill both my sadistic needs and my sexual needs, I decided I was destined to be alone. They don't cross paths. I have mistakenly believed I would never be able to have a serious relationship with anyone because I couldn't see how anyone would be able to accept my darker side as a separate entity."

She was starting to understand how his mind worked. It was warped, but she was catching on. "And Carter and my brother slapped you around a bit about this issue until you saw it more rationally?"

"Yes." He grinned. "They did more than that. I had several screws loose apparently. I've spent the last few days wrapping my head around the idea that anyone—especially you—could possibly get on board with my proposal."

She cocked her head to one side, confused again. "Especially me?"

He tapped her nose. "Well, you're the only woman I ever cared enough about to broach the subject. And, as I've said, I still have my doubts. I've never been this nervous. The level of trust and commitment it would take to make my world perfect is more than I've ever been willing to ask of anyone."

She set her palms on his chest and leaned into him, needing the contact. His willingness to so openly discuss this issue demanded her respect. "I'm here. I'm offering to try."

He set one of his hands on top of hers over his heart and squeezed. His voice was lower when he whispered. "And you have no idea what this means to me."

She had more questions. "Explain why you could never forge a relationship with a masochist? You've met so many over the years. Why none of them?"

"I've tried with several women. I simply don't get off when I'm topping someone. I can't. I need to concentrate. I could seriously injure someone if I were dealing with a hard-on while I flogged them. So, when the scene ends, even if I'm currently romantically interested in the woman I just topped, we're in different head spaces. She might be primed and ready to go. Maybe other men can drop the whip and get it on, but I can't switch gears that fast. I need some transition time."

Wow. He was serious about this. It had been a problem forever. Not to mention his explanation went a long way toward endearing her to him even further and eliminating any doubts she might have about trusting him with other women.

She constructed her next question in her mind. "What if orgasm is the goal of the person you're with? Surely that happens a lot. You can't stop them from getting aroused."

"True. I'd say my bottom derives pleasure from pain often. I usually negotiate what their goals are ahead of time. If they want to come, that's fine with me. It's just not going to end with my dick inside them. Or my tongue for that matter."

She cringed slightly.

He gripped her hand tighter. "This is new territory for me, baby. A totally new world. I promise you I would never do anything that made you uncomfortable. If you agree to be mine, we'll negotiate the fuck out of every detail of this until you're comfortable with everything I do with other submissives." He leaned forward, his face inches from hers. "And let me remind you, this entire thing is negotiable. If you watch me perform and realize you can't stand it, I'll walk away."

She swallowed her emotions. "I'm confident it won't come to that. I trust you."

"It's not just trust I need from you. I need you to be comfortable with everything I do, or I won't do it. Anything that makes you cringe is off the table. If I found out you withheld concerns, I would lose my shit. Then *I* would have trust issues with *you*. You have to be an open book when it comes to your reactions to my sadism, or you're likely to find yourself on the receiving end, strapped to my table with a very sore ass."

She sucked in a breath, gripping her pussy at his threat. She might not enjoy most of the aspects of sadomasochism, but the idea of him strapping her down and spanking her made her knees buckle. It was irrational since the only time he'd spanked her had been for punishment, and she hadn't liked it. But, somehow the way his eyes were narrowed at her now implied something entirely different. Having his hand on her bare ass didn't sound like a punishment at all at the moment.

He moaned, rolling his eyes. "I've created a monster." As if he needed space for self-preservation, he set his hands on her shoulders and stepped back, putting a few feet between them.

They needed to get out of his office. She took another step back and glanced at the door. "How about if we go downstairs to the club together and you show me around? Start with a tour. Pretend I have no idea what the inside looks like." She grinned. They both knew she was well-acquainted with the layout of the club.

He glanced down at her chest and then lower. "Okay, see, there's just one problem."

"What?"

"I've come to acknowledge that I have a possessive, jealous streak when it comes to you."

No sweeter words had ever been spoken to her. But she also intended to play this hand to her advantage.

He continued, "Half of me has been distracted ever since you stepped into my office, worrying and wondering about who saw you in that nonexistent outfit between your apartment and my office." He winced. "Don't get me wrong. It's sexy as hell. My cock jumped to attention immediately, but it's... lacking material."

Laughter bubbled out. "Seriously?" She glanced down. "I'm totally covered. Nothing important is showing."

"Sasha…"

"Are you saying you don't think I'm sexy? Are you embarrassed to show me off?" She was totally needling him.

He shot her a glare. "Of course not. You're the hottest woman I've ever laid eyes on, and twice as fucking sexy in that dress thingy."

He squeezed his eyes almost shut. His expression was comical. Not quite a wince. More like a grimace. Tinged with a nervous energy.

"See, like I said—and believe me, I'm new to this feeling—but, a possessive streak has raised its ugly head and taken over my body."

She worked hard to keep a straight face while he kept talking, curious to see how many words it would take him to explain himself sufficiently.

"I mean, I know I've been going to fetish clubs for over ten years now, and I'm clear that people attend in every state of dress and undress, but… What I'm trying to say is that I don't care how people dress. It totally doesn't faze me. I'm desensitized to nudity or any public display of affection. But…" He took a deep breath.

She bit the inside of her cheek to continue to hold a straight face. Her only movement was to lift one eyebrow to encourage him to continue with his four-page thesis paper on why she needed to be completely covered in public. What else could she do? It was too comical for words.

He groaned, tipping his head back and forth in order to work out imaginary kinks. "I don't want you to think I'm overly domineering or anything. It's not like I intend to start telling you how to dress or whatever. It's just that…"

And it kept getting thicker.

He lifted both hands, ran them through his hair, tousling it so that it fell in a sexy disarray across his forehead. "Fuck. Sasha, you can't wear that outfit in my club," he rushed to say, his words suddenly spewing out in rapid succession. "Every man would be leering at you, and I'd have to hurt a few people, and I really don't want to do that. Not today. My blood pressure can't take it. Could you put on a sweater or something?"

"A sweater." She cocked her head to one side, fighting hard to keep from laughing outright.

"Yes. Something. Anything." His voice rose. He waved a hand around in front of her, indicating whatever imaginary vision he had about her state of undress. "I'm fucking serious, baby. I don't care what other people wear or what other Doms let their subs wear. I don't even care what other subs I've worked with wear. But you're different. I'm not interested in sharing you."

"Different." She tried hard to repeat the word as blandly as possible.

"Yes, different." His voice rose higher. "Mine." He grabbed her arms and hauled her against his body. He was heaving for oxygen, but he slowly calmed down and swallowed. His next words were gentler, controlled. "You're mine, Sasha. I don't want to share you."

"Why didn't you just say so?" she teased.

"Woman…" he warned.

She set her hands on his chest. "First of all, it's super cute and kinda hot that you took ten minutes of stammering to tell me that you aren't comfortable with other people looking at me, which I might point out is seriously hilarious. Second of all, my brother is part owner of your club if you'll recall. I have no interest in him ever seeing any inch of my private parts. Gross. And third, I'm totally decent, so no, I'm not going to change. Not today. Get over yourself. I spent a lot of time picking out the perfect outfit to seduce you in, and I intend to wear it all night—unless you demand I take it off entirely at some point."

He gulped.

Cute.

She continued, "Lucky for you, I don't like to be naked in public, so this is a win-win for me. I was worried that being submissive to you was going to mean we went head-to-head on that topic soon. Obviously I don't have to fight that battle. The extent of my public nudity happened last Friday night when Master Colin lifted my skirt two inches. Don't ask me to do it. It makes me uncomfortable. Hard limit."

He exhaled. "Thank God."

"If you're really bothered by this outfit, I won't wear it out of the house again, but for tonight, let me enjoy one single evening in this rather conservative fetish wear. I feel sexy in it. Don't make me feel dirty."

His eyes widened. "Done."

"That's it? You're going to drop it?"

"Yes. You're right." He lifted a finger between them. "But only tonight. I'll buy you all the fetish wear you want, but after tonight, keep it in the bedroom."

"You didn't seem to mind having me totally naked in the living room, the kitchen, and even the backyard over the weekend."

"The bedroom is figurative." He grinned.

She rolled her eyes.

"And on that note, I officially declare this conversation closed. Put bossy, insolent Sasha away and trade her for demure, submissive Sasha for the next few hours, okay?"

At least he sort of asked. "Yes, Sir."

"That includes eye rolling, cussing, and disrespect."

"Yes, Sir." And just like that, the tiny strip of floss that constituted her thong was wet.

Lincoln had his hand on Sasha's back as he led her into the club. It was just opening when they got downstairs. Carter lifted a brow and smirked as they walked past him. Rowen was nowhere to be found. Probably for the best.

Sasha was shivering. She had one arm crossed under her chest, that hand grasping the elbow of her other straight arm. "You cold, baby?" he whispered into her ear.

"You wish," she muttered in response.

He chuckled. "Nervous then."

"A little."

The club itself had once been a living space. It took up the second floor above a strip mall, and the layout included a great room—where they were standing now—and a hallway that contained what would have once been bedrooms that were now reserved by members for privacy.

The lighting was dim and perfect. The walls and flooring dark. Blackout curtains covered the windows. Lincoln loved the feel, and he glanced around now, taking in the various apparatus spread out around the main space. There were few people in the main room yet, but in a few hours, it would be crowded with members and guests.

He led her to a darker corner, backed her against the wall, and loomed over her, blocking them both from anyone who might glance their direction. "I don't want you to be nervous. It's just me. We'll define this thing between us as we go along."

"Okay." She nodded. "Sir."

He shook his head. "It's going to be so much fun training you."

"You don't think you've trained me enough? *Sir.*" Snarky and insolent.

His smile grew wide. "Sweetheart, we're just getting started. And just so you know, there are plenty of private rooms in my club. No one will see your naked bottom if I take you into one of them to spank you into submission." He lifted a brow.

She bit the corner of her bottom lip, eyes wider. "Yes, Sir." And then she gave him exactly what he was hoping for. She fidgeted.

She pressed her thighs together and squeezed her arm across her chest. She was aroused.

Thank God.

"I'm pretty good at taking cues from subs, baby. I have years of experience. And you're an open book. So, don't even try to hide anything from me. You will fail. Safeword?"

"Red, Sir."

"You want to change it?"

"No, Sir. Red is fine, Sir."

He inched closer, crowding her space until she had to back into the corner. He set both hands on the wall above her head, caging her. "You're mine." If he said it enough, maybe he could will it into truth. Just because Sasha thought his sadism was no big deal, until he proved that, there were no guarantees.

Until he performed for her while she watched, there were no guarantees.

Until he saw her face and held her in his arms after working with a masochist, there were no guarantees.

Her breathing came in sharp pants. "I'm yours, Sir." God, he hoped she still believed that in a few hours.

"Trust me to take care of you."

"I do, Sir."

"I fucked up. It won't happen again. You have my word."

She nodded. "I know, Sir."

He lowered one hand slowly until he cupped the side of her face, and then he angled it to the left and lowered his lips to hers. He moaned into her mouth as she eagerly opened for him.

The kiss was deep and powerful. It made his cock stir again. But he needed to put an end to it before he got carried away. If she wanted to watch him in action later, he needed to get in the right mind frame. Thinking about what he might do to Sasha's sweet body later wouldn't serve his scheduled subs well.

He reluctantly ended the kiss, nibbling a path to her ear before whispering into it, "Hot. Sweet. Innocent. Pure. Mine."

She moaned.

He smiled. "She likes that."

"She *loves* that, Sir." Her hands went to his waist, grabbing on to his T-shirt and fisting it.

He loved that too. Keeping her slightly off-kilter was going to be fun.

He pulled back to meet her gaze. "You intend to test me all evening? I'm just asking so I can go ahead and reserve a room."

"No, Sir."

He lifted a brow. "You sure?"

She shrugged. "Well, I wouldn't mind if you got a room. It might be fun to try that other kind of spanking you told me about."

His dick was not going to survive the night.

She must have thought he didn't understand her meaning. "You know, the kind where the sub gets off on it. Not the kind where it hurts."

He smiled slowly. "I know the kind. You ready for that?"

"Yes. I mean, I'd like to try but not with an audience." More squirming. She was ready.

"I'll reserve the room. But it's up to you what it gets used for. Understood?"

"Yes, Sir." Her face flushed. Beautiful.

"Come on. I'll show you around a bit, and then I need to get ready. I'll need a few minutes to meditate a bit, clear my head of the sexy vixen tempting me with her eye rolling, and concentrate on my job."

"Okay, Sir."

CHAPTER 24

Sasha stood as far away from Lincoln's scene as she dared. Far enough that she could see everything without threat of being a distraction to him. She didn't want him to know where she was or what she was thinking.

Carter was with her, his huge bulky body standing behind her in the shadows like a secret service agent. He made her giggle inwardly. Lincoln had asked him to keep an eye on her—code for making sure she didn't freak out and need her own aftercare in the middle of the scene.

Lincoln was in a zone. Mesmerizing. She couldn't take her eyes off him. The sub he was working with was a pretty redhead who had negotiated the entire scene ahead of time. She wore a blindfold, but other than that, she was completely naked.

Lincoln had already landed several warm-up strikes on her butt, faint pink lines barely visible from where Sasha stood. She had tensed a bit with every swish of the whip at first, but as time ticked by, she grew more accustomed and at ease.

It truly was an art. Lincoln stalked around his sub gracefully, carefully plotting where to place each thin welt. It was hard to look away.

Carter had given her a play-by-play in the beginning, until she assured him she was fine. She knew he was still eyeing her closely.

As the strikes landed with more force, closer together, Sasha tensed, but she wasn't worried. He knew what he was doing. That went a long way toward soothing her. She might not experience the same level of calm watching a Dom she didn't know, but this was Lincoln. Not a stranger.

He'd prepared her earlier, letting her know there would be a lot of welts and exactly where he intended to place them. But there wouldn't be blood. That hadn't been negotiated into the scene, and besides he did that only rarely and only with select submissives he was incredibly well acquainted with.

As she suspected, it didn't bother her to watch him top another sub. She knew it wasn't sexual for him. He'd also made that abundantly clear. It gave him a certain kind of release and a satisfaction she would never understand, but it didn't give him a hard-on.

He'd also assured her this particular submissive was only interested in the endorphin release from a whip. She didn't use it to reach orgasm.

His entire concentration was focused on lining up his next strike and then ensuring it hit precisely where he intended. He never missed. Every once in a while, he paused to touch base with the woman, speaking into her ear, soothing her with a gentle hand to the back of her head or her shoulder.

Sasha felt a sense of pride. She smiled. He was indeed a professional. This was as intense a scene as she'd ever want to watch, but it didn't make her doubt his commitment to her. There was no distrust. She knew he was hers. It didn't matter that they were in the beginning stages of their relationship. In a way they had been dancing around each other for so many years that she felt an instant connection.

She wondered if he would want to take her home with him tonight. Every time she thought about the possibility of being alone with him again, her heart beat faster. He had indicated they should take things slow. How slow? Going backward wasn't reasonable in her mind.

He was a bit possessive it turned out, so she couldn't imagine him dropping her off at her apartment later and calling next weekend for a date. He hadn't taken his hands off her since they left his office until he needed to prepare for the scene.

His gaze was intense. Always. He made her pussy leak with just a look. Her nipples had stood at attention the entire evening too, brushing deliciously against the silk of her bodice, which also kept them alert.

He had looked at her with that same intensity for years. She simply hadn't been able to read it for what it was—his inability to rein in his feelings. In fact, the look had often turned into a scowl in the past. She hoped he wouldn't feel the need to glare at her in frustration anymore. Not if the reason for his frustration had stemmed from wanting more from her.

She was his. Did he realize that now?

She drew her attention back to the scene to find dozens of pink lines up and down the sub's thighs and butt and shoulder blades. The woman was humming rhythmically, deep in subspace.

It was almost over.

Sasha backed up and turned to Carter. "I think I should let him finish without me hovering."

Carter's eyes came closer together. "You okay?"

"Yep. But I know she needs aftercare, and I don't want Lincoln to feel awkward about me being close by."

Carter nodded slowly and took her gently by the arm. "I'll escort you to his office."

"I can manage that on my own," she teased.

"I'm sure you can. But that isn't what I promised Lincoln."

She smiled. *Of course.*

As they headed toward the stairs that led to the third floor, they passed a woman with thick blond hair. Distinct blond hair

Sasha would recognize anywhere because it was the sort of blond that came naturally. Almost white. Definitely not from a bottle. Sasha remembered her as the dungeon monitor from Breeze. "Faith?"

The blonde lifted her head and met Sasha's gaze. If it weren't for her stunning hair and her mesmerizing blue eyes, Sasha wouldn't have recognized her. She was not wearing the head-to-toe black clothing from the last time they'd met. Tonight she wore a red corset and a short, tight, black leather skirt. Deep red heels made her several inches taller than her five four.

Sasha met her eye to eye since she too wore heels.

Faith smiled, but it didn't reach her eyes. "Hi." Her voice was soft.

"You two have met before?" Carter asked.

Sasha nodded, her gaze still on Faith. "Yes. At Breeze."

"Ah. Then I guess introductions aren't necessary."

"What brings you to Zodiac?" Sasha asked, intrigued to find herself staring into the same sorrowful eyes of the woman she'd met several weeks ago at the competitor's club.

Faith licked her lips. "I'm thinking about switching my membership."

Sasha nodded slowly when Faith took a step back, obviously not interested in expounding on that statement. "Well, I hope you enjoy your evening."

"Thank you." Faith's heels tapped lightly on the floor as she hurried away.

A light touch on Sasha's arm drew her attention back to Carter. He smiled. "She's stunning, isn't she?"

"Yes." That was an understatement. It wasn't that she had the classic beauty of a model or actress or anything. But that hair… And those eyes… Sasha wondered if everyone else could see the sadness behind them. She shook herself back to the present as Carter continued to lead her to Lincoln's office.

When they arrived, the brighter lights of the upstairs room

making her squint, she was surprised to find Rowen sitting on the loveseat. "Hey," she murmured.

Carter left her at the door, shutting it behind him as he headed back to the club.

"Hey, yourself." Rowen patted the space next to him, but he turned his face away from her and held out a blanket from the arm of the sofa.

She tried not to laugh as she tucked the throw over her shoulders and draped it across her front.

She hadn't spoken to him in over a week, so she wasn't sure what to expect. As she lowered onto the cushion next to him, she noticed the scabs on his angry red knuckles. "You have an accident?"

"Run-in with a wall."

She grinned. "I heard about that."

He leaned back against the couch and sighed. "You okay, Sasha?"

"Yes. Better than."

"I feel a bit responsible for backing you into a corner."

"I'm a grown woman, Rowen. I can make my own decisions. And I have to take responsibility for my own actions. You can't beat yourself up every time I make a choice you don't agree with, even if I get hurt. You have to let me live my life."

"I know." He sighed again. "I'm trying."

"I owe you everything. If it weren't for you, I have no idea what would have happened to me. You were a great brother and father figure to me when I was vulnerable and too young to make any decisions, let alone good ones. But you did a good job. I turned out okay." She nudged him with her shoulder.

He smiled. "You turned out amazing. And I wouldn't change a thing."

"Thank you."

"So... Lincoln, huh?"

"Yeah."

"Couldn't you pick some medical student who's been studying for so many years that he has no history?"

She chuckled. "What's wrong with Lincoln's background?"

"Nothing. Oh, except for the sadistic part," he joked.

"I'm in love with him, Rowen."

"I know you are. I don't know why I didn't see it sooner. I just want you to be happy."

"He makes me happy."

"You mean, he's made you happy for the last three hours? Because you weren't even close to happy the last time I checked in with Rayne."

"She's amazing, by the way. Thank her for me."

"If she's speaking to me this week."

"Off again?" She winced.

"We'll see."

The door opened, drawing Sasha's attention across the room as Lincoln stepped in.

Rowen stood. "My cue to leave." He sauntered across the room and met Lincoln at the doorway. "Make her happy, man."

"I promise to do everything in my power."

And then Rowen was gone and the door was closed. Lincoln leaned against it. "Come here, baby."

She stood, dropped the blanket, and made her way across the room until she could lean into him, putting her hands on his chest. She looked him in the eye to make sure he didn't doubt her sincerity. "It was like a piece of art. Beautiful. Mesmerizing."

His shoulders relaxed. "You were okay with it?"

"Yes. I trust you. Not saying I'd want to watch all the time or that I ever want to see a scene where there's blood involved, but that choice has nothing to do with you. I'm just squeamish about pain and blood." She shuddered.

One corner of his mouth lifted. "Still uncertain if you're a masochist?"

"No." She shook her head. "Not even close. You still sure it won't bother you? Do you need that from me?"

He smiled. "Never. Turns out I need way different things from you. I may do scenes with other people who need that sort of thing, but it doesn't suit you, and it's not who we are together."

"And who are we together?" she prodded, grinning.

He set his palms on her hips and then ran them up her back under her hair. She shivered at the contact to her bare skin. "We'll figure that out as we go along, but I have a pretty good idea." He lowered his face to claim her lips. When he pulled back, he spoke. "You still want to play? We don't have to if you're tired. It's late. I've put you through hell this week."

"Don't you have other subs scheduled?"

"Nope. I canceled a few and another Dom took a few."

"Then what are you waiting for? Take me to your private room and make my body hum, Sir."

Lincoln's heart was full to overflowing as he led his sub to the private room with the spanking bench. He dimmed the lights, locked the door, and pointed at the maroon, leather-padded bench.

He was anxious to get started and didn't want to make her any more nervous than she already was by dragging out the process. Another day he could ease in slowly. But not today.

He suspected she would calm as soon as she was in position. "You've seen other subs on one of these before."

"Yes, Sir."

With a hand at the small of her back, he led her to the end. He had a plan in mind, and he didn't intend to discuss it with her. "Trust me?"

"Implicitly, Sir."

He stood behind her, set his hands on her waist, and lifted her onto the bench so that her belly rested on the center padded section and her knees and elbows lined up with the four other leather kneeling pads.

She shuddered, but he soothed her with a hand on her back, applying the right amount of pressure to ground her and calm her nerves. "Safeword?"

"Red, Sir."

He released her back and gathered her hair into a ponytail, tugging the band from his wrist to secure it in a messy, loose bun at the top of her head.

She giggled. "Cosmetology school, Sir?"

"You think now is the time to make jokes, little girl?"

She pursed her lips. "No, Sir."

"Didn't think so. You *are* a little girl tonight, aren't you? *My* little girl."

She licked her lips slowly, her face flushing, her back arching subtly, thrusting her breasts toward him. "Yes, Sir."

Damn. What was he doing? This was unchartered territory they had not discussed. "I assume it's a role you don't mind playing since you showed up dressed for the part."

"Yes, Sir."

Okay then. Deep breaths. Lincoln had brought her into this room so she could experience an erotic spanking. He hadn't considered role-playing, but now that he had her sweet body on his bench wearing that teasing, pink, little-girl outfit... He kneeled in front of her and caught her chin. "You understand role-playing, right?"

"Yes, Sir."

"Can't say I've done it often myself, but I'm up for it if you're curious."

"Okay, Sir."

"I want to make it perfectly clear that when we play like this, it's strictly a scene. In no way do I think of you as a little girl outside of this scene." He knew it bothered her that their relationship had begun on the wrong foot with him publicly humiliating her about her youth. He wanted to be damn sure she wouldn't resent him using that same theme in a scene.

The moment those words had slipped out of his mouth—*You are a little girl tonight, aren't you? My little girl*—had not been planned. But he couldn't have anticipated her reaction either. Thank God she didn't call him *daddy*. He was pretty sure that would squick him out.

Time to play. He stood, intentionally putting his bulging cock near her face. "Have you been a naughty girl this week, Sasha?"

She licked her lips, her gaze on his crotch. So fucking sexy. Her ass wiggled a bit as if she was trying to get comfortable. "No, Sir."

"Did you touch my pussy?"

"No, Sir."

"Hmm." He trailed his fingers up and down one arm for a while and then rounded to the other side to do the same, watching her relax in increments. Finally, he slid his palm down to her hand and gently eased a Velcro cuff around her dainty wrist.

She whimpered beautifully.

"You like being restrained, little girl?"

"Yes, Sir." Her voice was barely audible. Breathy.

He did the same to her other wrist. "Too tight?"

"No, Sir."

He cupped her cheek and dragged his thumb across her lower lip, pulling it from between her teeth. "Don't hurt my little girl's lip."

"Okay, Sir." Her eyes were huge as she looked up at him.

He decided to test the waters. "If you need something in your mouth, I'll find something for you. Not this lip." He tapped it again.

Her eyes widened as her face flushed further. "Yes, Sir."

Fuck me.

As he released her chin to trail his fingers down her shoulder, he stepped to one side again. Without warning, he yanked the front of her bodice down several inches.

She gasped as cool air hit her tits. They swayed for a moment. Her perfect nipples were dark and puckered. He flicked one hard enough to make her gasp.

"So pretty, little one. Do you know how long I've dreamed of seeing these perfect tits?"

"No, Sir."

"Years. Ever since that day you showed up at the beach wearing that scrap of material you called a bikini and nearly thrust yourself at me with your sunscreen."

She sucked in a breath. "That was your idea, Sir."

"Mmm." *She remembers.* Instead of continuing to play with her nipple, he grazed his fingers down the side of her breast, across her belly, over her hip, and down her thigh. As he bent behind her to secure her ankles in the same manner as her wrists, he lifted his gaze to see her delicious pussy glistening with arousal.

He almost choked when he noticed she wore nothing but a thin thong. He hoped she didn't have an attachment to it, because he was going to shred it with a yank of his hand in a minute.

As soon as he had her ankles secured, he stood, easing his palms up and down her inner thighs.

Her breaths came quicker. Her head lolled back and forth. "You're an amazing submissive, Sasha." He broke the scene slightly to tell her that, but he thought it was important that she have the reinforcement.

"Thank you, Sir."

It would take some time to figure out exactly what made her tick, but they had the rest of their lives, and Lincoln couldn't wait to experiment.

He knew Rowen had been kidding when he joked about Lincoln taking BDSM 101 classes, but the man also had a point. It was time to put everything Lincoln had ever taught or learned about the various aspects of the lifestyle to use. He'd spent the last decade concentrating on sadism. There were so many other avenues to explore with his voracious new sub.

He continued to stroke her thighs, moving from the inside to the outside and then back again, inching closer to her pussy with every pass until she was a ball of nerves about to explode. "My little girl is so responsive. Why is that do you think?"

"I don't know, Sir." Her voice was strained. "I think it's only for you though, Sir."

"Hmmm. We'll never know, will we?" The thought of another man ever touching her made him grit his teeth.

"No, Sir."

When did he get so fucking possessive that he felt the need to claim her every few minutes? He had no idea, but she squirmed more with every mention. She had all night. "Whose little girl are you, sweetheart?"

"Yours, Sir."

"That's right. My good girl." He smoothed his hands higher to cup her ass, molding it in his palms while she moaned. His thumbs were intentionally close to her tight forbidden hole. He would never touch her there this soon, but he did intend to tease her and make her wonder.

He pulled her skirt up around her waist and tucked it under her belly to secure it out of his way. "My little girl's bottom is so smooth and white. It's going to be so sexy when I color it pink in a minute."

She whimpered.

He took the opportunity to stick one finger under the elastic strip of her thong at her waist and gave a sharp tug.

She squealed in shock.

"I love the noises you make, sweetheart. My cock gets so hard."

She didn't respond. He doubted she could. He hadn't even landed a single palm on her and she was about to explode.

"Is my pussy wet, little girl?"

She made an undainty noise before responding. "Yes, Sir."

"Let's see." He eased his flat palm down between her butt cheeks, applying slight pressure to the crack as she drew her cheeks together. When his fingers stroked through her folds, they came away soaked with her juices. He lifted them to his mouth and sucked her flavor off each one as she wiggled.

"What a naughty girl you are, so wet and swollen. You shaved your pussy for me. I like that."

"Yes, Sir." Her voice was so wobbly she sounded like she literally might come.

"You don't have permission to come, sweetheart. Not until I say so."

"Sir?"

"You heard me. Can you hold it back, baby?" He didn't want to ask her to do the impossible, but he did want her to learn to control her orgasms. Wait for them. Let him decide when she came and didn't come. It would heighten her arousal and keep her guessing all the time.

"I… I don't know, Sir. I'll try."

"Good girl. That's all I ask. I won't punish you this time if you fail. I know it's hard. But I want you to try your best. In the future I'll expect you to comply. Understood?"

"Yes, Sir."

He continued speaking simply because he knew he was driving her mad with lust. "I own your orgasms from now on, little girl. You're mine. And your pleasure is mine to dole out when I see fit."

"Okay, Sir." Her voice quivered.

"If you get too close, you need to stop and tell me. Don't come without permission." While he spoke, he teased her outer lips with almost nonexistent strokes of his fingers.

"Yes, Sir."

Stepping closer between her legs, he pressed her thighs wider and flicked a fingertip over her clit.

She moaned. Her legs stiffened.

"Don't come yet, sweetheart. I'm not done exploring." God, this was hot. The hottest scene he'd ever participated in. This one was on fire. If he lived through it, it would be a miracle.

He hoped she wasn't too sore from the rough way he claimed her virginity the other day because he wanted inside her again tonight.

"Such a good girl," he crooned as he pulled her lips apart and dipped the tip of one finger into her warmth. Goddamn, she was tight. His cock jumped in protest as if pissed off that he would dare enter her with something other than its swollen head.

"Sir, I'm going to come, Sir." Her voice was strained.

"Okay, sweetheart. Come for me." He thrust two fingers into her channel.

She screamed, her orgasm pulsing around his finger. Good. He needed her to get the first one out of the way or she would never survive the spanking.

CHAPTER 25

Sasha squirmed against the soft leather bench, silently pleading with her Dom to continue touching her. She knew better than to ask, but she wanted more.

The orgasm had been amazing, but it barely took the edge off her arousal. She was burning up. No wonder people enjoyed this lifestyle. Being restrained and helpless while her Dom teased her was the singularly hottest thing she'd ever experienced—far better than watching others play, and that was hot too.

She knew she gave off an air of innocence to most of the world, but underneath the conservative dress, this preschool teacher had always been hyper-aware of her sexuality. She liked to come, and she liked to come often. And she'd like to come again right about now.

Her pussy gripped at nothing as Lincoln's fingers eased from her channel and lightly stroked her swollen lips. "Such a greedy little girl." He set one hand on her lower back, making her shudder at the pressure.

Oh, yeah, she was totally into bondage.

"My naughty girl broke several rules earlier tonight, didn't she?"

Sasha's heart raced. *Shit.* They hadn't been in D/s mode when she'd broken most of his rules. Would he punish her for offenses committed when they weren't playing? She hoped not. It would get confusing. And for as much as she enjoyed him dominating her, she also recognized she wasn't the sort of submissive who would enjoy a twenty-four seven arrangement. It was too intense. Draining. Too many things to remember all the time.

She hoped he would be willing to negotiate something part-time. She also hoped he would be willing to spend the rest of their time engaged in normal vanilla life. Easy laughter. Meals together on his back porch. Watching television. Going to dinner. Regular things.

He can. She felt confident. After all, he'd told her he would give it all up for her. Every single aspect of BDSM. So, surely it would be easy to negotiate something in the middle.

Suddenly he was kneeling in front of her face again. He'd taken off his T-shirt. His six-pack caught her attention when his abs flexed. She wished she could run a hand over all that hard muscle. Later.

He stroked her cheek with his thumb. "What's going on in my little girl's head?"

Ah, he was so observant.

He smiled. "Nothing gets by me, sweetheart. I told you I'm good at this. Now, you clenched up when I suggested punishing you. What happened?"

"Shouldn't there be a distinction between when we're playing and when we're not, Sir? I mean, it doesn't seem fair that I be disciplined for perceived disobedience I committed when we weren't in the role. That would imply I'm always really your sub, and it would be too stressful. I don't think I can do twenty-four seven, Lincoln."

He smiled wider. "Ah, such good questions. I'm proud of you. Never hold back that curiosity. If you have a concern, bring it to me immediately."

"Yes, Sir."

"To answer your question, no, I will never punish you for anything you did while we weren't playing. You have my word. Won't even bring it up. In this case, I was just pretending as part of the role-play." He winked. "Pretend offenses will be followed by a pretend punishment that will be nothing like the last time I spanked you."

She blew out a breath, relieved. "Okay. Thank you, Sir."

"Little girl, I'm about to rock your world. You have no idea."

Heat rushed over her cheeks. If he did anything half as erotic as what they'd already done, she would die happy.

"Shall we resume?"

"Yes, Sir." She relaxed into the bench once more, deriving comfort from the cuffs at her wrists and ankles. They kept her from having to proactively hold still for him which was also hot in some circumstances, but could be stressful at the same time.

For this scene she was relieved to have the option to escape him taken out of her hands.

For several minutes he said nothing as he resumed petting her, stroking her skin everywhere. He even unstrapped her heels and slid them off to tease the soles of her feet. She giggled.

Finally, he was back between her legs. He adjusted something on the bench between her thighs and they spread open farther. Obscenely farther. "Oh, yeah. That's better. I like my little girl's pussy wide open so that it drips onto the floor with nowhere else to go."

She moaned. *Please touch me.*

She got her wish when he dragged one finger slowly through her wetness. "So wet for me. Do you know how hard my cock is, little girl?"

"No, Sir. Show me?"

He chuckled. "Sassy, aren't we?"

"Sorry, Sir. I just thought you'd like me to maybe lick it." She was definitely testing the waters with her smart mouth, but it was a scene after all. She might as well tempt him to either give her the contact she needed or spank her.

Not to mention the fact that she had yet to take his cock into her mouth. She was anxious and curious about doing so.

Lincoln's palm squeezed her butt cheek so hard she winced. "I warned you about trying to top me."

She swallowed. Had she tried to top him? Oh... yeah... probably. Apparently she shouldn't make suggestions during a scene based on what she craved.

"I'm gonna have to spank this sweet bottom until you show me proper respect."

"Yes, Sir." Was he still playing the little-girl scene? Or was he really going to punish her?

Two seconds later she found out when his hand lifted and came back down on her bottom right at the junction of her cheeks and her thighs.

She lost her breath and then held it, not sure she could move an inch or breathe without coming.

"I think she sees the difference," he teased, again slipping out of the scene. No. It wasn't that he left the erotic D/s scene, it was that he had occasionally pulled away from the sub-scene in which they were role-playing that she was his little girl. Confusing, but it didn't matter because the same rules applied. They were in D/s mode no matter what.

His hand lifted and swatted her again two times, once on each cheek. Again, low. Not as hard as he'd struck her to discipline her on Saturday. No, this was more sensual. Erotic. And it was working.

She would come a second time if he struck her again. "Sir, I need to come."

He soothed her cheeks with his palm, molding them and squeezing them, pulling them apart. She tried to ignore the fact that he could see her rear hole every time. She knew when it was visible because the cooler air in the room hit the puckered flesh.

"Good girl. Catch your breath. I'm not done yet. You don't have permission to come. Not for a while."

Not for a while? Shit.

"Did you just cuss at me in your head, little girl?"

Shit.

He must have taken her silence as affirmation because his hand swatted her again right between her cheeks.

She gasped, squeezing her eyes shut to keep from coming. He wasn't even touching her pussy or her clit.

"Is it appropriate for little girls to use four-letter words, sweetheart? Even in their heads?"

"No, Sir. I'm sorry, Sir."

"You know I won't tolerate your pretty mouth being soiled with inappropriate language. Understood?"

"Yes, Sir." She gritted her teeth.

He might have thought he could bring her back from the edge if he stopped spanking her to engage in conversation, but he was wrong. Every time he insinuated she was a disobedient little girl she grew hornier.

Who knew she would enjoy any of the things she was experiencing tonight? He had unleashed a monster.

While he smoothed his palm over her warm cheeks, he kept talking. "Someday I'm going to use a flogger on your bottom, little one."

Her breath hitched as she squeezed the muscles in her ass.

He chuckled. "Yeah. I haven't forgotten the way you squirmed while you watched that first scene at Breeze. I thought you were going to come from the voyeurism alone."

Oh God. He saw that? How long had he been at Breeze watching her? Duh. Probably the entire time.

Now both his hands were on her ass, molding it, parting her cheeks. "If you like being spanked, you're going to love the soft thump of my flogger."

She had no doubt.

"I would never use a tool that left a mark on your skin, but I can't wait to lull you with thick strands of soft leather."

She really needed him to stop talking. If he thought this short break from spanking her was meant to draw her back from the edge, he was wrong. Talk of flogging her sent her heart racing. So much wetness between her legs.

He leaned forward and kissed a line up her spine. When his lips reached her ear, he whispered, "Here's what we're going to do, little one. I'm going to spank your bottom rapidly until you come without me touching your pussy, and then while you're still screaming out your release, I'm going to fuck you so hard you won't know how many orgasms you had in the end."

She nodded, unable to speak. Wanting what he offered more than anything in the world.

"I need words, little one. Repeat back to me what I just said. Paying close attention to me is an important part of the lifestyle. I expect you to do so when we're playing."

Was he kidding? How was she going to utter a syllable, let alone repeat his erotic suggestion?

"Did you like what I said, little one? Did it turn you on?" He brushed her hair from her face.

"Yes, Sir." She hardly heard herself.

"I'll wait for you to repeat it, and then I'm going to make it real."

She swallowed. She had to do this, because she really wanted the end result. "You're going to spank me until I come without touching my pussy, and then you're going to... have sex with me."

He chuckled. "Good girl. I like the way you didn't use forbidden words." He righted himself.

She didn't have time to think another thought before his hand lifted off her bottom and he swatted her rapidly, over and over, spraying the lowest part of her ass with so many blows she couldn't count. Not hard. Just right. Every single one made her arousal rise.

He spanked her upper thighs too and then struck several times right in the middle, hitting both cheeks and her thighs. The vibrations went straight to her clit, and she came hard, screaming out her release.

True to his word, she was still pulsing around the orgasm when she heard the distinct sound of his zipper lowering followed by the rip of a condom wrapper. And then he slammed his cock into her channel.

She lifted her face, gripped the pads under her fingers, and shouted, "Lincoln. Sir. Oh. God. Oh. God."

He pounded into her, his grip on her hips. Her legs so obscenely wide that she couldn't do anything but take every thrust and enjoy the best orgasms of her life.

CHAPTER 26

Sasha was burrowed so far under the covers of his bed that Lincoln had to dig around in the tangled mess of sheets and comforter to find her small body. He was laughing by the time he found bare skin.

She moaned, swatting at him as he cupped her breast.

He chuckled again, sliding his front along her back and settling her against him with a hand around her waist. He kissed her temple as he pulled the comforter away and kicked it to the foot of the bed.

She was a heater. He would burn up if he let her continue to snuggle so deeply like that. She shivered. "Lincoln..." she pleaded. "I'm cold. And I'm tired. Let me sleep."

He propped himself on his elbow to look down at her. Her bottom hand was pulled in tight to her chest, her fingers fisted. Her top hand lay between her tits doing the same.

His cock was hard. He needed her again. Now. And he felt confident he could get her easily on the same page even though he'd only let her sleep a few hours and it was still dark out.

He teased the skin of her arm until goosebumps rose. She groaned in protest, but he wrapped his fingers around her wrist and pulled her arm above her head to trap it between his chin and his shoulder.

Her eyes finally opened. "Lincoln…" She didn't sound as disgruntled anymore. That was good.

"Go ahead and sleep, baby. I'm just going to explore."

She tipped her head back to blink at him. "Seriously."

He nodded. "Yep." With her arm trapped, her breast was high, her nipple puckered. He tweaked it slowly until she shuddered and her eyes fluttered closed.

Oh yeah.

He wedged a knee between her legs, pushing the top one up to her chest. Opening her pussy. It had been less than a minute, but when he touched her, he found her soaking wet. "Sleeping?"

She whimpered.

He pushed two fingers into her. "Insatiable."

She said nothing, but she rolled farther forward and pressed her face into the pillow.

He circled her clit and then pinched it.

She writhed, tugging on her arm and pushing her leg against his thigh.

He kissed her neck. "Need you, baby."

"Okay."

He chuckled. "Just okay?"

"Whatever." Sass. Pure sass. Did she think he wouldn't fuck that sass right out of her?

He thrust into her again, still so tight. She gripped him as his thumb landed on her clit. He fucked her warm pussy with those fingers so fast she caught her breath. "Lincoln…" This time his name on her lips was pleading. The sass and the sleep were gone.

"Yeah, baby?"

"Stop teasing."

"Whatever." As he repeated her word, he pulled out his hand, rolled her onto her back, and slid down between her legs. His cock was rock hard, but he needed his mouth on her first.

As he sucked her clit between his lips without warning, she gasped, her hands grasping at his shoulders. "Lincoln..." Her legs trembled, and her fingernails dug into his skin.

Oh yeah. Drowsy Sasha was delicious. He flicked his tongue over her clit and then suckled it again.

Her legs clamped around his head.

He released her clit and dipped a finger slowly into her tight pussy. "You saved this for me, didn't you?" he whispered. Ever since he'd found out she hadn't penetrated herself with anything in her life, he'd suspected as much, but he wanted to hear her say it.

"Yes..." The one word was barely audible. She didn't meet his gaze.

"Sasha, baby, look at me."

She swallowed as she dipped her chin to meet his gaze in the near darkness.

"Baby, you intentionally saved yourself for me. Not just your virginity, but you let me be the first to enter you at all."

"Yes," she repeated, shivering beneath him. "I wanted it to be you. Maybe that sounds ridiculous, but I wanted everything to be you."

"I'll never take that for granted again, baby. It humbles me. I hate the way I treated you the first time I took you. It won't happen again. You deserved better." It would take a lifetime for him to forgive himself. "I didn't even use a condom. If—"

She stopped him with a tight grip to his shoulders. "It wasn't the middle of the month or anything. Don't worry."

He sighed and kissed her clit reverently. He wanted to tell her how committed he was and that he would do right by her no matter what, but it seemed she understood without him saying more.

She reached with one hand to cup his cheek. "Stop punishing yourself for the way you took my virginity. It was amazing. In my wildest imagination I couldn't have come up with a scenario that hot. Maybe in the future don't walk away from me after you fuck me against the wall, but before that part, you stole my heart and made me the happiest woman on earth."

He closed his eyes. He didn't deserve this woman, and yet he had her anyway. Needing to taste her again, he lowered his face and sucked her sweet pussy lips, dipping his tongue inside her.

She writhed, bucking her hips as he held her down.

He thrust his tongue in and out of her until she cried out.

But he didn't want her to come yet, so he released her, licking her sweet taste from his lips. "Legs open, baby," he murmured. It was difficult to focus. He couldn't wait any longer. He grabbed a condom from the bedside table, rolled it on, and climbed up her body to fuck her. On a bed. In the most basic of positions for the first time.

It was earth-shattering. He knew this was as true for her as it was for him because she screamed loud enough to shake the foundation.

Sasha awoke to the smell of coffee and bacon. She smiled and stretched out against the sheets. She sighed, determined to make sure the first thing she and Lincoln did today was talk.

After he'd fucked her into the next month last night at the club, he'd driven her sleepy body to his house, put her in his bed, and then reached out to fuck her again at some ungodly hour. She sighed as she remembered his mouth on her pussy. So hot. She had yet to wrap her lips around his cock, and she intended to rectify that as soon as possible. Somewhere in between the talking they needed to do.

At least he'd let her sleep after sucking on her sex and then filling her pussy again, but there hadn't been much time for conversation yet.

She winced as she eased from the bed, every muscle in her

body sore. And then she glanced around to take in Lincoln's bedroom for the first time. As she would have guessed, it was bland. Dark wood, black and gray accents, thick gray carpet. He seriously needed some color.

She padded to the attached bath and nearly giggled at finding the same décor. After making quick work of using the toilet and cleaning up from middle-of-the-night sex, she found a new toothbrush on the counter, brushed her teeth, and headed back to his bedroom.

She considered remaining naked, but then grabbed his black tee from last night and pulled it on. It gave her some level of protection. Not much. But some.

It wasn't hard to find him. He was in the kitchen looking like a master chef instead of a Master Sadist. His body made her mouth water even more than the scent of food. No shirt. Bare feet. Low-hanging gray sleep pants. He must have sensed her because he turned as she approached, reaching out his arm and pulling her into his side. "Hungry?"

"Starving." Would he let her feed herself? They had so many details to iron out. Here she was in his home on a Thursday morning. What was next?

He kissed her forehead. "Sit, baby. I'll bring the plates over."

She slowly made her way to the table. What did he mean when he commanded her to sit? She was afraid to guess wrong, so she stood near the table and waited for him.

He set two plates on the table, glancing at her quizzically. "Sore bottom?" he teased.

"No. I wasn't sure where you wanted me to sit."

He shrugged. "I don't care. I don't have some special chair I prefer. You pick."

She nodded. "That wasn't what I meant," she stated as she chose a chair and lowered herself onto it.

He plopped down on the one diagonal from her and picked up his coffee, staring at her over the lip of the mug. Finally, his eyes widened and he set it down. "Right. Shit. Sorry. We have discussed nothing. You're confused. And you have two thousand questions."

"Yes." She left her hands in her lap, worrying them together. His T-shirt barely covered her ass.

He reached across the table and cupped her face, holding her chin steady with his thumb as he often tended to do. "We aren't playing right now, Sasha. In fact, I don't think we should play today at all. I was hoping we could spend the day getting to know each other better. Run a few important errands. Swim. Talk. Eat. Watch TV. Normal stuff."

She chuckled. "You can do that?"

He laughed. "Yes. I can do that."

She reached for her fork. "So you want to spend the day with me? If you have errands, I could go home while you do them. I need to do some things around my apartment. It got rather neglected the last few days." She wasn't kidding. It was a disaster. Laundry. Dishes. Take-out boxes. Luckily she'd had the wherewithal to call Mrs. Lopez and let her know she was home for a few days. Even luckier, she'd gotten the woman's voicemail and hadn't had to field fifty questions.

He set his fork down, his throat working before he took a deep breath. "You want to go back to your apartment?" His expression looked like she'd suggested a two-week vacation to Hawaii without him.

"Well, I mean, I do have some cleaning to do. And I need to find a summer job of some sort. I don't make enough money to support myself without it."

He leaned back in his chair, his gaze on his plate, not seeing it.

They really did need to talk. Their entire relationship consisted of ignoring each other for five years, her submitting to him full-time for twenty-four hours, and fucking hard in his club last night. There were holes all over this picture. "Talk to me."

He lifted his gaze, but he looked scared. "I thought it was pretty clear last night that I'm in love with you, baby."

She stopped breathing, her head moving slowly from side to side. "I don't think you specifically said that." *She* had said it. The word had been tossed around. *He* had most definitely not said it.

He held her gaze, his voice gravelly when he spoke, not mincing words. "I'm in love with you, Sasha. You're mine."

She nodded, her heart rate picking up. "I'm in love with you too. I'm glad it's mutual. But, you're going to have to connect the dots for me. We still have to work and make money and pay rent and all the other adulting things."

"I was hoping we could do them together."

"You mean run errands? Okay, I guess we can. You need to hit the store? What sort of errands?"

He hesitated. "In my mind we would start with packing up your stuff and moving you into my house."

She flinched. *Shit.* She didn't even know how to respond to that. She was blindsided. "You want me to move in with you? Like today?"

"Yes. We wasted years acting like idiots—mostly me. I don't want to waste more of them talking on the phone on Tuesdays and going to the movies on Sundays. I'm in love with you, Sasha. I want you in my house. My bed. I was hoping that started yesterday."

"Oh."

"That's it? Oh?" He looked worried now.

"I'm processing. Give me a second to catch up. Nobody's ever asked me to live with them. And they certainly haven't ever assumed it without asking me." She might have snapped a bit, but she tried not to.

He pushed his chair back and reached across to snag her around the waist.

She yelped as he pulled her onto his lap sideways, his hands threading into her hair at her temples. His eyes were inches from hers. "Move in with me." He threaded his fingers into the back of her hair, gave a slight tug, and then tipped her head toward his.

She smiled. She didn't want to smile. It just happened.

"We'll figure out all the details together. But I want you in my bed. I want to be able to reach out and know you're there, feel your heartbeat, hear your breathing, touch your skin, smell your shampoo." He kept going, not taking a breath. "Then you won't have to find a job. Financial problem solved. If you want something to do for the summer, you can work for me."

He made it sound so simple. She was leery. "At the club?" It suddenly occurred to her that she had no idea what else he did. The club was only open three nights a week. Surely he didn't spend the rest of the week balancing the books or ordering more spanking benches.

He shook his head. "No. My other job."

"What do you do?"

He furrowed his brow. "You have a point about us needing to talk. We don't know much about each other. I flip houses."

She pulled back a few inches, notably not dislodging him. "Like, you buy then and fix them up and sell them?"

"Yes. Well, not me personally. I'm not a carpenter. But I hire people to do it, and I manage it. So I have to visit the sites every few days and pay all the bills and that sort of thing."

"Okay, then. You flip houses."

"What else is keeping you from moving in? Name it. I'll fix it."

"I have a lease."

"We'll get out of it. Next."

"I haven't even met your mom." She was reaching now. But it was kinda fun.

"I'll call her after breakfast. We'll do lunch. Next."

Her heart was racing. She set her hands on his forearms and gripped them next to her face. "I have no idea what you expect of me."

He frowned. "Expect of you? I expect you to be happy. To do whatever you want that makes you happy. I don't have requirements."

"Lincoln, you have so many requirements I can't even list them all on one piece of paper."

"D/s you mean?"

"Of course."

"Our lives are not going to revolve around D/s, baby. We'll negotiate how much we want to play and when and where and all that as we go along. I'm not worried."

"*I'm* worried. I don't even know that much about the lifestyle. You haven't let me cook for you or clean up or even give you a blowjob." That last part was maybe overkill. Her mind was running through all the things she'd expected to do under his control. None of which had happened.

He tipped his head back and laughed hard.

"I'm not being funny."

He still held her face steady, and she dug her nails into his arms to get his attention.

"I'm sorry."

He didn't look sorry. He looked mischievous.

"Sasha, you're not a domestic sub. Or if you are, I don't care. I never looked at you like that. I don't need you to cook for me or clean up after me or kneel between my legs sucking my cock—though that last one is totally on the table for discussion any time you want." He winked.

"What exactly *do* you want me to do?"

"Just be you. Be Sasha. Be my little girl on occasion. Play nurse if you want. Maybe even teacher. No. Not that one. Stick to role-play that doesn't make you the Domme. I can't do that. All I'm saying is that I would be honored to dominate you as often as you want. Nothing makes me harder than watching your face and entire body come alive when I top you. It's sexy as hell. You love it. It's not our entire world."

She chewed her bottom lip.

He leaned in and kissed her, biting down on that same lip.

When he pulled back, he set his forehead against hers. "Move in with me. We'll fill in the blanks as we go along."

"It might be a bit soon to meet your mom."

He grinned. "Agreed. Next week."

"Maybe in a few weeks." She slid her hands down to his waist and snuggled closer. "I stole your shirt." Why she felt the need to comment on that she had no idea. But it was easier than answering the looming question.

"It looks great on you. Better on the floor. But I can live with it if you want to wear it." His eyes twinkled. "Move in with me."

"Would you expect me to call you Master?"

"Nope. Unless you want to. But only when we're playing."

She leaned in closer. His chest was so warm and hard. She loved feeling it against her in the night. She could get used to sleeping with her head on his shoulder, her hand on his abs.

"Sasha."

She met his gaze. Stalling was over.

"I love you. Maybe it feels sudden and too soon, but it's not really. I've loved you for a long time. I'm not perfect. I'll make mistakes. We'll argue. You'll set me straight. We'll make up naked. I don't want to waste another day without you in my life. Move in with me."

"Okay."

One second she was sitting on his lap, the next second she was in his arms in the air, and the next second her butt was on the kitchen island. Lincoln's mouth was on hers, devouring her. He tugged her to the edge, his cock pressing against her bare pussy through his sleep pants.

His hands were everywhere.

She was so aroused so fast she couldn't catch her breath.

The man could dominate her like she was putty. But, holy shit, he could also make her body hum without a single command.

Just Lincoln Walsh. The first man who'd ever awakened her

sexuality. The only man who'd ever awakened her sexuality. The only man who ever would.

She couldn't think of a good reason she shouldn't move in with him, not while his hand was between her legs stroking her to a maddening height. Not while his shirt had disappeared so that his mouth was wrapped around her nipple, suckling it. Not while her hands were buried in his hair, feeling the softness of it like silk.

She cried out as she came. So fast. So easy.

He was totally going to take advantage of that knowledge.

She was totally going to love it.

EPILOGUE

One week later...

Sasha was on her knees, naked, her hands clasped behind her back, her shoulders thrust back, making her breasts jut forward. Just the way Lincoln liked her. Often.

She didn't argue because damn the position made her at least as horny as him. Or perhaps it was the look in his eyes when she submitted to him like that. Like he wanted to devour her.

But it wasn't his turn to do the eating. So far he'd permitted her only a few fleeting tastes of his cock, muttering something about preferring to be buried in her pussy and not wanting to come prematurely in her mouth yet.

A half an hour ago, they'd been at the site of the house he was in the middle of flipping. She'd lifted onto her tiptoes, set her hand on his ass, and whispered in his ear. "You have two choices."

He'd flinched and then lifted an eyebrow, a smirk playing with the corners of his mouth. Before she knew it, he had her fingers threaded in his and he was hauling her into what would one day be a renovated bathroom. At the moment it needed a lot of imagination.

But it had a door, which Lincoln had shut. He flattened her to the surface, pressed his cock against her belly, and cupped her face. "Do you have any idea how hot it makes me when you do that?"

"Do what?" she'd asked, trying to sound innocent. She knew him well enough after one week to grasp that while she damn well better not top him when they were playing, she could get under his skin easily when they were not in the role.

He'd shook his head in dismay. "You're not fooling me. Lay it on me, baby. What are my two choices?"

She'd almost lost her nerve, but steeled herself and licked her lips. "Either you agree to let me suck you off at home tonight, or I'm going to lean over your lap during the drive and make it super difficult for you to stay on the road." Bold. Brazen. Risky?

For a second, she wasn't sure how he would react, and then he'd pushed off the wall, taken her hand, and tugged her out of the small bathroom as fast as they'd entered.

Carter had been working in the kitchen. He'd lifted his head as Lincoln ushered Sasha toward the front door.

Lincoln had barely paused to speak to his friend. "Gotta go. I'll see you here tomorrow to go over the tile samples for the bathroom."

Carter had chuckled as he shook his head and bent back to his task. "Whatever."

Sasha had been completely flushed and rather embarrassed as she nearly jogged to follow Lincoln to the car. Maybe her plan hadn't been a great one.

Lincoln had opened the passenger door of his SUV and lifted her around the waist to set her in the seat as if she weren't capable of doing so herself—or he was too impatient to wait. He even reached across her, buckled her in, and tugged the belt tighter. His gaze met hers, his eyes burning. "Do. Not. Move."

She had correctly assumed he'd chosen option number one.

Twenty minutes later, here she was, on her knees, ready to service her Dom. He was stripping slowly, circling her, making her pant with the desire to suck him. The only thing was he hadn't taken her home. He'd brought her to the club. It was closer. She'd fought the urge to giggle over his impatience when he'd pulled into the parking lot.

His shirt hit the floor first, his shoes were kicked off next, and then he popped the button on his jeans.

Her mouth watered. Twice he had permitted her to lick a line up his cock. One time he'd allowed her to slide his thick length between her lips. All three times, he had stopped her too soon.

Honestly, by today, no matter what he murmured about how talented she was with her lips, she had a bit of a complex.

"You're nervous," he pointed out as he lowered his zipper, standing two feet in front of her. "You don't have to do this, you know. You can back out."

She lifted her gaze to meet his for a moment before jerking it back toward the floor. "I know I'm not very good at it, Sir, but if you'd teach me." She wanted to please him. Men liked blowjobs. She knew they did. His reticence about this topic unnerved her.

He froze, his hands on the sides of his jeans now, tugging the denim over his hips. "Baby, you're totally misunderstanding."

"Enlighten me," she told his crotch.

He continued to remove his jeans, finally kicking them aside to reveal his unbelievably sexy naked body. And then he stepped closer, his cock bobbing in front of him. He cupped the sides of her head and tipped her face back, forcing her to look up at him. "You can do no wrong in that department, Sasha. As long as you keep your teeth off me, there's nothing I won't enjoy the fuck out of. The reason I haven't let you suck me off has nothing to do with your skills."

How would she know?

"My cock is greedy. It likes to be buried in your pussy."

She smiled. Maybe his motives were legitimate after all. "I'm glad, Sir, but I bet I can tempt you to enjoy my mouth too."

"I'm certain you can, sweetheart. And I'm going to grant you this. Your terms. Your call." He released her and stepped back to sit on the loveseat. "Explore all you'd like, baby." He set his hands at his sides.

Would he really let her do whatever she wanted? She released the tight grip she had behind her back and crawled forward on her knees.

His face was tight when she glanced from his thick length to meet his gaze. He fisted his hands at his sides on the couch as if he thought she might bite him. "Can't promise I'm going to have enough control to keep from coming in two seconds all over your face, baby."

Ah, so this was about control, not pain. She wrapped her hand around his cock and gently stroked from the base to the tip. Precome dripped from the head, and she leaned in to flick her tongue through the slit.

Lincoln moaned.

Emboldened, she lowered her face, sucking him into her mouth as far as she could while inhaling his scent. Clean fresh soap and Lincoln. Intoxicating. She tightened her lips around his cock as much as she dared, experimenting.

His thigh stiffened under her other hand, but the soft groan coming from his mouth told her he was the complete opposite of uncomfortable. "Baby…"

She sucked him in again, her hand still wrapped around the base, her cheeks hollowing as she lifted off a second time. On the third pass, he lifted his hips into her mouth, deepening the blowjob. She forced her throat to relax and let him in. It was awkward, but she managed.

She enjoyed the power she felt. This man who was always in control, making her body hum, was completely at her mercy.

Maybe he'd known that would happen, and that's why he'd been reluctant to permit her to suck him.

It was heady. She wanted more. Perhaps too much more because after sucking him a bit deeper with a few more bobs of her head, he grasped the back of her neck. "Sasha…" he warned.

Her pussy clenched. She let her nipples rub the edge of the leather sofa with every move. If she thought he wouldn't break the scene and punish her, she would have reached between her legs to masturbate while she sucked him.

She shook the thought from her mind, not wanting to risk his reaction, and lowered her face again, farther, deeper, tighter.

His hand tangled in her hair, gripping, though she doubted he was aware of his actions. Besides, she loved the feeling of having him hold her like that.

And then he stiffened, deep inside her mouth. He groaned loudly as he came, every pulse of his cock shooting his come into her mouth.

She swallowed, working hard to keep up. She wanted to catch every drop and leave him empty. It was important to her for some crazy reason. And she succeeded.

When he finally lowered his hips to the couch, sighing, his hand slid from her hair to her shoulder. "Jesus, Sasha."

She licked a line up his length as she lifted her head. He was staring at her, his face relaxed, his lips turned up in a smile. "Next time I'll choose option two and pull over to the side of the road," he teased.

She grinned. "Glad you liked it, Sir." She was relieved and pleased with herself.

Suddenly, from one second to the next, she was no longer on her knees, and Lincoln was no longer lounging languidly. He grabbed her by the waist and hauled her up to settle her straddling his lap.

Her legs were forced wide, her pussy so wet she thought it might drip on him.

When he reached toward the end table next to the loveseat, she giggled. A glass bowl filled with a colorful array of condoms sat in the center of the table. She'd never seen it there before. He snagged one. Purple. Apparently he'd made a few changes to the office. She shivered at the way he'd so obviously become Mr. Prepared.

As he opened it and then reached between their bodies to roll it down his length, she watched. How the hell was he already erect again? And then he grabbed his still-stiff cock, rubbed her slit with it, and lowered her over the length.

She gripped his shoulders and let her head fall back on a moan. "That's it, baby. So sexy."

When she started to lift off him, needing the friction, he stopped her with a hand on her hip. "Don't move. My play now."

She lowered her face, her vision clouded with lust. A whimper escaped her lips before she could stop it.

He chuckled. "Don't worry. I'm gonna let you come." His hand reached between their bodies to find her clit, and then his fingers worked their magic. His other hand held her firm, his cock buried inside her, thickening, filling her, so tight.

She wanted to move.

He had other plans.

"Greedy girl. Stay still. Stop fighting me." His fingers kept circling her clit, teasing it, flicking over the top and then retreating. "Hold still and I'll let you come."

Was she moving? She glanced down. Yes, she was squirming, trying to get the friction she desired from twisting since he wouldn't let her lift off him.

"Look at me, baby."

She met his gaze, blinking. Her mouth hung open. She was panting. Sweat had built on her forehead. "Please," she begged. She rarely took that risk. It often didn't end up in her favor.

But this time he smiled. "My girl likes to suck my cock."

"Yes, Sir."

"I think she deserves to be rewarded then." He released her hip, set his hands at his sides, and nodded. "Go ahead. Fuck me, baby. Make yourself come. I want to watch."

Her eyes flitted shut as she braced herself on her knees and lifted halfway off him. She didn't waste time. She set a pounding pace, needing the friction more than her next breath. In moments, she was coming around his cock. It wasn't enough. She didn't stop. She held on to his shoulders tighter and kept bouncing over his length.

He was so thick.

"That's it, baby. Come for me again." He grabbed her hips then and helped her, lifting and lowering her over his cock.

When she blinked at him, her second orgasm so close she couldn't breathe, she found his teeth gritted tight. That was all she needed. She tipped over the edge, her entire body shaking with the force.

Lincoln was right behind her, burying himself deep. He set his forehead against her shoulder when he came, a deep moan filling the room. She had no idea which one of them had made the sound.

An hour later, Sasha lay curled against Lincoln's chest on the loveseat, a soft throw covering her lower body. She wore his T-shirt. He wore his jeans. He was smoothing her hair from her forehead while he used his free hand to flip through different sites on the laptop that rested against his thighs.

She had never been so content. Peaceful. Perfect.

They didn't need conversation. The silence was comforting. Normal.

A knock at the office door caught her attention.

Lincoln swiveled his head toward the door as he tucked the blanket securely around her body. "Come in."

The door opened and Rowen stepped inside. When his gaze landed on the two of them, he hesitated.

"It's okay," Lincoln said. "Everything vital is covered," he teased, hugging Sasha tighter against his chest.

Rowen's brow was furrowed, raising an alarm in Sasha's mind. She started to sit upright, but Lincoln stopped her with a firm grip.

"I saw your car outside when I pulled up. Didn't realize you were both here. I can come back." He started to back out through the doorway.

"No need," Lincoln said as he sat up straighter and closed the laptop. "What are *you* doing here in the middle of the afternoon?"

Rowen stepped farther into the room and then lowered himself onto the armchair across from them. His brow was furrowed, but he forced a small smile. His gaze searched Sasha's. "You look good. Happy."

"Thanks," she whispered. "You look like shit." He did. His face was a dichotomy of expressions. But his eyes looked sad. Distant.

He tipped his head to the floor, and, ignoring her comment, spoke again. "It might take me a while to get used to seeing the two of you together, but I'll get there. Give me time. It's weird."

Sasha shifted her gaze toward Lincoln, her brows lifted in question.

Lincoln responded. "We'll do our best not to rub it in your face, and I promise we won't play in the club in front of you. I wasn't expecting you to be here this afternoon. I'm sorry. It won't happen again. It was insensitive of me to come here."

Rowen shook his head, glancing up. "No worries. This is your office."

"I should have locked the door. I wasn't thinking. It's the middle of the day. I didn't expect you. But, Rowen, what's going on? You're here for a reason."

Rowen smiled wanly, closed his eyes, and leaned his head back.

"We must have had the same idea. I thought I would be alone in the office."

"What's wrong?" Sasha asked tentatively. Something was definitely not copacetic.

"Rayne and I broke up."

She blew out a breath. "You and Rayne break up about once a month. That's not news."

He met her gaze. "This time it's over."

She stiffened. He seemed serious. Definitive.

So did Lincoln, his arm trailing down to her waist. Stiff. "What happened?"

Rowen shrugged. "We realized we just aren't compatible. It's amicable. I mean, I think we're both mature enough for her to remain a member of the club. We're friends. But something's always been lacking in our relationship. It's time to stop pretending otherwise."

"I'm so sorry, Rowen," Sasha stated. She flattened her hand on Lincoln's chest. "I know she isn't really into the lifestyle." Rayne never had been completely comfortable at Zodiac. Sasha couldn't imagine why her brother's girlfriend would continue to be a member if their relationship was over.

Rowen shook his head. "It's not that. For a long time, I thought the same thing. So did Rayne. But the truth is not quite as simple."

"What do you mean?" Lincoln asked.

Rowen sighed. "I mean, I think she really is submissive. We've had some intense scenes together. Just a few weeks ago, we did a spanking scene that was smoking hot. She has it in her. It's like we just don't click with each other. I think there's a Dom for her. It just isn't me."

"Are you okay?" Sasha asked.

He nodded, forcing another smile. "It's sad. Not going to lie. We've been dancing around each other for a long time, but I'm also relieved, and so is Rayne." He set his hands on the arms of the chair and pushed to standing. "Didn't mean to bring you guys down. I've got some paperwork to take care of in my office."

"Okay," Sasha whispered. She felt bad. For both Rowen and Rayne. Rayne had been so kind to her the last few weeks. "Let me know if you want to talk."

Rowen headed for the door. He turned around before leaving, his hand on the doorframe. "Do me a favor." His gaze was directed at Sasha.

"Of course."

"Don't act differently around her. I meant what I said about this being amicable. I know you two have gotten close lately. Don't let my break-up get between the two of you and your friendship."

Sasha nodded.

Rowen left, the door shutting behind him.

Sasha slouched against Lincoln's chest. "How could it take one couple over a year to figure out they don't belong together while you and I managed to know what we had was special within a few days?"

Lincoln set the computer aside and pulled her sideways onto his lap. He cupped her face and tipped her head back. "I don't know, baby, but you're half wrong."

She cocked her head to one side as much as his grip allowed. "How?"

"I knew you were mine in less than a few minutes. Not days."

She furrowed her brow. "That makes no sense. You chased me out of your house after one day."

"I'm not talking about last week. I'm talking about the day I first laid eyes on you." He kissed her forehead, and then her nose, and finally her lips. "Five years ago, I walked into this club, spotted you across the room, and knew. I might have been too stupid to admit it, but I knew."

She slowly smiled, her heart soaring. "I was a little young back then."

He winced. "Yeah. I had no business lusting after you. That's for sure. So, I kept it to myself. But waiting five years might have been overkill. I intend to make up for lost time starting now." He angled his head to one side and kissed her again, this time deepening the kiss into something far more heated.

She held on to his biceps with both hands, the blanket sliding down to her lap as his hands eased from her head, down her neck and shoulders to her breasts. His thumbs teased her nipples mercilessly as she arched into his touch.

When she whimpered, he broke the kiss to murmur against her lips, "You're mine now, Sasha. I will never let you go."

"I intend to do everything in my power to ensure you never want to." She meant those words. Every one of them. She was committed to this relationship in a way she'd never sensed from Rowen and Rayne. Perhaps their break-up was for the best. After all, Sasha never would have settled for less than what she had in the arms of Lincoln Walsh. She never had, and she never would.

AUTHOR'S NOTE

I hope you enjoyed this first book in the Club Zodiac series. Please enjoy the following excerpt from book two in the series, *Obeying Rowen*.

OBEYING ROWEN

CLUB ZODIAC (BOOK TWO)

"She's amazing, isn't she? It's like watching a moving piece of art."

Rowen didn't acknowledge Carter's statement. In fact, he wasn't sure he'd blinked in the last ten minutes. His mouth was too dry to speak.

Carter was right. The petite woman currently circling the man lying over a spanking bench was spectacular. Her thick blond hair was pulled up in a high ponytail that swayed across her back as she moved. Her skin was alabaster pale, standing out in stark contrast to the black leather skirt and corset she wore.

She wasn't tall by any stretch of the imagination, but the black heels she wore made her legs appear to go on forever.

Faith Robbins. He knew her name, but he hadn't had the pleasure of meeting her face to face yet. Subconsciously, he had to admit he'd probably steered clear of her out of self-preservation.

From his vantage point, Rowen didn't think she had a single flaw. He'd caught a glimpse of her clear blue eyes on occasion since she'd joined the club a few months ago, so he also knew a man could get lost in those orbs for days.

But none of that mattered at the moment. Not her beauty or

her legs or even her fucking fantastic cleavage pushed high under the corset.

What mattered right now was the way she moved, the way she held the long black flogger, and the way she kept her gaze locked on her submissive as she slowly glided around his body.

She could easily star as the Domme in any movie and make millions. Anyone watching this scene would agree in a heartbeat. But Rowen sensed something was off. He couldn't put his finger on it. But he knew.

"Is this the first time you've watched her perform?" Carter whispered from about a half a step behind Rowen.

"Yes."

"Breathtaking, isn't she?"

"Yes. I don't know the man subbing for her. Are they a couple?" he asked, trying not to sound too interested.

"That's Levi Calloway. He's also a new member. I think the two of them met recently, though. I don't think they're together." Carter nudged Rowen with his shoulder. "You interested in having her hands on you?" He chuckled softly.

"Hardly." *But I wouldn't mind getting my hands on* her.

"It's been months since you and Rayne broke up. Maybe you should get back out there. When was the last time you scened with someone?"

Rowen glanced at Carter, his brows raised. "What are you now, my dad?" He let his gaze roam back to Faith as she dragged her fingers across Levi's shoulder blade. They looked fantastic together. Levi's skin was dark against Faith's nearly white complexion.

Levi was resting on one cheek facing Rowen. His eyes were closed, but his mouth was open, and he licked his lips every time Faith stroked his skin. He wore nothing but a black G-string that left his butt exposed. He gripped the padded section of the bench where his fingers wrapped around the edge, and it appeared it took an incredible amount of energy for him to remain still as Faith circled behind him and gripped his butt cheeks.

When her small hand smoothed down between his legs to cup his cock, Levi moaned.

Rowen almost moaned too. Luckily he managed to bite the inside of his cheek instead. Carter would never have let him live that down.

But Carter Ellis knew Rowen well. They'd been friends for years, ever since they met as enlisted men in the army when they were eighteen. Now they were business partners, each owning a share in Club Zodiac with their third partner, Lincoln Walsh.

Carter chuckled again. "Not gonna lie. She makes my dick hard too."

Rowen didn't comment. His own cock needed to be adjusted inside his jeans, but no way in hell was he going to reach around and touch his junk in front of Carter and risk hearing the man's laughter again.

Faith was a piece of art. Nothing more. Anyone would be mesmerized by her scene. Her clothing alone was mouthwatering. Lots of women wore corsets and skirts similar to hers, but none of them wore the two pieces quite like Faith. It was as if the black leather was custom made to mold to her body.

Finally, she took a step back, lifted the flogger in the air, and let it sail down to land on Levi's ass. It wasn't hard. She was warming up. But it was enough to make Levi flinch and Carter groan.

Rowen turned his head to smirk at his friend. "You gonna become a bottom now?"

Carter rolled his eyes. "Hardly. Not any more than you are. But you can't deny she's smokin' hot wielding that flogger. There's something super sexy about a confident female dominatrix. Not saying I want to be on the receiving end, but I can appreciate beauty when I see it."

Carter was not wrong.

Faith exuded a level of authority no one could dismiss. But something was still off...

"Did Lincoln say she transferred her membership from Breeze a few months ago?"

"Yes. There's a story behind that, but I don't remember what he said."

I bet there is.

Carter kept talking. "You should see the SUV she drives. That tiny ball of power drives a fucking ninety-thousand-dollar Range Rover. I saw her pull up in the parking lot."

Holy shit. Rowen's eyes widened, but he kept it to himself. Maybe the thing he was noticing about her that seemed off was simply that she was wealthy and carried herself in that manner. It would sure explain the clothing.

Rich people had a tendency to rub Rowen wrong. Or, more accurately, pretentious people. He'd met many over the years— both members of the club and clients of his accounting firm. He found that frequently the richest clients were the most entitled, nickel and diming every single cent to avoid paying their share of the taxes. And wealthy men and women who came into the club often thought they knew everything about BDSM because they googled it and had the cash to buy thousands of dollars' worth of toys.

In his experience, wealth did not make someone a good Dom. He and his partners went out of their way to ensure rich visitors didn't overstep their bounds in their exuberant desire to master the art overnight. They were statistically more likely to have a safeword called on them.

And rich submissives could be worse. Sometimes it even hindered their ability to let loose and be authentic. If they treated the lifestyle like it was a game, they also stood a higher chance of getting hurt—emotionally or physically.

But damn, Faith moved fluidly, like a seasoned Domme. She might have money, but she took her role seriously and didn't mess around.

"I didn't say that to put you on edge." Carter leaned closer. "I've seen no evidence that Faith is anything but the perfect Domme."

Rowen nodded, not glancing away from the scene.

Carter spoke again, lowering his voice. "She's not like that Brenda woman."

Rowen winced.

How did Carter remember the names of people from as far back as five or more years ago?

Brenda had come to the club while John Gilbert was still the owner. Rowen was unfortunate enough to be the one to greet her at the door. She'd flung her wealth around and demanded an "experience" as if the club were a place people paid for services.

To this day Rowen had no idea what the woman had hoped to get from her "experience," but he suspected she thought rough sex was on the menu. She was loud and belligerent and demanding. She'd disrupted the entire club before John escorted her out.

Rowen would never forget her because she was shouting that she was going to sue Zodiac for treating her unfairly. Apparently Carter hadn't forgotten either.

"Nor is she like that woman Lori. Not everyone with money is undisciplined," Carter added.

Lori. Lori had joined Zodiac soon after Lincoln bought the club. He'd been a little too lenient about vetting applicants in the early days. Lori had slipped through the process and then brought her own "Dom" one night to play.

From the moment Rowen saw the man, he'd rubbed him wrong. He was cocky, too loose, and he swung a whip around beside his leg like a crazy man would walk through a department store swinging a semi-automatic weapon while shouting about his second amendment rights.

And the unease had been warranted because Lori let the man tie her to a St. Andrew's cross and blindfold her. She'd insisted she didn't want him to go easy on her, and he did not. Within minutes she had blood running down her belly from two long cuts. Rowen had rushed forward to intervene, but he was about two seconds too late to stop the damage.

Lori had glared at Rowen with the most evil eyes he'd ever seen and blamed him for not doing a better job monitoring the scene. She had *also* threatened to sue.

Luckily neither woman had sued the club. But they had both left a sour taste in Rowen's mouth that would never fully go away.

"Rowen?" Carter interrupted his thoughts.

"Yeah?" He glanced at his friend. Had he missed a question?

Carter frowned. "You good?"

"Yep." He turned his gaze back to Faith. Carter was right. She was not Lori or Brenda. She was totally in control. Calm. Stunning.

When she lifted the flogger a second time and rained several blunt strikes over her submissive's butt cheeks, she bit the corner of her bottom lip.

Rowen's breath hitched. He watched her expression instead of her movements for several minutes. She was good. Well trained. Exacting with every strike. She took the time to soothe Levi's skin with her palms at perfect intervals. She kept him on edge by lightly grazing her nails over his cock every once in a while too.

Her perfectly manicured nails... So, not just the SUV. She literally carried herself like someone born with a silver spoon. They had a "look." The way she moved, walked, held her head, her hands. So...proper. Stilted. Or maybe that was part of her act? Was he judging her too harshly?

So what if she had money? It shouldn't bother him. She didn't belong to him. Besides, she was no slacker in the world of D/s, so Rowen needed to stuff his judgmental side down and give her a break.

Levi was in subspace within minutes. His head tipped back, elongating his neck as his body relaxed. The only time he stiffened was when Faith touched his cock through the bulging material of his G-string.

Rowen's gaze went back to her face. That lip…

He wanted to bite that damn lip. Pink. Swollen. Lush. Her perfect white teeth gleamed where they pressed into the soft flesh.

She exuded power. Except for that lip…

The room was so silent watching this piece of artistic perfection that every small noise coming from Levi echoed.

It had been nearly half an hour when Faith circled to Levi's head, set her flogger on his back, and leaned down to whisper in his ear.

Levi groaned, his torso squirming on the bench, as he rubbed his cock against the leather edge. Suddenly, he moaned loudly, arching his back as his hips thrust forward in the sharp rhythmic movements of an orgasm.

"Fuck me," Carter murmured. "I've never come on command."

Rowen hadn't either, but if Faith Robbins sauntered over to him at that moment and demanded he come too, Rowen was fairly certain he would comply instantly. He was that hard.

Carter wandered away, muttering something about needing to jerk off in private.

Rowen didn't move a muscle as he watched Faith help Levi off the bench and over to a loveseat. She wrapped a blanket around his shoulders and then squatted in front of him with her hands on his thighs and her head tipped back.

Rowen couldn't hear what she was saying, but her body language spoke volumes. When she leaned closer, her breasts rubbed against Levi's knees, but she didn't seem to notice.

People moved away to watch other scenes happening in the corners of the main play room at Zodiac. The lighting was dim. The walls and ceiling and floor were all black. But Rowen continued to watch from his vantage point partially hidden in a dark corner.

Levi nodded a few times and accepted a water bottle from

someone. After he drained half of it, Faith stood. She didn't stroke Levi's face or run a hand through his hair or caress his chest. She didn't take a seat next to him either. Instead, she waited until she was certain he was okay, and then she left.

Rowen's breath hitched again as she headed his direction. Her face lowered. She bit that lip again. And then she lifted her hands together at her waist and threaded her fingers delicately.

She didn't acknowledge Rowen as she passed. He doubted she even noticed anyone was standing there. She was in her own world. But she was not satisfied. The air around her was tense. Frustrated.

The beauty that was her dominance for the better part of the last hour had disappeared, replaced with uncertainty and...sorrow.

Faith Robbins may very well have been the best actress in the world, and her performance was breathtaking, but was it authentic? He didn't think she was a Domme. It didn't suit her. He had his doubts about her even being a switch.

He'd bet money Faith was a submissive.

If Rowen's cock could get any harder, it did. As he watched her back—shoulders squared, head tipped toward the floor, feet spread slightly farther apart then necessary—he finally gave up the battle and adjusted his dick. Not giving one solid fuck who saw him.

Reviving Bianca

Reviving Olivia

Project DEEP Box Set One

Project DEEP Box Set Two

SEALs in Paradise:

Hot SEAL, Red Wine

Hot SEAL, Australian Nights

Dark Falls:

Dark Nightmares

Club Zodiac:

Training Sasha

Obeying Rowen

Collaring Brooke

Mastering Rayne

Trusting Aaron

Claiming London

Sharing Charlotte

Taming Rex

The Art of Kink:

Pose

Paint

Sculpt

Arcadian Bears:

Grizzly Mountain

Grizzly Beginning

Grizzly Secret

Grizzly Promise

Grizzly Survival

Grizzly Perfection

Arcadian Bears Box Set

Sleeper SEALs:

Saving Zola

Spring Training:

Catching Zia

Catching Lily

Catching Ava

Spring Training Box Set

The Underground series:

Force

Clinch

Guard

Submit

Thrust

Torque

The Underground Box Set

Saving Sofia (Kindle World)

Wolf Masters series:

Kara's Wolves

Lindsey's Wolves

Jessica's Wolves

Alyssa's Wolves

Tessa's Wolf

Rebecca's Wolves

Melinda's Wolves

Laurie's Wolves

Amanda's Wolves

Sharon's Wolves

Wolf Gatherings Box Set One

Wolf Gatherings Box Set Two

Claiming Her series:

The Rules

The Game

The Prize

Emergence series:

Bound to be Taken

Bound to be Tamed

Bound to be Tested

Bound to be Tempted

Emergence Box Set

The Fight Club series:

Come

Perv

Need

Hers

Want

Lust

The Fight Club Box Set

Wolf Gatherings series:

Tarnished

Dominated

Completed

Redeemed

Abandoned

Betrayed

Wolf Gatherings Box Set

Durham Wolves series:

Rescue in the Smokies

Fire in the Smokies

Freedom in the Smokies

Stand Alone Books:

Blind with Love

Guarding the Truth

Out of the Smoke

Abducting His Mate

Three's a Cruise

Wolf Trinity

Frostbitten

A Princess for Cale/A Princess for Cain

ABOUT THE AUTHOR

Becca Jameson is a USA Today best-selling author of over 90 books. She is most well-known for her Wolf Masters series and her Fight Club series. She currently lives in Houston, Texas, with her husband and her Goldendoodle. Two grown kids pop in every once in a while too! She is loving this journey and has dabbled in a variety of genres, including paranormal, sports romance, military, and BDSM.

A total night owl, Becca writes late at night, sequestering herself in her office with a glass of red wine and a bar of dark chocolate, her fingers flying across the keyboard as her characters weave their own stories.

During the day--which never starts before ten in the morning!--she can be found jogging, running errands, or reading in her favorite hammock chair!

...where Alphas dominate...

Becca's Newsletter Sign-up:
http://beccajameson.com/newsletter-sign-up

Join my Facebook fan group, Becca's Bibliomaniacs, for the most up-to-date information, random excerpts while I work, giveaways, and fun release parties!

Facebook Fan Group:
https://www.facebook.com/groups/BeccasBibliomaniacs/

Contact Becca:
www.beccajameson.com
beccajameson4@aol.com

facebook.com/becca.jameson.18

twitter.com/beccajameson

instagram.com/becca.jameson

bookbub.com/authors/becca-jameson

goodreads.com/beccajameson

amazon.com/author/beccajameson

Made in the USA
Las Vegas, NV
12 December 2020